Sary's Gold

by

Sharon Shipley

Sary's Gold

COPYRIGHT © 2015 by Sharon Shipley

Cover Art by *Debbie Taylor*

The Wild Rose Press, Inc.
PO Box 708
Adams Basin, NY 14410-0708
Visit us at www.thewildrosepress.com

Publishing History
First Cactus Rose Edition, 2015
Print ISBN 978-1-62830-701-6
Digital ISBN 978-1-62830-702-3

Published in the United States of America

The stage-halt proprietor, a fat man in a greasy apron and thick ginger sideburns, hawked her. "Can't hardly doss 'em here, uh, lady!"

She turned, raising her face, and shyly held out her hand. "It's Sarabande, Sarabande Swinford, but—"

"Don't make no matter if'n you're Queen Victoria—"

He stopped, awkward. The face before him was blooming, fresh, young, her translucent green eyes cutting through the dust, even after the ravages of the trek up-mountain, and especially so for Big Bear, where womenfolk coarsened up quickly in the thin, sere air.

"Yes, of course." Sary carefully counted coin from a thin purse.

Enigmatically shaking his head, he watched Sary drag their odd jumble of baggage across the dust to McAdams Hostelry, cheek by jowl with Delacorte's Saloon. Behind her, the layabouts mugged, nudging each other as their attention trailed her.

Praise for *SARY'S GOLD*

Dedication

To Loren G (Skip) Shipley,
my Angel,
for his grace and generosity.

The Beginning

This is my story, whether you like me or no…whether you approve of me or no, or of what I did—or *had* to do. Yet it happened this way…

Think on a wood surrounding a cornfield. It was winter. 1897. Stark trees, a skeleton rattle of dry corn stalks, and snow dirtied with daubs of Indiana clay…

Sebastian, a weakly handsome man, crouched behind a tree, sucking a flask, smirking out at men in hunting gear toting shotguns across the dried stubble. Blearily, Seb mumbled as he re-read his scrap of frayed newsprint dragged out with his flask:

Holcombe Valley ♦ Big Bear ♦ Belleville!
GOLD RUSH !
1,000 Men follow the Gold!

Seb peered out again, his smirk still in place as the hunters neared his hiding place. Grumbling, he stuffed the newsprint back in his pocket and grabbed his shotgun, tripping over the stock. Twin blasts disturbed a sky of winter crows winging away as one, like the grim reaper, cawing *Death*. Seb watched, befuddled, as one hunter—Jonathan—crumpled, firing his own gun. The startled men ran across the stubble to him as the handsome blue-jawed face dimmed in agony and brilliant red crept across his jacket and the snow beneath, and he bled his life away.

Seb's grin was like a guttering candle with a queer

flicker behind his eyes as he trotted out, leaving his own telltale gun behind. The hunters eyed him but seemed to think Jonathan died by his own hand.

****

The farmhouse was plain, wood, and very neat. Sary, a healthy girl in country dress, kneaded biscuit dough for supper, already thinking of a fat rabbit roasted on the spit and the canned runner beans and fried sweet potatoes she and Jonathan would share, and the sweet night ahead. Clear eyes the color and sparkle of pale green glass clouded as she squinted out the window; then she tore out, with her feet bare and her coppery gold hair coming all undone, a splash of color against the leaden day, to the hunters carting Jonathan's body home. Weeping, she clasped his head in her arms, while Seb avoided looking at her.

****

The church, plain as the house, was weathered, and if it ever had paint was innocent of it now. Tilted stones and gray wood crosses marked the raw earth that smelled of false spring. Sary started to pluck a lone jonquil struggling through the snow, but let it be. It was alive.

A hole marred the snow where mourners lowered the coffin on ropes that slid through horny palms streaked with blood as the hunters eased it down.

Sary tossed in the shotgun and stormed back alone to the line of waiting wagons.

****

It was late afternoon that day, and still bleak outside. The farmhouse parlor, kerosene-lit and spare, the few ornaments lovingly displayed, held a fierce family argument as elders tried to convince Seb of something, with much finger stabbing and body English.

Seb vehemently shook his head—"No!"—while his elders thrust Sary at him, indicating she was now his responsibility.

He stared at his sister as if seeing her for the first time. Her face...waist...hips...bosom...

Chapter 1

Big Bear, California. It was spring in that rough mountain mining outpost when the crude stage, little more than a buckboard with canvas flaps, rattled into a clutter of stables, mercantiles and saloons.

One saloon, Delacorte's, seemed rather grand.

As Seb and Sary—her dusty black mourning gown and black straw bonnet could never hide her stellar face and figure—stepped stiffly down, layabouts kept them in their sites, while proprietors, like predators, and at least one pair of hardened female eyes belonging to Handi McAdams, followed them from the dens of their establishments. Sary slowly surveyed the bleak mountain mining town.

****

From the halt, Seb, shivering in the thin mountain air, belligerently assessed the raw straggle of Big Bear, too. He gripped Sary's arm and, loud enough for all to hear, ordered her, "A room! One night, now, mind!" Striding to Delacorte's saloon, he spun when halfway there. "And don't let 'em gyp ya none!" he bellowed. Seb checked for onlookers. "Got business! *'Portant* business."

Sary gazed after him, stoic, cheeks flaming as she watched Seb halt by the swing doors.

Seb sneered at a yellow poster depicting a flamboyant but handsome man in tights and the proclamation:

"Sleight of Hand! Jugglers. Fire Eaters!
Feats of Strength!
Rousing Recreations of William Shakespeare's Hamlet!
Starring Headliners of All Europe!
Seen by Royalty!"

Blotches of yellow poster seemed to be everywhere. Seb eyed them and spat on the grimy plank walkway. "Painted-up *Molly!*"

At the halt, Sary turned wearily from Seb—*never mind what he's doing; it won't be to our good*—to a tatty gaggle of baggage, and once again helplessly assessed the drear strip of Big Bear.

The stage-halt proprietor, a fat man in a greasy apron and thick ginger sideburns, hawked her. "Can't hardly doss 'em here, uh, lady!"

She turned, raising her face, and shyly held out her hand. "It's Sarabande, Sarabande Swinford, but—"

"Don't make no matter if'n you're Queen Victoria—"

He stopped, awkward. The face before him was blooming, fresh, young, her translucent green eyes cutting through the dust, even after the ravages of the trek up-mountain, and especially so for Big Bear, where womenfolk coarsened up quickly in the thin, sere air.

"Yes, of course." Sary carefully counted coin from a thin purse.

Enigmatically shaking his head, he watched Sary drag their odd jumble of baggage across the dust to McAdams Hostelry, cheek by jowl with Delacorte's Saloon. Behind her, the layabouts mugged, nudging each other as their attention trailed her.

****

Seb thrust through swing gates, posed, and sauntered big to the long, polished slab of plank where Ratchet, a rangy hatchet-faced man of forty—a chilling presence—lounged, elbows on the bar. He turned, lazily sized up Seb, and included everyone when he snorted, "You just keep pouring in like rain, locusts, and bad liquor"—he nudged Seb—"don't you, you ignorant plowboys?"

Seb pinked up. "Bad corn's got more kick—but prob'ly the likes of you wouldn't know." He rapped the bar. "Barkeep!" The barkeep shot a knowing glance at Ratchet.

Across the room, Julian Delacorte, an elegant but dissipated ruin of a man, presided over a gaming table with two buffalo-shouldered men—Orvis O'Malley and Aaron Doheny, chinless, with a beak of a nose anchoring thick glasses through which he worried his cards—and a fourth, a mountain of a man, who was more tolerated than a part of the group, for Ev'ret played his own game, arranging a messy pile of chips in pretty colors and patterns.

Julian Delacorte, coughing subterranean mines of phlegm—Seb neither knew nor cared whether from consumption or syphilis—spared Seb a look, instantly forgetting him as Ratchet slugged back Seb's drink, flipped the shot glass over his shoulder, and grinned.

"I mean to say…you keep the stagecoach company in bizness. They just keep findin' the same blame nugget over and over in you." Ratchet leaned and thunked Seb's arm as Seb lifted his new pour, sloshing out the precious whiskey.

Seb beeted up again, white-knuckling his shot glass.

Ratchet jabbed a thumb at the meek man. "Aary there, he runs the mercantile. That's where gold's at. We just seed that same old nugget so some sod-bustin', mule-humpin', inbred country manure picker can stumble on it all over again." Ratchet had pulled the room in with him and shoved Seb again.

The room waited for Seb's reaction and then eyed him dismissively.

Seb, flaming by then, hunched over his fresh pour. Even the few soiled doves trailing down so early in the day, the doxies—looking no better than they should, still, reasonably clean—openly grinned past yawns.

"Like, maybe, someone like you." Ratchet smirked at the room and kept on, straight-fingering Seb's shoulder.

Seb slammed the glass down. His hand shook. He half-raised it gripped tight like a rock, ready to throw at his tormenter. "You telling me I can't cut tobacca? I earned these!" With flaming eyes, Seb showed how huge his stringy muscles were.

Ratchet's snigger sounded like rats crawling a drain.

"How? Being your own mule? Field hand?"

"If gold's in this heap of manure you call a town, 'at's as good as mine!" Seb yelled, flashing a thin roll tied with dirty string. "Whiskey! Whiskey for every man-jack 'cept him and that tarted-up dandy over yonder who don't seem to have no manners to welcome a stranger!"

Julian Delacorte cut Seb a glance.

Giving the great man one more look, Seb faltered, slapped a third of his wad on the bar, tossed back a fresh pour the bartender had provided, and strutted out, a man on a mission.

****

Sary, puffing, yanked the last bundles beneath the McAdam's Hostelry sign and into the lobby. Blinking in the cool dimness, she approached a desk, leaning the better to see the lurid yellow poster on the wall nearby, a twin to the one Seb had been so intrigued by. She blushed. It depicted a raffishly handsome man, if a bit flamboyant. Rather embarrassing tights clothed the lower half of his shapely body, illustrating he was very much a male. She peeked again, with a shy secret grin, and didn't see Hannah McAdams watching from a half-open door beyond the desk until the ravaged woman imperiously cupped her hand. "Come!"

Sary tore her eyes away from the poster.

Trying for elegance, Handi missed, by the depth of her cleavage and the amount of her makeup. Age-ripened to rot, Handi owned a vein of common lead running through her matronly silver exterior, or so Sary might have guessed.

"Beg pardon? I am looking for rooms. Isn't this—" Sary sized Handi up. "Perhaps I'm in the wrong place. This…is much…too grand!" she finished awkwardly.

"Got the only place. Come!" Handi jerked her head to the room behind her, opening the door enticingly. Her lips were a glittering red invitation, and so Sary entered a room of European grandeur, missing nothing. Her gaze discreetly flicked over gaudy paintings: "Pompeii," "The Rape of Europa," "A Venetian Bridge," and one, where a lady casting smoldering glances was apparently clad only in wet gauze.

Sary looked away. Certainly it wasn't biblical, or even Æsop's Fables.

Through other doors, she saw glimpses of a rather mannish office and an over-lavish boudoir, yet she could not leave the exotic paintings, glittering with oily richness, jewel color, and promises of unknowable worlds.

Sary stroked one. "Are these…real? I mean, the places? Not fanciful like…like fairy tales?"

Handi snorted.

Sary turned in time to see Handi watching her, peeling Sary's clothes off with her eyes, before she indicated the room. "Want 'em to be?" she barked in a rather coarse voice. "Sit! Last long enough, might discover this is Big Bear's rarest privilege. Sit! Call me Handi. Hannah McAdams," she ordered in the brusque way that was apparently her manner.

Sary looked anxiously to the lobby. Seb would be waiting. She murmured vaguely, "Sarabande. Folks call me—"

Handi waved her off. "Call yourself anything you like. In a few months you won't be the same anyways." Enthroning herself, she poured something amber and painfully propped a puffy ankle on a tufted stool while stuffing a long, slim pipe.

"Only whiskey cuts the dust in your veins or your—" Handi poked Sary through her black dress, at the V of her thighs, with the stem of her pipe. She raised the decanter. "Want a tot?"

Sary jumped back at the poke of Handi's pipe. The woman laughed harshly and drank deep. "Suit yourself. Spell since I've had a lady here."

Sary's look swept the room. "You're here."

"Hunh! No lady! Ladies have blue milk running through their veins and vinegar in their…" She started

9

to poke Sary again, snorted a laugh, poured herself another drink, and rang a small ornate bell. A slattern, an oddly wanton-looking old woman appeared, in a low, loose-necked dress despite her age, glumly toting in tea and cakes and another of the long slim ivory pipes. Handi winced at her appearance. "Belle? You wash your funsies and your fancies today?" Belle snorted. Slamming the tray down, the woman threw Sary a knowing leer and shuffled out.

Sary looked in puzzlement after the elderly servant in the alarmingly low bodice from which her withered dugs threatened to spill out; however, Sary inhaled the tea like life-giving nectar, watching over her cup in alarm as Handi vigorously clawed an ankle.

Still clawing, Handi made a face. "Gift from a French gentleman. Won't kill me. Till I want it to," she amended and licked the knife. Slicing fruitcake, she placed it with her bare fingers on Sary's plate. When Sary demurred, Handi shrugged and ate it herself.

Sary half rose. She looked with some panic to the door. "My brother," she stammered. "We—we need a room."

Handi stared into the distance and puffed her pipe with a bemused look Sary couldn't interpret.

"Brother? Could be." She hitched a shoulder, amused by something. "Once the door's closed?" Handi guffawed.

Sary frowned, puzzled. The woman made little sense, but Handi changed the subject in the maddening way she had. "Own this place. Mine! Only way to own anything, if you're of a female persuasion." She continued clawing her leg while scrutinizing Sary, narrowing her eyes.

"Look like a schoolmarm. Could be the best doxie I got. Teachers make tolerable whores," she reflected. "Always wash up after. Talk nice, too."

Sary stared. *Is she—? No, surely not. She's so— elegant.*

Handi continued, oblivious. "Miners, bless 'em, prefer girls like their sweethearts back home. Get to thinkin' love is listening to bedsprings, though!" She chuckled again.

Oh! She is!

Sary jumped up when Handi gestured something, surely obscene, and nudged her back into her seat with a cane Sary hadn't before seen. Slick, black, like a snake, with a gold knob on the end. Sary stared at the cane, seeing it for what it really depicted, as Handi bored on.

"More gold in mining back pockets, ehhh? While men are otherwise…occupied?"

The heavily made-up woman sucked her pipe and coughed. When she was through, she demanded, "Well? What say?" Slitted puffy eyes almost concealed Handi's rapaciousness.

Sary, seeing the black glitter, felt a chill and stiffly gathered her skirts. "My brother and I…have other plans."

"Wager you do!" Handi barked a laugh. "Wait! That's right. Keep your skirts yanked tight and safe-keep those valuables. Might change your mind."

Bewildered, Sary watched Handi hobble to an ornate dresser to withdraw and lovingly heft a petite pistol, all ivory and silver, and a small sack.

"This little darling's already shot its quota. Might be a few killings left in it." She aimed it at an ornate

11

cloisonné vase. "Pulls a tad right. Want to blow a hole through some scoundrel's cranium, aim for the left ear. Go on!" She thrust it at her. "You'll need it. Take it. Called a Derringer."

Sary shied away. "I don't mind if it's called Gabriel's trumpet on a plate. A killing's already killed me. I don't intend—" Sary stood.

"Huh!" Handi snorted. "Here trouble stalks like sickened bobcats. Won't need to scout it out for it to find you. Take it," she cajoled, "for me." She thrust the pistol at her again.

Sary gingerly reached for the toy-like gun. Didn't seem so bad in her hand, more like comforting, the way it fit, the warm ivory matching the smooth curve of her palm as if made for it. Pretty. Gleaming, engraved silver and old ivory. *Like an objet d'art.* "Might take a dollar for it." Handi grunted.

Sary blushed. "I'm—grateful. I can't remunerate you now," and handed it back. Handi fussed with the tray. "Take it, 'fore I lament it. Secure it in your knickers," she barked.

Sary hesitated, then slowly raised her dusty travel-stained skirts, half-turning away. Oh, why hadn't she better petticoats and underthings? Handi eyed her with clinical interest as Sary revealed shapely darned black-stockinged legs, tucking the silvery weight in a petticoat pocket, where it banged, bothersome and alien, on her thigh.

Handi grimaced. "Black scarcely favors you. Get shed of it. Makes you all peaky, like clabbered milk."

"Yes, ma'am. Thank you for your—concern." Sary bobbed a conflicted curtsey, taking one last look at the room and the tea and cakes.

****

Across the street, Seb, to the registrar's open amusement, studied a plat map tacked to log walls. Behind Seb, a balance scale winked a dull gleam and a champion nugget sat in solitary splendor under glass. Map trays and other paraphernalia proclaimed the room to be the Deed and Assay Office. Men still garbed in heavy flannel shirts, thick canvas Levis, and well-worn boots lounged around a crude stove stuck in the fireplace even though it was spring. Others pored over plats. They all were winking behind Seb's back, sharing the diversion the greenhorn provided.

The first niggling glimmer that this enterprise mightn't be as easy as plucking nuggets from the ground slick as eggs from a mad hen flitted uneasily across Seb's brainpan as he scrutinized the staked-out map full of squiggly lines and color. He started when the registrar finger-tapped the map.

"Sure it's this piece right here? Old Elijah—that be Elijah Lucky K. Baldwin—well, he kinda still owns it—still. Though some *do* say our esteemed Mr. Delacorte—that be Julian Delacorte—stakes some claim. Then, Julian Delacorte stakes most all of Big Bear. Including the bears."

An old jest. There was general agreement.

He tittered. "Wouldn't take kindly to it being sold twice"—the registrar winked at the men—"I should opine."

"See here!" Seb felt his cheek flame. "Fella told me it were just laying to waste—for the taking. You bait-and-switchin' me here?" He squinched his eyes and reared back.

"Heaven forefend!" the registrar said. "Wouldn't

try that on a shrewd Jasper like you—tell that right off!"

Seb smirked. "More like it—"

"That what you heard must be so!" The registrar stabbed the plat map. "I hereby give you...let's say..." The registrar pinched his lip. "Claim to the 'Lucky Strike Mine'—provisional, mind you, till we do proper provenances."

"Yeah. What you just said—the provnunces. You do that." Seb tucked his hands under his armpits and rocked back on his heels, self-satisfied.

With a wink over Seb's shoulder, the registrar added, "And I'll toss in this bitty section of creek rights. Might do, to get your feet wet some first."

Seb signed the paper put before him and snatched up the deed. "And I'll jus' be taking this along—case you be thinkin' on changing it some."

****

Safe on the plank walkway, Seb rubbed his hands, chuckling, surveying the raw panners, ranchers, and trappers, all stalking by with some mysterious manly purpose, all in muddy, cracked, flaking gear and of brownish-gray appearance—flannel faded to dun, Levis bleached and dirtied the same, boots scuffed to rawhide—but to Seb, they might as well have been gold-plated. Seb yearned mightily to join their ranks of hardened masculinity.

He ignored the few women scoured plain and reddened by heat, dust, and chilblains, but then he was jostled aside by a flamboyant and chattering tribe distinct in all their peacock colors, fuss, and feathers. He glared, disgusted, after the rowdy noisy bunch. Greasy clownish faces—*too orange to be what nature give 'em, too red in the cheeks and mouth—and is those velvet britches?* "Tchaaa!" Seb spat. Moreover, their females were either booming or trilling. One swatted him with her fan, winking broadly, and the men had a trace of what Seb was dimly aware of...the *Oscar Wilde.*

Seb sneered and shied away as a tall man with long thick brown hair and a spit curl drooping over his forehead like a dad-burned trained cowlick brushed shoulders with him. Had Seb been more literary, he would have recognized the Lord Byron influence, but he did suddenly realize it was the same damned catamite he'd seen in tights on the yeller poster. "Tchaaa!"

Chapter 2

That night, Seb and Sary picked through a plate of limp fried potatoes and greasy fatback Sary wouldn't have fed her dog, back in Indiana. From the crude dining hall, Seb sullenly pushed Sary through the swinging doors of Delacorte's saloon and into an explosion of noise and color.

On a far stage of set-up planks, Sary glimpsed a man in what looked like sagging long johns and a leopard-spotted loincloth, spewing fire from his mouth. The bad dinner forgotten, she clapped her hands. "Oh, look, Seb!"

A battered sign she could barely read, proclaimed:
"Luigi
Dines on Cinders for Breakfast!
and Lava for Luncheon!"

Seb scowled as Sary rose on tiptoes.

Her gaze danced across the room to the far stage. Oh! It was all so cheerful! There were a few other women here, too, in their Sunday best and all curled and corseted, with ribbons and brooches. She wished she had better and was vexed at her vanity.

Best to be modest, even though she would lay down sadness like an old quilt to pick up this new crazy-patch one of bright colors, if only just for now. Just for one last evening.

More cheers. Sary craned to see.

Now it was Strong-Man Caine parading about, all draped in hefty-looking chains. After much plum-faced straining, posturing, and flexing biceps under yellowed sagging cotton, challenging all to test the vigor of his strength, Caine casually dropped the chains in a clanking puddle about his feet, finishing to puzzled but good-natured guffaws. She clapped loudly too.

Seb looked on, sneering.

She ignored him. Seb always had a poor face.

Oh, but wonders! A male midget garbed in a patched-quilt costume bounced on stage, and more women, in fancy dress, lustily emoting. The handsome poster-man, Sary noticed shyly, was all in bottle-green velvet, with lace, and a real crown on his head. She frowned. For some reason the handsome thespian carried a skull.

She risked a glance at her brother. She could just imagine how he viewed the balloon drawers with colored stripes poofed out over—as Seb would say—long johns.

Viewing the muscular legs of the man on stage, Sary twinkled. They were almost as good as hers.

Seb whirled on Sary, shaking her out of her good humor. "Here, now! Satisfied?" He yanked up her already high collar. "Supposed to be mourning!" he carped. "And don't get used to this livin' high on the hog, neither!" Seb scowled out at the crowd, holding her back, hissing, "Scrunch down by the door," as he pulled futilely again at her already modest neckline. "And don't be making a spectacle of yourself!"

"No, Seb." Sary bit back. "I wouldn't be doing that anyways, without your help!" Seb narrowed his eyes, about to say more, but much of the audience had turned toward him, to see what the ruckus was about. Sary moved away, in his inattention, and strained to see and hear above the cheers and stamps before Seb spoiled it all. If only she could regain her cheerful feelings. *I shouldn't have mouthed off.*

Seb calculated the mob—especially the old fart with silvery pomade hair leaning over the gallery above the fray. Delacorte! Seb spat. Julian Delacorte, Mr. High-Muckety-Muck, straightened with effort, once more a king surveying his realm. Seb squinched his eyes, focusing on a huge turnip watch winking out from that fine silvery tailored waistcoat up there. Seb's eyes fixed on other bits of jewelry. A fat gold ring and stick pin with a diamond big as a turkey egg. Mesmerized by the watch, Seb yanked Sary's arm.

"Hold on, Sary. Let's just not be in such a tear here. Reckon it wouldn't hurt none for you to stand on a chair where they—*you*—can see, like."

Sary looked at Seb oddly as he helped her up, turning the chair just so, all while casting feverish glances at the gaunt old man with the face like a long gray dishrag let to dry, up on the gallery. Seb seemed to will the old man watching the crowd from beneath hooded eyes to look their way.

Strangely highlighted in black, Sary was a glistening, iridescent raven in a field of songbirds, the dark dress a foil for her translucent skin and gleaming coiled hair. She'd added a tad of lace and a brooch with a lock of Jonathan's hair, but she could have dressed in flour sacks and still been noticed.

Julian's uninterested regard still roved the crowd, the jaded emperor. He eyed Sary and passed smoothly by, but his gaze kept returning. Beside him, Jules

Delacorte also lounged, a younger, slighter version of Julian—unused to sun, effete and fine-boned—flicking bored glances at the stage. Jules's gaze was caught on the actor's laces and feathers, not Sary, until he noticed his father's focus, and his eyes bored into Sary as if sucking her bones.

****

The play was in fulsome swing. Enraptured, Sary watched the actors' flamboyant flourishes. The stage was her world right then, not Julian Delacorte or Jules or even Seb, who finally left her and wended his way to the bar.

Seb, scowling at the fancy man, mumbled to his drink, "For some reason the popinjay's jabberin' to a skull, while a fat old redhead, bustin' her stays, simpers from under a cockeyed crown, and a dyspeptic old long-bearded fart who looks like he et somethin' tainted wallows in a big chair alongside the redhead. Tchaaa!" The sign read "Hamlet" now.

Seb shook his head, muttering. "Hey Lacy-Drawers. What *you* all tarted up for?" He sneered. Then he recalled Sary. He'd left her alone in the back and now he hotly followed her gaze, admiring the same fancy man he so disdained. He flicked back to the stage. There, Lacy-Drawers shielded his eyes and leered out at the mob.

One more drink. Seb motioned the barkeep, overhearing the actor: "And who shall deign to play my beauteous Ophelia for the night?"

Seb mimicked him, *"An' who shall..."* sourly watching sporting girls and a few ugly ranchers' daughters elbow each other on their stampede to the stage, smirking when Lacy-Drawers fended them off.

The doves swung around, discombobulated, as the actor held his hand out past them.

Seb swiveled too, with hot suspicion, and choked on his drink as the crowd parted for his own sister. *Well, we'll see about that!* Actually, they were dragging her forward, but that didn't matter. He'd put a stop to it. *Seen cats in heat actin' more modest!*

Sary thumbed her wedding band and smoothed her stained dress. Her lips twitched and her eyes, unused to sparkling, lit up. Flustered, laughing and demurring, her black dress billowing, Sary was seemingly levitated by the crowd as it parted in waves before she vanished in their midst and the mob pulled her to the stage. Above, Julian also riveted on the ethereal girl glowing in widow's weeds. Rheumy eyes darkened with interest. He almost seemed alive.

Sary shuddered. *What's that chill...? A goose walked over my grave!* As she passed beneath Julian's presence in the gallery, something compelled her to bend her neck, and her white face looking up was directly below the old man's. Their eyes locked. His cloudy gray marbles, cold, mucous-y...dead. She shivered again—hot—cold—faintheaded—as those rheumy eyes bored into hers. *Must get to the stage—* laughter there, and color and life! Why had this old man shivered her so? She didn't even notice the effete young man named Jules next to him, but she should have.

Plunging forward, Sary grasped sweaty hands, all reaching out. Then she was hauled above the crowd, and someone thrust a sheet of paper at her. Oh! She must read this! And thus Sary became a part of them, this friendly, under their fearsome paint, troupe. The actor, not handsome as she'd first thought, his brown eyes heavily ringed in grease pencil like a raccoon, yet in molten-honey tones emoted: "And you, fair dam-sel shall grace my stage…and my heart." And bowed, sweeping a rather molting cape.

Her face warmed like a flatiron on the stove as the perspiring actor grinned, patting his grease-stained cheek.

"Supposed to buss me here," he invited, waggling his brows as he grabbed Sary's waist.

Sary gave him a shy, self-conscious peck.

He spun at the last minute and thoroughly kissed her mouth. The tip of his tongue and the faint taste of onion and peppermint intruded, sending heat lightning to her toes, but it wasn't unpleasant. It wasn't like when Jonathan had kissed her, strong and filled with urgency but brief. Too brief, oft times, for her liking, if shameful truth be told. She could feel her cheeks warm. She stood in the middle of the stage as seconds passed, unaware of color and sound and sweat and the perfume of the actors around her. In the brief pause as they watched, she reflected his kiss was warm and strong and—and pleasurable in ways she hadn't known, even if it was just—playacting. Still, shocked by the sensation, she almost responded, but he mugged to the crowd, dropped her, backed dramatically, and pointed a finger.

"My Ophelia!" he bellowed. "Get thee to a nunnery! Be thou chaste as ice!" Sary blinked.

The mob stomped and whistled, but then Seb bulled in, red-faced, tripping onto the stage. Halting at the fringe, he leaned far over and stage-whispered, "Sary, get on over here! Git!" and spoiled it all.

Seb finally clambered all the way onto the platform

and snatched at her, but the troupe got in his way, whether by design or happenstance. They tried to include Seb, but it turned to ugly burlesque, making Seb even more the fool. Suddenly aware he was in the spotlight, Seb grinned a sickish grin, bowed clumsily, and stumbled off to the accompaniment of catcalls, alternately dragging and shoving Sary. Above, on the gallery, Julian Delacorte looked on enigmatically.

****

Once outside, Seb hauled off and slapped her, roaring, "Well—*you* sure looked a bitch-dog in heat!" and shook her for emphasis.

Sary pushed him hard, holding back the tears. "Sebastian! I'm a woman married! I'm not a girl, or a—a *whore!*"

Seb leaned in, hissing, "Not any more, you ain't! Till you're properly joined up agin, *I'm* your man." He jabbed his chest, looking her up and down as if she were tainted. "My own sister! Actin' the harlot!"

"Seb. There were other women. Some not as old as me!" Sary protested, but Seb open-handed her cheek again. "Don't give me your sass!"

Sary slapped back, and it rang sharp against the night. She stopped, stunned, then waded in, beating at him with both fists to ward off what surely would be retaliation, but Seb's eyes glowed with strange excitement—it wasn't ire. "Them's my words," he growled in an odd throaty voice. "Don't make me lose my temper. You *know* what I can do."

"Yes, *Se-bastian!*" Sary bit the words as hard as she dared, but stepped back.

"Don't push me with your brazen ways, neither!"

Seb's eyes held that stormy look, as if he would do

anything with no thought as to where he was. Sary averted her face to put out that fire and, yearning to say more, clamped her teeth. *Seb's nervy. Things will be better, once they've settled.*

"No, Seb. No, I won't," Sary said, feeling restless and strange, like before a bad Indiana storm blew through and the air turned green and sulfurous, even though this air was mountain dry. She dawdled down the wood walkway, finally looking back wistfully at the gaiety, light, and laughter faintly trailing her as she returned to Handi's.

Seb had already rejoined the frivolity inside the saloon.

****

That night, fully clothed, Seb and Sary lay back to back in Handi's hostelry bed, as if an invisible board lay between them. Both had bleak faces as they studied the dark.

Chapter 3

At dawn, Sary and Seb rattled out of Big Bear in a weary wagon with scanty new gear, a few hogsheads of salt pork, bags of dried beans and peas, some meal sacks, and their worn baggage.

The rowdy theater troupe also made a grand and exuberant departure in their own gaudy wagon train piled higgledy-piggledy with props and costumes, trunks, plus the midget, with a long plume in his hat, riding a mule.

From an upstairs saloon window, Handi gazed down hard at both of the departing groups.

Sary turned her face, showing a slight bruise, as if she felt her watching, or perhaps just looked back for female kinship.

She waved up, tentatively smiling, and stealthily patted her skirt where the Derringer lay nestled.

Handi closed the curtain. Julian halted her and looked out. His dead eyes warmed.

"Nice piece. Angel on a Christmas tree."

Handi stiffened. "You're worse than Jules."

Julian studied her raddled face in the harsh light.

"We're a long time over, Hannah."

"You made me this way." She squinted at Sary's back. "Already asked her. She'll *beg* to empty my whores' slops jars, once she claws her way through a Big Bear winter."

"Keep your filth off this one."

Handi looked slapped, turning away while Julian tracked Sary until the wagons rounded the feed store across from the stables and disappeared.

****

At a dusty, rocky crossroads, the troupe waved royal goodbyes to Seb and Sary. Tommy, for Sary had learned that was the actor's name, tipped a flashy fedora. *"Ophelia!"* he sang out, and blew her merry kisses.

Sary grinned back, half-standing, and wildly waved, with the oddest urge to just leap out and run to their wagon. She unconsciously brushed her lips recalling the tingle of his touch, and wondered how she would look in the redheaded woman's purple velvet turban with the feather and jewels…

"Owww!" She looked down at a sudden pressure on her knee.

Seb pinched it—hard—nailing her in place.

The actor mugged, "Sorry!" He almost toppled as the wagon jolted on, but laughed uproariously and kissed his hand, waving it at her.

And so the long moment passed. Sary watched until the troupe rounded a bend and became just a cloud of pixie dust, and even watched that as if Tommy might magically appear out of it, as a genie from a fairy tale, the boisterous singing still in her ears—and long after in her mind. She smoothed her black dress as if holding in her emotions. Perhaps it was for the best. She clenched her jaw. She must be a helpmeet, not a naysayer or a loose woman or a flibberty-gibbet.

****

Mesmerized by the mule's patient jog, Sary

nodded, fanning from her nose the thick yellow dust heavy with pine pollen, dully scanning last year's dead weeds lining the trail like children's pickup sticks, and endured the new-hatched swarms of gnats without noticing them anymore. Dust spurting from the rattling wheels coated her face with dun powder. The trail was steeper and less defined now; the mule labored. Sary jolted with the wagon, trying to hang on and stay seated as the iron-rimmed wheels bumped and clanged over a trail that was more rocks than dirt.

She spared a glance at Seb. He too looked tired—or worried. Then…Sary heard an almost joyful sound of rushing, gurgling water, still unseen. They must be close! Seb licked a dry mouth. She hoped he would stop and not mulishly keep on—but Seb flicked reins and the mule spurted ahead. They rounded a bend to come upon a lean man hunkered over a frigid-looking rushing creek. Apparently he was panning. She watched with curiosity.

A thicket of beard covered most of his jaundiced face like a pelt, right up to the man's black watchful eyes. He seemed an animal peering through a hedge. The panner hungrily hawked Sary beneath a shadowed brim, but he held a cocked Colt in mute warning for Seb to just keep on going.

Seb, sunk deep in his denim collar, shrugged nervously. "Reckon—reckon our claim's on down a ways," he muttered, throwing haunted looks back at the man.

Sary looked back, too.

The man with the wide silver pan and deep hat brim still followed her with his shadowed eyes. Sary shivered and shrank down on the plank seat.

****

Later, the sun poured gold honey on their faces, light swallowed beforetime by jagged conifer peaks. As night sucked twilight dry, a scrap of pink bandanna fluttered like a faded flower on a skeleton clump of gorse.

"Calculate this be it," Seb grunted.

Seb was as uneasy as Sary. Why did that give her little comfort? She *must* be a helpmeet—not a Doubting Thomas. Yet as Sary surveyed her new home there was little to give her hope.

Seb attempted to hop from the wagon with vigor, but his knees crumpled as he furtively checked out the cheerless clearing at the edge of a straggly-treed foothill, with the requisite creek running through it.

Chapter 4

A tarp was slung over a tree branch. Sary ducked out of it, holding her back, and looked around, sighing. *We've been here a month, and what have we got?* There was a crude fire pit, and their scant belongings stored and stacked as neatly as Sary could approximate a home. She should wash out her bloomers and petticoat and Seb's mud-caked shirt before dark, she thought, yet there was more important work to be done. She heartened. Stimulating chores this time…the reward for slogging snow-melt streams from dawn till dusk, chafed red hands, and draggled wet skirts.

After a plate of beans, Seb lounged by the fire, blankly watching Sary, sweating, heft a bottle of mercury and start to prepare the copper plates. He called lazily, "Hot enough now for ya, Sary-girl?"

She wiped her face and pulled at the underarms of her shirt in answer. Somehow, Seb couldn't do this. It was delicate, woman's work, he said.

"Tole ya to wear trousers," he continued to harp as she struggled with the awkward plates. "How can ya drag all them skirts around anyways?" he observed.

"I won't give up my skirts. I need something to remember I'm a—a lady." Old arguments. But Sary smiled to take the sting out. No bad feelings tonight. She turned back to the plate. "Sure this is how to do it, Seb?"

"'At's what a man tole me." Seb yawned and leaned closer. "What's 'at yer doin'?"

"If you helped me, you'd know," she snapped—she couldn't help herself—and continued scraping sludge from the completed plate, carefully lifting the hot gold-rich mercury sludge and pouring it into a kettle with a drain.

"You gettin' mouthy?" Seb almost stirred himself and then sank back. "Hunh," he groused. Soon losing interest, Seb dozed in the heat of the enterprise.

Grimly Sary salvaged the hot mercury. Her arms shook as she dropped the heavy kettle, waking Seb up.

****

Later, grinning and shyly triumphant, their faces glowing from heat and fire, Sary and Seb in rare companionship hunkered over a trickle of molten gold spreading out to fill the lozenge-shaped ingot.

Then Seb jumped up and war-whooped a victory strut, crowing, "Didn't I tell ya I'd be rich? Didn't I? Hot *dang!*"

Sary trickled the last of the molten gold into the lozenge. She bit her lip. "Yes, Seb. You did."

****

In Delacorte's saloon, O'Malley trickled gold dust on a small balance.

Julian Delacorte, his gray satin waistcoat matching his slicked-back mane of hair and brocade vest, assessed, nodded, and dealt cards to O'Malley, Ratchet, Orvis, and young Cooley with his flaming acne. Julian winced at Cooley's face. When he turned, something just as distasteful entered his view: The green flatlander riding by on a mule.

But just then Biskits snuck past with a tray, headed

to the gallery stairs, further distracting him—something about it wasn't right—and Delacorte forgot all about Seb.

"Hey, Biskits?"

Biskits grunted.

"Just when do *we* get any a your culinary treats?" Julian gave a laugh, scowling, when Biskits averted his head and continued up without answer.

"Around here, I'm first served!"

Biskits nodded, fearful, hunching a shoulder up. "Pearl. And—and, with *Jules*." He studied the tray. Looked anywhere but at Julian.

Delacorte brushed past, up the stairs. Ratchet, smirking, re-arranged his lanky body and followed, lounging outside the room of masculine opulence Julian had just entered, where a bronze sun seeped through drapes muddying the bright day outside.

****

Biskits stepped in with the tray, all eyes.

Pearl, a battered dove with a torn chemise, was dimly seen huddled in a corner behind the bed curtains, whimpering and mewling. "Mr. Julian, sir…?" She began to crawl to him across the coverlets.

Julian snatched the tray, glaring Biskits out. He spied Ratchet, lurking outside the door and hissed, "Fuck off! He catches this filth from you!" And kicked the door closed.

Ratchet called from the hall, "Can't catch the contagion if you already suffered the bite, Delacorte! Jules don't scratch the itch," he singsonged. "Neither do you when you need tidying up."

Julian grunted under his breath, "And who has ta carbolic the place after?"

Pearl whimpered as Ratchet's laughter echoed down the hall.

Julian spun to Jules, who wore an olive-green silk robe embroidered with dragons and poppies, and seemed oblivious to the commotion. He sagged when he saw his son consumed with heating a knife blade in a candle flame, while young Pearl, bearing spade-shaped burns on her arms, still mewled and rolled her eyes at Julian like a frightened colt.

Julian sat on the bed, earning a frown from Jules, and calmly went through an elaborate cigar-lighting ritual, ignoring the other two. He eventually murmured, studying the end of his cigar, "Jules? You are gainfully employed. And what is this in aid of?"

Jules turned eagerly. "Gonna show Pearl a good time, Dad!"

Julian blandly examined one of Biskits' sandwiches—delicate slabs of ham and bread with trimmed crusts. A small wildflower lay by the side. "Asked Pearl?"

Jules ignored him and sulkily turned to Pearl, who backed to the headboard of the bed, giving little mews of distress. Julian laid down the sandwich. Taking cards from his waistcoat, he riffled and cut, apparently unconcerned by the happenings on the bed.

Jules reacted in irritation at the distraction.

"Play you for her, Son."

Jules looked from Julian to Pearl, intrigued, but—"No."

Julian snapped the cards. "What'll it be? Five out of five? Loser takes the new stallion. That *black* stallion. Winner takes Pearl."

Jules's eyes glittered like the onyx ring he sported.

"One you said I cain't ride, less the devil was my stable hand?"

"The very one."

Jules dropped the knife. The bedspread smoked.

Julian palmed the scorch and laid out the cards.

Jules fiercely concentrated, and eagerly lost game after game.

Julian finally gathered the cards. "Now, I believe a *true* gentleman—a cultured gentleman—unties Pearl and honors his wager, Son. Give me the knife."

Jules looked stunned as he deciphered his father's stratagem—his trickery. Pushing his lower lip out, he threw a sulky nod at Pearl. "But can I still have a good time?"

Julian wagged his finger. "No bruises. Not around the face. Customers don't like their doxies used-looking."

"Those ruffians wouldn't recognize a whore from a slag-heap," Jules mumbled.

"Get that way soon enough without our help," Julian rejoined with a faraway look.

Jules sighed and handed over the knife. Julian froze halfway to the hall when his son murmured slyly, "I saw you eyeing that girl the other day, eyes green as my jade stick pin. Awfully fetching. She wasn't a slag yet"—he paused delicately—"either." Sliding a glistening eye toward his father, he giggled, tongued a slice of ham, and rolled over to Pearl. "Now, where were we?'

Once Pearl saw Julian was not going to remove her from Jules' presence, she tried to jolly Jules by smiling and adjusting her petticoat.

Jules offered Pearl the wildflower from the tray

and kissed her cringing toes. Pearl ventured hopefully as he reached the door, "Mr. Delacorte…sir?"

However, Julian was already in the hall, flipping the knife to Ratchet.

"Yours, I believe. Ya lost this one." Julian brushed past.

"That boy could use a little roughing up." Ratchet displayed lupine teeth and hung on to Julian's arm. "What ya pay me for."

Julian flung him off. "Off the payroll."

"He needs to know how to treat women." Ratchet's words were calm, but his eyes gleamed wet. He subconsciously licked his lips.

Julian looked off. "Not from you, he don't."

Ratchet cackled, tucking the knife into his belt with a flick of his rangy wrist. "Too late, Julian. Your boy's a pure-born natural."

Julian started to reply but then swiveled at a thud of boots and laughter exploding from below.

"What in thunder's going on now?" He peered over the gallery and his lip twitched, releasing the tension. Seb, the greenhorn peeling bills off a roll, stood in the midst of a ring of men, and Delacorte's liquor flowed.

Chapter 5

Sary could hear Seb from the campsite, not that she hadn't been listening, one ear cocked against the rattle of pines and howl of wind between the rocks. Seb's faint voice! She gathered skirts and raced, stumbling in the dark, up the rise overlooking more dwindling ranges of peaky forests, and there was Seb, drunkenly caterwauling, leading the mule and riding a scrawny horse.

As they approached. Sary ran alongside and called up to him in excitement. Catching the horse's mane, she distractedly scanned the animal while searching saddlebags. "Did it assay? How'd it assay out, Seb?"

Wearing a flash new hat, Seb slid off, flicking a new whip. "Feller at assayer's tried ta gyp me. Said it was so puny he had to haul out his false eyes." He chortled.

Sary jumped back, avoiding Seb's random whip flicks. "But you got something? They gave you something?" Sary still grinned, as Seb wavered about, lashing his whip. "Assay fella was goggle-eyed. He says to me, 'Plague take it! Where you get this at?' "

"I said, 'Why, a place you told me warn't enough gold to stick in your jaw.' "

"He says it warn't much, but pretty dang pure!"

Sary distractedly lifted and prodded the mule's saddlebags. "Anybody hear you, Seb?"

"He'll keep shut. Tighter'n a hen's egg-chute."

"But—you didn't go in the saloon?" Sary rummaged the horse, increasingly frantic.

Seb looked to the fire. "Maybe told a few folks."

She ran to the other side of the mule, tugging and unbuckling straps. "Meal? Seb? The flour! Where's the provisions? Beans, at least! Seb!" Sary finally screamed.

Seb aimed for his bedroll.

"Already et," he mumbled, flopping down.

She tugged the saddlebags off the horse—*nothing*—and spun, snatched the whip but ran up and kicked his backside instead. "Damnation, Seb! Hell's bells! Six months for a dead horse! What do we do? Eat it?"

Seb rubbed his backside and rolled over, petulant. "No respect, man don't own a horse." Squinting at Sary, his eyes shifting as though she wavered in his vision, he slurred, "Ain't purtiest star in the firma-ment, Sary Swinford. Still, men'd pay hard eagles for what you got." He sank back. "Wha' a fancy feller told me."

Sary cracked the whip. Splitting the air, it sang out her anger. "Did he also tell you what we *eat* this winter?"

Seb still gaped bright-eyed at her like he'd seen a vision, ignoring the whip. "Hey! 'At's right. 'At's right. I could be a fancy man steada lookin' after you. God-dang it, Sary. You're a God-danged anvil round my neck. I'd be somebody—*make* somethin' of myself— weren't for you, by gawd!" He swiped his nose. "Maybe it's *my* turn." And he peered blearily at the fire and spoke as though remembering. "Fellow at a saloon don't guzzle scag-end beer. Aged whiskey! Rum! Alla way from Carri-be-an."

Seb sniffed himself, wrinkling his nose. "Stunk good, too!"

"That would be a treat!"

Seb scratched under his arm, tracking Sary. "You mouthing off?" He sucked a tooth. "Peculiar, ain't it? I'm slavin' away, and all you'd hafta do is wallow in some big ole feather bed."

"What!" Sary scrambled for a branch.

Seb snaked up, darting for the whip faster than she thought possible, but he tripped, tangled with it, fell over, and wrenched the branch away instead.

"Stop it, don't, Seb!" Sary flinched, holding her arms up, and waited for the blow.

He grinned, instead poking her with the branch. They tussled, circling the fire until she was dizzy; Seb leaned over and retched, losing all the Big Bear whiskey he'd treated himself with. He looked up with mean eyes. "You know what's between the kivers! He's dead and molderin', but you sure ain't!" He stopped, swaying, distracted by Sary's bosom blooming between torn buttons of his shirt. *His shirt, by gawd!* He finally slung the branch on the fire.

Sary, shaken, breathing hard, took up her book—she had been re-reading *Æsop's Fables*—and tried to sit calmly by the light of the fire.

She ignored him. Ignored her hunger. Scarcely felt anything but an odd cold fear dropped like an icicle down her neck.

Seb scowled and tossed pebbles at her, whining, "Dagnab it, Sary."

Chapter 6

Sary strode by boulders tall as a man on her way to the creek. *Strange furniture.* At first, the rocks had seemed as if she lived in an airy, half-ruined castle. Those fanciful days were long gone. She hardly felt like a princess, or looked like one, now. Back in Indiana the cornstalks would just be turning from vibrant green to the first dulling wither, from juicy sweet corn to field corn fodder.

Now cold rain bucketed down, and the rocks became misty nuisances she must navigate to perform the simplest chore.

She'd bolted last night's biscuits with a mug of precious coffee before it cooled. Seb would be impatient, calling for her. Wouldn't do if he actually roused himself and worked till she got there. The rain had ceased for now, a small blessing.

As she scoured a pot with gravel, she eyed their scant foodstuffs that had seemed so wastefully bountiful at the beginning. A long way to Big Bear and a short way through their coin. Up at dawn—no change there from the farm, but now she must crouch by a creek, trying to keep heavy dragging skirts from the icy mountain runoff, calf muscles stiffened with ague like an old arthritic farmer's wife—the constant dipping, swirling, searching, bending…

She grimaced, checking her long fingers, no longer

expecting the cleaned, trimmed nails of before. Her hands were scraped raw, worse than when she'd husked and shelled corn.

Oh, do shush up, Sary! Seb's right. She heartened. *Haven't we already scooped up some of that fairytale dust from the water? Months ago, though.* Duller than supposed, yet glinting with the promise of dreams, she thought, as she thrust through the last of the undergrowth, stoically tucking up her skirt. Maybe today. Sary watched Seb shovel grit into the sluice, obsessively sorting the lower cleats, before she entered the chill rushing creek. Seb was already on the near side. She had to cross to the other.

Halfway there, her skirts came undone, and she dragged sodden layers of petticoats clammily slapping her ankles to the other side. He scowled over as she rolled her sleeves.

"Yes, yes, Sebastian. Here now. Someone needs to red up camp."

"Always house-proud, you women. Find us some gold, you can build you ten houses," he sneered. They hadn't found a salt-grain of gold in two months. An hour later, Sary still uselessly panned with fingers so numbed they were one with the metal. The water was still bone-cold from rain and early snowmelt. Even Seb floundered, shivering, wet to the waist. Sary hid a grin. Seb fell on his backside into the creek. No doubt giving him leave to sit by the fire and dry off.

****

Sary arched her back wearily, eyeing the dry weedy bank. *Hard to believe after all the cold rain of a few weeks ago.* The earth blotted up moisture like cornstarch, and the creek itself was a lazy trickle, with broad islands of bone-dry stone alive with lizards baking in the sun. The sluice box, a narrow chute with ridges to separate gold from gravel, still squatted by the creek. She squinted at the sun—closer here in the mountains. Back home, the sun would be shimmering through layers of Indiana humidity. The last of the ears of corn on the stalk would be hard as bullets for the cows to graze on, and the leaves brittle. Harvesting soon, but that brought back pictures of Jonathan. Sary waded to pan the opposite side in nothing but her chemise, pantaloons, and petticoats, already sweating under Seb's critically judging scowl and odd secret looks.

"Gold's heavier!" Seb sorted and flung gravel as Sary bent, dipped, scooped, swirled, and flung, and bent again. His exclamation broke into her musings. Jonathan, she thought with a stone chill, was fading. Were his eyes blue or—?

And the new day started stretching till dusk—at least for her.

"Yes, Seb." *Maybe he'll hush.* Forlorn hope.

Seb slung his pan. "Stays on the bottom like a God-damned carp!"

Holding sodden skirts, Sary once again dipped her large round pan, aware Seb still judged as she shook it in searching circles.

"Gets caught in slow-movin' spots. Around bends. Along the shore!" He stopped, eyeing her meanly. "Dang it! Sary, are you deef? Swirl it!"

Sary swirled harder. "Easy as plowing fields. Said that, Seb." He was more intractable as the profitless days ground on.

He waded over and knocked her in. She sat hard in

the gravel. "That hurt, Seb!" Water rushed over her legs and splashed her chemise. Seb looked down at her, raging. She covered her wet chemise; it was distressingly sheer, but Seb seemed beyond that. "Shakin' it too rough! Losin' half the gold!" He grabbed her pan. "Tip to the side where the dang riffles are! Just keep doing that—Christ, yer thick! No wonder we ain't having any luck!" Seb clenched his fist and swayed there, rocked by the water, just staring. Finally, he looked away befuddled and splashed to the bank. Sary shakily stood and wrung out her petticoats, limping to the shore. At least he was leaving.

"Goin' for a smoke," Seb announced. "You just keep—*practicin'*." Sary waited till he was gone and picked up the pan.

"Yes, Seb, and a solid gold nugget's going to hop right down my corset stays," Sary muttered sitting on the bank. "And if that occasion does occur, you'll see my apron strings."

Chapter 7

The creek was a narrow corrugated ribbon now, meandering past gravel bars and broad islands of scalding rock. Days stretched under drought, the air thick, choking and mustard-yellow with pine-pollen haze. Both Sary and Seb grew leaner, browner, like fall leaves. Her eyes were lighter, like clear water in her tanned face, and her red-blonde hair paled to the gold they were seeking. Back home the musky grapes would be sweetly harsh going down, and fulsome ripe, and it would be harvest time, she mused. Sweet October.

Seb idled more and more betwixt manic harmonica playing, morose whittling, or vanishing for long stretches in the woods, returning mostly empty-handed.

Their flour sacks hung limp. The hogsheads rolled empty. Bleakly Sary stirred a pot.

"Where's 'em biscuits at, lazybones?"

"Soon, Seb." She muttered, *"Biscuits!"* Then louder said, "Sebastian? Why not play us a tune?" Sary smiled bitterly, throwing him a dark look. "While you're waiting."

Seb perked up at any hint of slander. "Had your nose in them books again, didn't ya! Man quits work, he's hungry."

"Work! Who scrounges greens and…and—oh, never mind."

Seb flopped back, sucking a tooth. "What ya see in

41

them dry dead things?"

Sary paused from stirring the bilious greens and chickpeas and lighted up like a Christmas cathedral. She laid down her spoon, *seeing* it. "Oh, Seb! It's like walkin' through a door into this rich world! Europe's all gold and pretties and fancy things!" She looked down at the broth, seeing the lagoons of Venice instead, in the steaming green depths.

"Seb?" she mused. "There's this place in Italy where houses float on water and long skinny boats takes you everywhere you want to go. Imagine!"

"Don't get much plowing done then, I reckon." Seb too casually sauntered to Sary's things, rummaging. "Need more fire."

He picked up a book, thumbing it. Sary stared at him. *What's he up to now?*

"I-dylls of the King. By Alfred Lord Tenny-son. Well ain't he a swell! This one a them *European* books?" Seb ripped pages out and tossed them in an agonizingly slow motion, into the flame. Sary froze as he chucked the whole book in. Frozen, she watched the colored cover picture brown. "Keep your mind on your knittin' now."

Sary scrambled too late. Grief-stricken, she raked the scorched book out, sucking her fingers.

Seb scratched his jaw reflectively. "Scrapple. Turnin' winter soon. Now, think I'd like me a mess a scrapple."

"Need pork for scrapple," Sary hissed. "We'll be gnawing barrel staves next, and the meal?" Sary thrust a tin under his nose. Weevils writhed in a scant inch of corn meal. He batted it away, twisting his face.

"You could hunt!" She pressed hands to her breast

in frustration. "Or teach me!"

Seb sniggered. "Learn you to shoot? Like I'd trust a *female* with a gun. Hunh!"

Sary gripped Handi's pistol beneath her skirts, resisting the temptation to shoot Seb's toes off. Seb would just sell the comforting weight she'd grown used to bumping against her thigh, if he knew of its existence.

Sheepish, Seb picked up his harmonica and brassily ripped scales, swung into "Camptown racetrack five miles long, doo dah, doo…" and then slid into a jig: "Put your little foot, put your little foot, put you little foot right down…"

Sary couldn't help tapping her feet. Then, grin flashing, she whirled about the fire pit faster, *faster* as Seb played more manically, watching his sister with green fire in her eyes twirl about, all blurring skirts and flashing ankles.

Sary finally staggered, giggling, out of breath. Somehow, she hadn't the stamina of old. The cooking pot flew as she bumped into it, spraying chickpeas and broth.

"Oh, no!" Sary dropped to her knees, scooping peas back into the pot. "Broth's all gone. Oh, sugar! Seb *look* what you made me do!"

Later, the two morosely picked at their plates.

Every now and then, Sary plucked a pebble out of her mouth.

How long can we go on? Seb's so pigheaded stubborn he will never admit failure. Yet Seb always had a scheme or two. His eyes followed her everywhere now. It made her uneasy without kenning why. She looked at the trees pressing round. *Is this my life?*

Chapter 8

Snow spit spitefully and pine needles that had turned brittle skittered across the top. The leanto had a tarp flap now, with rocks piled along the sides and a marginally better firepit. Sary pottered about, leaning into each step, wearily picking up a dishtowel—a rag really, but made for a hope chest a lifetime ago—wedged between rocks.

A dried bit of corn cake dropped out.

They eyed each other and dived, fighting, clawing for it.

Seb triumphantly gnawed it down.

Sary retreated to the small fire. *Oh, my stomach is too friendly with my backbone.* She shook herself, muttering. "Hot water. Maybe won't feel s' hungry."

Seb, now hunkered in a quilt by the fire, didn't stir himself. Shivering, Sary dragged herself up, grabbed the bucket, and headed to the ice-plated creek, where she smashed the ice, dragging the bucket through the water.

In the gloaming, bright color flashed, surreal in the dun and gray-green background, catching her eye, and a vision appeared. Handi, stuffed in a lavishly fur-trimmed purple habit, rode down from the knoll on a shining, supple-flanked horse, sitting an elegant sidesaddle.

She watched Sary without moving. Then, with a

contemptuous flick of reins, Handi was gone. Sary, shivering in her drooping, shapeless dress and sagging petticoats, with a holey shawl wrapped tight around hunched shoulders, gaped after her. She stumbled back, pale cheeks flaring red, water sloshing, to Seb hunched over the fire. Skidding short of drenching him, she plunked the bucket down.

Seb moved fastidiously aside, annoyed at the splashes on his breeches. "'At's cold, Sary!"

"How long, Sebastian? How long are we going to last?"

"Do I have a fortuneteller cape on? Do I have one a them big pointy hats with stars all over? Hell's fire and spare the matches, Sary. How do I know *when?*"

Seb rubbed his toes, pouting up from the corner of his face. When he did look at her, it was through eyes rimmed red, and Sary was shocked at how sunken they were. Seb looked right through her, then narrowed pink watery eyes. "I tole you. While there's gristle still on the bone." He said, desperate-sounding, "That old man! He's important, Sary."

Seb smirked with his old fire, settling back with arms behind his head, and nodded knowingly. "You jumped the broom for love, Sary girl." He made a dirty gesture. "Now do it for cold hard *cash.*"

"Se-bastian. *What* old man?"

"*That* old man! I seen him. Eyes pecking you all over like crows in a cornfield." Scandalized, he jabbed his finger. "I seen *you* lookin' up at *him,* too." He nodded vigorous, pointing. "That time! That *time!*"

Sary gaped. *That old man! The one in the saloon.* So, *that* was brother's grand scheme. Her inner eye cringed from the one occasion she'd beheld the old

45

ruin. *Dragged-down jowls, corded neck, crevices grizzled with bristle, eyes cold as greasy dishwater sunken under bony brows, and a skeletal body, as if the elegant coat drooped on coat hangers, his back all hunched and shattered with coughing... Uhgggn!* She shivered involuntary.

Worst of all, Sary recalled the bony hinges on those long spatulate fingers, horn-nailed, thick with yellow crust, gripping the gallery that night, no matter how big the diamond in the massive gold ring glittering from his arthritic little finger.

Sary's stomach roiled as she tightened her shawl, spun, and ran until she was leaping, stumbling over rock and scrub. In the end, heaving, gasping, she rotated in place, scanning for a breach in the horizon and seeing only a solid fortress of trees—everlasting *trees,* not full-leafed and warmly green, but dull, spiky, and harsh. No place to go—to hide, to *flee!* The ranges and peaks forming her prison, so distant when first she and Seb arrived at this place, crept closer every night until a jagged wall encircled like a warden's arms, cordoning Sary from life itself in this land of suffocating pitfalls and preternatural nightfall, where unseen animals snuffled, yowling and rarely seen— *"Abandon all hope..."* She squinted past the ranges.

Long, barren seasons stretched ahead with not a solitary soul but Seb to talk with...no other womenfolk, not a scrap left unread. She had hidden a few books, but varmints got to them, leaving a Morse code of chewed-up words. The way out was barred by Seb until her heart froze over, icebound as the creek, and her spirit and body were skeleton-thin as the bleak-to-the-bone seasons while the two of them plummeted to lunacy.

What youth was left her would be sucked dry in the desiccated air, like brittle parchment, her body to become as insubstantial as a dandelion thistle, thanks to her brother's vainglorious dreams.

Chill tears tickled her neck. She didn't even know when the joyous, lifting spirit of Christmas might be, she thought. She started up again. Frantic this time.

Sary gasped to a halt, crouching, exhausted, way beyond the creek, even beyond the knoll and the farthest safe edge of her existence. She shuddered, clutching the shawl about her dress, the one with the torn sleeve. Her warmest. Thick wool plaid taken out for festive holidays...*with Jonathan. Cornhusking, Thanksgiving barn dances with chaff flying and feet bouncing...the heat of dancers' smiles, bright colors... cider and rich wild-persimmon pudding singing in her veins...*

She focused, vainly seeking a light out there in the unrelieved wall of mountains. All was flinty gray-green, dun, and bone-white, suffocated in an everlasting purple haze.

She wandered back to the creek. It was full dark. Stars glittered off black water like winking eyes. *Can't go back. Not yet.* Suddenly, her fingers fumbled buttons. They wouldn't work. She ripped the bedraggled dress down the front, finding it too soiled and scratchy to bear against her flesh, as if by shedding this dirty garment she could toss away the shackles of wilderness, hunger, hopelessness, and grinding boredom. Then, hunkering naked, she eased into the creek, relishing the bite of acid-chill water on her bare fanny.

She laid her body full-length, allowing the stream

to sluice over her, around her breasts, flensing her with frigid sterility until icy shock numbed her heart. Maybe it would stop beating and she would lie there in a watery grave, clean and pure, and be taken straight up to Jonathan in a chilly rapture. She sat up, suddenly scared, and grabbed a handful of gravel, with which she scrubbed her flesh—*hard.*

She wanted to hurt, to *feel* something!

Stupid—stupid!

Seb had cut wounds of remembrance as open as the day Jonathan died. For a moment, Sary glowed with remembrance, once more warmed—*gilded by late afternoon sun, slanting through blowing curtains.*

Lately she had revisited this bedroom more and more. This time, *piercing spring corn waved green susurrations through curtains newly starched and blued with Argo, over Sary and Jonathan's bare flushed skin. His rough legs sliding against her silky smooth ones. The weight of his body…The urgent completion…hot, lingering kisses, fervent whispers, and the soft chuckles after.*

She blinked awake.

It was only the evil ripple of black water whispering cold nothings. Goose flesh prickled her arms. Yet it wasn't that that numbed her. She *heard* something. A crack of wood, the death-rattle of weeds as she whispered, *"Jonathan…"* Tensing at a sound, she covered her breasts.

A figure stood mute.

For a moment, she felt as if Jonathan had formed a fleshly shadow to re-materialize…saving her.

No, not Jonathan. Too short. She scrambled out, shocked anew by the wind whipping her limbs, and jammed her cold slippery body into her petticoats, the briar-like dress sticking to her flesh with barbs of wool.

And then Seb slowly swayed into the moonlight, his eyes queer and glittery as the creek and somehow *nearer*—silent, except for his odd breathing.

She edged past, clutching her gown closed. "Seb?"

He shot his arm straight sideways, blocking, dipping his head to hers, nuzzling her hair, as she stood rigid and confused. "Seb! What are you doing?" She shook, and her teeth chattered. This was her *brother*...pigheaded, lazy, and *wrong. He's my brother!*

Seb rubbed her arm, softly at first.

"Don't. Don't!" Sary eased away, fumbling to close the buttons of her wet gown, though they persistently kept sticking and she got them all crossways.

For long seconds Seb's white face with the deep, haunted, shadowed eyes followed her. Then he faded into the trees, his faint words floating back, *"I don't know..."*

****

Sary, in the same dress, boots half-buttoned, bound with her thickest shawl, recklessly yanked the horse and a small carpetbag through snow-scrub to the highest ridge west of camp; stumbling at the brink, she scrutinized the same distant endless layers of gray, filtered with moon mist.

How did we get here? How the Hades did we get here! Seb was always promising a trek down to Big Bear and its bleak amenities, if even for a spell, but always there was some excuse—the horse was lame, wait till the weather cleared, he was feeling poorly that morning. When they found a few more slippery flashes

49

of gold in the creek, he slipped off by himself. The months evaporated.

Their sketchy wagon trail was overgrown. Open patches between brush and fallen limbs could be a true path or meander into dead ends on a precipice. She could wander hours—days—lost and starving till she and the horse dropped in their traces, hoping she'd glimpse some spark in the wilderness, *some* glimmer of another living creature heralded by campfire, a lantern, smoke. All was black like a wall two inches before her nose, dense and secretive. All she knew was she must get away. Which way was that God-forsaken outpost of Big Bear? Vaguely north, she thought, looking in vain for the North Star, recalling they'd veered off-trail after coming across the panner—didn't they? Seb had forged the mule through close-set pine, following the sound of water, before they found that bandanna scrap. Laughing bitterly, recalling how green she was and how she'd feared bears, she paid more heed to the underbrush than to her surroundings. She would almost welcome a bear now as another living creature.

The horse balked. Its knees stiffened. Sary looked down, aghast.

Her toes were two inches from a steep drop. As the moon sailed beyond a cloud, she made out a thin ledge about three feet below. In the next pass of the moon, she saw another shelf, like a stair step, and perhaps a gentle descent beyond?

She yanked the horse's unyielding scrawniness. "Come on! Move!"

The horse dug hooves at the brink, threatening to jack-knife itself over, when, from out of nowhere, Seb whacked the horse's legs. *Seb!* The horse staggered to its knees.

Sary sagged. *But Seb was asleep. And I was so careful.*

Seb jerked Sary, bending her out into space. Yanking her back, he screamed against the wind into her face. "Know what they do with horse thieves? Twenty-five miles to the next train halt! Big Bear? In the dark? Hah! And you ain't got no where-with-all. Don't see how you're gettin' where you're goin', sister-mine. Skinny crow bait. That's what! Couldn't last the night."

He stopped, heaving and murderous—*and scared,* she saw—and hauled his hand back.

****

Seb looked down, stunned, his hand still poised for the stinging blow to her face, where Sary huge-eyed but determined, steadied Handi's pistol against his midriff. Seb chuckled shakily. "And where'd ya get *that* fancy little gewgaw?" He walked into it, pressing his belly hard against the tiny cold muzzle, grinning down at her.

Sary's hand shook. *How did things get this far?*

"Here." Seb didn't fail to read her hesitation and snickered, cricking his neck—and grinding her gun-hand up, he dug the Derringer deep in his own jugular.

"Stop it!" She twisted her hand.

"Or here!" Seb sniggered, unrelenting, forcing her fist clutching the tiny pistol grip to the other side of his neck. He seemed to have regained his backbone if not his imagination. She could kill him if he didn't stop!

"Blood gushes good from the neck. Have to step back lively, though." He giggled and wrested the gun to his temple, grinning from shadowed pits of eyes. His head blotted out the moon, with a pale blue corona about his unreadable face.

"Or here," he breathed hoarsely drawing the misery out. "Nice—big—black—hole. Brains just *ooze* out," he whispered, "like long—bloody—worms." He gripped her chin with his other hand, forcing her head back. She couldn't speak.

"Bone chips'll spatter, stickin' all over your purty face."

Seb released her and slid her gun hand down to his belly, pressing the barrel into it, as Sary struggled to regain control. *How can Seb be so strong? He doesn't do anything!*

"Or here," Seb whispered intimately in her ear. "Gut shot. Ever seen a man gut-shot? Oh, the pain…! Guts just pop out, all coiled up in there—"

Sary gagged. "Stop! Don't, Seb! It's enough!" But it wasn't. She recalled Seb's jests and teasing always were one or twenty steps too far to be funny or clever. He wouldn't stop. She remembered the tickling sessions as children, when she supposed she would faint. The rodents and dead snakes in her underthings, in her drawers. "Just leave me alone!" Sary cried out, wrenching the gun free.

He'll end up killing himself or me, she had time to think, when a shot blasted the night and Seb's mouth formed a hurt O.

He stared down at the toy-like gun Sary still held, his expression almost comical, and grabbed his side. His hand came away all bloody. He snatched at the Derringer with hands so slick they slid off, and he tottered back, with a wounded look. His hand drizzling red, fingered a bloody kiss on her mouth before he theatrically slumped to his knees and toppled at her feet.

As she watched Seb drop, howling, making a great fuss, Sary smeared her lips dry with the back of her hand. "Help me, Sary," he whined.

****

By the fire's light, Sary roughly daubed a raw streak that glanced across Seb's ribs, while Seb moaned, casting mournful looks.

"Hurt me, Sary," he whined.

She almost replied, aware he watched with a calculating hangdog look. Sary mutely wiped the wound, binding it with a scrap of old petticoat.

"Thank your lucky stars I ain't dead," Seb prodded.

Sary roughly smoothed his shirt down. "You're not dead—not even hurt—but it was a fool-headed thing!" And, later, she told him, "You shouldn't press me, Seb."

Seb awkwardly patted her shoulder. "Won me a hand a whiles back, Sary. Squirreled away. It's yourn. Take it, or however much you need. But not too much," he mumbled. "And we *ain't* going back."

****

Seb wended their horse down the mountain next dawn—the right trail commenced just beyond a dead branch Sary noted that looked mighty like a resting squirrel—to the outpost of Big Bear City. Sary kept her eyes peeled, scribing each twist and turn in her head, every odd-shaped boulder and lightning-struck conifer, cursing herself for being starry-eyed and woolgathering on her maiden trip to the camp when all was new and filled with wonder, either for good or ill. She'd remember it all, and just maybe she could escape.

Chapter 9

Big Bear City. As Sary and Seb rode in, Jules watched the world pass, with a bit of the "Emperor" his father owned, from his usual place of eminence on the veranda, fronting two sides of his father's saloon. Bored. Listless. Usually bad news for Pearl, or one of the other "slags."

His lizard eyes flickered mild interest over the weak spectacle of two flatlanders riding in on a horse he wouldn't feed his hounds. His eyes flared like dying stars as he watched Seb hand a wallet over his shoulder to the too-thin-for-his-taste girl, he who liked their flesh plump and moist, mottled with bruises like over-bloomed roses. Still—his gaze traveled her lithe figure. Her hair was rough, and her dress hung from her shoulders, with the small points of breast moving gently beneath, he fancied like small warm kittens—still there was a vulnerable beauty in the pure-honed features and long neck…and those huge eyes, like water sparkling from the sunburned face.

"And don't be spendin' it like you're a danged Carnegie!" he heard the weak man carp. The girl said something back that Jules couldn't catch.

"'Course not, Seb. Only what we need." Sary muttered under her breath, *"Everything!"*

Sullenly, Seb hitched the mount at the saloon post, hawking his sister as she rushed to the nearest mercantile. Finally he wiped his mouth and clomped up the steps, stopping dead at the top.

That odd cuss Jules just sits there, grinning like a fool. Seb was aware too of a hulk of a man tilted in a chair beside Jules, but next to Jules's eerie presence, he was a mere cipher. *A big barn with nothin' much ta stable.* Seb snickered to himself, uncomfortably aware the big man's—*the buffalo's*—feet stuck out, blocking his dignified way. With cold sweat tickling his back, Seb calculated he needed to go past Jules, and he needed to piss. Seb wavered, already committed, one foot raised to reach the step.

Jules giggled as Ev'ret stuck out an anvil-sized boot and played foot games with Seb.

Seb wobbled. *Lordy, I want to avoid the pair of them.*

Jules smirked wider at the hick grinning sickishly as he hopscotched over Ev'ret's feet darting in and out. Finally tripping, the clumsy oaf bowed himself into the saloon. Jules smirked again and sighed, boredom once again descending.

Ev'ret, Jules's new, huge, dumb-as-a-plank, goon/bodyguard, zealously watched everything Jules did, to Jules' annoyance, including Sary as she crossed the road, for Jules recalled her name now.

Jules was not alone. His father also hawked her from his bedroom window.

As Julian slicked his hair, his yellow-toothed grin drew neck wattles in strings of flesh up from a starched collar. He tugged his new velvet waistcoat, straight from Chicago via the train to Redlands at the foot of Big Bear Mountain. He slapped his jowls till they stung, checked himself in the mirror, and glanced once more out the watery panes before leaving. Feeling foolish and denied, Julian ducked back.

Jules and Ev'ret tracked the Swinford girl as she walked into view from under the saloon veranda…*his angel on a Christmas tree.*

****

Jules slammed back into Ev'ret, who dogged him as close as a coat of paint. Ev'ret, rooted like a rock, rubbed his chest, sulking as Jules snarled, pushing at him. It was like shoving the horse *and* the wagon. "Don't you bathe? Soap? Stay away from me! And where the hell's Ratchet, anyways?"

"Un-hunh." Ev'ret vigorously shook his head. "Julian said—"

"*Mister* Delacorte to you!"

Ev'ret breathed though his mouth. "Yah. Julian says, stick to you like plaster on a saint. Like plaster on a…" Ev'ret blinked.

Jules skimmed past him while he ruminated and was already strolling into the mercantile after that female by the time Ev'ret lumbered after. He looked like an ox pulling a cart.

****

Inside Delacorte's, Seb thumped the bar, seeking attention. One or two drinkers glanced over, but the joint was disappointingly empty, with only three card players.

Seb sniggered.

"My woman's gonna buy store out over yonder," he tried.

Men mocked with their eyes.

"Doncha know!"

The men went back to their cards.

His neck grew red as a turkey wattle. "Gotta watch her ever' minute. Man, can she siphon my money. Barkeep!" Seb rapped again. "That stuff you keep under the bar!" Seb morosely sipped alone. *Hadn't been so durn big-hearted, spoilin' Sary, he woulda had enough to buy a round. She'll pay! By gum, she'll pay.* He raked the bar under his eyebrows for Delacorte, half-fearful, half in hope.

Glory be! The Great Man himself nodded Seb over.

Seb gestured, "Who me?" and swaggered big to Julian.

****

In the mercantile, Jules fitted on Homburgs and Trilbys imported from England especially for him, if he cared, tracking Sary in a hand mirror while Ev'ret hovered over a hard-candy bin.

Sary breathed the store in. It was scantily stocked, but wide in variety, from laces and dress goods to tobacco and harnesses, but it seemed like Paris and Rome and even London, like in that Dickens book. She sucked in scents of cloves and peppermint and sage before absorbing color, patterns, and occasional flashes of mirrors and cheap trinkets among the odd kitchen ladle. She roamed, happily oblivious of watchers, holding up ribbons of satin and grosgrain, fingering cheap lace collars, and thrilling over brassy bits of jewelry. Eventually she dawdled to the L-shaped counter where a proprietor intent on toting bills sucked a pickle and cast nervous flickers at Jules.

Sary watched the pickle. Her mouth watered. She swallowed.

"Sir?" she tried. Her voice was the caw of a crow, rusty from lack of discourse.

"How much might the twenty-five-pound bag be? The flour?"

"Could be ten dollars."

He looked her up and down, eyeing the frayed bit of lace tatting at her neck, taking in the deterioration. *Still, a dime's a dime, and there's a faded prettiness under the tan, and those eyes...* He dismissed her then. She clearly had no scratch.

"Oh." Sary calculated. "The meal?"

"Five."

"Oh, um, I, could I purchase three pounds each?"

She gazed hungrily at a molasses tin.

"Might come up with some"—the proprietor sucked the pickle in—"accommodation."

****

Whistling to himself, sprawled in a chair, and tilting his hat rakishly, Seb checked out Delacorte's office. "Yes, Captain. And what can I do ya for?" he offered expansively.

"Your sister, for starters." Julian hacked a cough, waiting for breath. "Handi's off emptying her whores' slops jars."

Seb looked confused.

Julian laughed and shakily poured shots, proffering a cigar box.

Seb chose one, warily venturing, "Ummm. Well. That's good…. A—a good thing…I reckon."

Julian snorted a laugh. "A small wager with Miss McAdams," not explaining further. He puffed. Seb tried to look interested.

His eyes roved the office as if trying for some clue as to why he'd been summoned.

"Thought she mighta died. Your sister. Buried up

there somewheres. Made up my mind before that turns absolutely true."

Delacorte held a Lucifer under Seb's cigar. Seb preened, lighting up from the flame Delacorte held—*for him!*

****

Suddenly Jules reached over and shoved Sary's money off the counter.

"*Give* it to her…" His eyes were spent bullets.

Sary looked down, clutching her purse tightly. A very pale and frail hand is in her view, a glimpse of lace cuff. When she looked up at Jules's pale pretty face, his eyes had a hot, liquid look, burning right into her like a faggot of firewood dropped on a tablecloth. There was a hint of the old man, Delacorte, about him too, but in an attenuated form, as if he were a fragile painted-doll image of the older man.

****

Inside Julian's office, Seb tilted his chair and drew deep on the cigar. "What 'xactly you got in mind, Cap?" Seb winked broadly.

Julian brushed a flick of ash, hiding his disdain. "Not what you think." His eyes looked down. "Pure?"

"Only by rights!" Seb sat upright. "Preacher-contracted," he blurted. "Hardly touched. Husband died young—warn't that a tragedy? But for a right dainty morsel, my sister's a real wildcat." He winked once more. "If you git my meaning."

Julian removed a wallet.

Seb's gaze followed it like a hunting dog would a rabbit, licking his lips. "Feller could do worse. Lot worse."

"Tell her—" Julian looked off. "Tell her I'd treat

her good. And all. Real good. Won't need to fret. Ever." He held onto the wallet.

Seb grabbed for it but let go like it was on fire. His chair banged the floor.

"Hold on now! You mean for good? For good and *all*?"

"A fuckin' queen," Julian growled.

Seb half rose but fell back, backhanding his mouth while tracking the money.

Julian leaned close. He watched him with pity. "How's that?"

Seb looked to the door as if seeing someone. *Perhaps Sary.* He licked his lips and grasped the wallet Julian still gripped, and he whispered huskily, "Maybe. Maybe it be best."

Julian frowned. "Any—hindrances with which I should be acquainted?"

Seb shook his head, dazed.

Julian released the wallet. "Have her redded up"— he hawked long and hard, gagged, breathless, and spat pink into a handkerchief—"for me."

Seb sat up. "Don't you worry none, Cap. I'll git Sary all spit-polished and shined to a fare-ye-well!" Seb waited. Nothing more was proffered. He jumped up to leave, but halted at the door. "You done us an honor, Mr. Delacorte. Uh—*Julian.*"

Julian waved him off. After Seb's footfalls clattered off, he fingered a velvet box rubbed bald at the corners. He opened it and removed yellowed India rubber tubing and a long hypodermic with the silver worn off to brass at the plunger. He unrolled his sleeve, revealing his once muscular arm riddled with purple welts. After a pause, Julian Delacorte sighed and sank back. After a time, he snapped open another velvet box to reveal a pair of pearl-drop earrings. He turned to a drawing and added a pencil line to a surprisingly good image of Sary's face and sketched in a pearl drop earring.

Underneath, a crude half-finished architectural drawing of a sprawling Victorian house lay on his desk.

****

Carefully not looking at Jules, Sary slid back her coin the proprietor had stooped for and shoved at her. "Take it!"

Behind her, Jules ripped his hat tag off and let it drop to the floor, fitting the Homberg back on. His small white teeth flashed, as if daring the proprietor. As he turned, the proprietor bent low as if getting something from under the counter, while hissing to Sary, "Your trade I ain't courtin'!" He glanced fearfully at Jules. "Hear? No more."

Sary blanched, nodded, and turned to rush out with her small bundles.

Jules allowed her to brush by, but she ran smack into the wall of Ev'ret, holding out hard candy for her in his meaty, dirty palm.

Jules looked on indulgently as Sary hesitated. She darted a look up at Ev'ret, ducked a curtsy, and snatched at the candy. She could hardly wait to get outside. Jules selected one too, tonguing it, watching Sary cram hers in her mouth once she was outside. He whispered, "Show you a good time..."

Ev'ret, drooling candy juice, wiped his chin. "Like now, boss?"

Jules studied Ev'ret long moments before switching his view back to Sary. "Soon. There's an exquisite sense of timing."

"Like when *he* ain't around?" Ev'ret nodded to a dazed-looking Seb just leaving the saloon.

Jules lashed out at Ev'ret's Adam's apple. Ev'ret choked on the candy and looked after Jules, hurt and confused.

****

Julian eyed the silent show from his upstairs bedroom as Seb dragged Sary, clutching provisions, from a shop window where she leaned nose to the glass to better scrutinize a cheap sprigged pink gown. "Oh, sweet girl, you'll have more than cheap dresses."

Julian brushed an unexpected hardening in his nether region, welcome in its rare delights. *Till she's all mine—or as long as it takes.* He chuckled with embarrassing candor. *She'll have all my attentions, warming my bed.* He rubbed his hands and wiped his mouth.

I'll be gentle, not like with Handi. His hands cupped air—he could almost sense the silkiness of her thighs under that misbegotten skirt she wore, and the soft weight of her breasts.

He tore his gaze away, puzzled as he noted with frowning interest that, almost as they reached their sad prospect of a horse, Sary broke away, running to Handi's. For a second he supposed she ran to the saloon —*and to him*—while Seb looked stunned, gaping after her.

Julian's chuckle was like scuffed gravel as Seb's boot tangled in the stirrup as he tried to dismount. Soon he'd think of something suitable for his rapacious new brother-in-law—like mucking stables.

****

Inside Handi's place, Sary looked around wildly, peering in the empty parlor, pressing the office door—locked. *Handi, where are you?* Outside, Seb smacked the poor horse. She looked up a staircase. *Perhaps I can hide…no, too late.* Seb had spied her. She studied the little Derringer, then, shoved it back into her petticoat.

Grabbing paper and inkpot, Sary scrawled a note. *'Money for gun—S.'*

She wadded the coin in the paper, shoving them both under the ledger. Later she pondered if that was the beginning of all the rest. Racing out, she glanced up.

Behind a window in the saloon, Handi raised heavy green brocade skirts and performed a slow, rude grind. Sary joined Seb, who had turned oddly sweet and amenable.

For some reason her mind flashed back to when Seb had helped her up on that chair…

"Sister. *Dear.* Come right on up here…" Seb dismounted, crouched, and cupped his hands for her foot, which had never received such help before. "Best we make haste for home…"

"Se-eb?" Sary stared at him queerly.

"Sorry if I was a little rough on you back there, Sister." Seb glanced up for Julian, but he was gone.

Sary studied her brother from the corner of her eye. *Perhaps things will go better. Seb seems so…chastened. Still, it is odd…* She had a queer unease, as if she were coming down with something—or maybe he was. Her heart thumped at the notion he might be ill or…*even die. And…* No. What a wicked, self-serving thought. Grief flooded her with remorse. What did the preacher say? *We all have thoughts that would shame Hell.*

****

Biskits wielded a straightedge razor over Julian's grizzled jowls where whiskers studded crevices like trees in raddled ravines. His boss gazed inscrutably at his own reflection, swiped the last foam away, and nodded him out.

Julian sucked in a concave belly, raising his chest, before he selected a set of engraved brushes to sweep silvery wings of hair, his one righteous vanity. Then, with a jar of pumice and a pig-bristle brush, he vigorously scrubbed long yellowed tusks, grinning experimentally.

Pleased.

He had no rotted teeth—good, for his age, or they didn't show. He sucked a loose one, and spat blood. Flashing a horse-grimace, Julian checked his breath, mouth-swished Bay Rum, and rubbed it over his face. After a swipe of it under his arms, he carefully slipped into crisp tailored gabardine, fresh from the Chinese tailor, so smooth it was like silk. He tugged on an ivory brocade waistcoat, shot his cuffs, and inspected moonstone links and a handsome cravat pin, then the hefty turnip watch and chain.

Stiffening his slightly hunched back, Julian gazed regally into the mirror and nodded curtly to himself. *He's still a fine figure of a man—any woman would feel lucky to be chosen.*

Julian crossed to his son's room, hesitating outside, almost passing. Entering, Julian sat by Jules's bed, watching his beautiful son sleep for a few moments, then tenderly covered him as if he were a small child. *She might be young for a mom, but she may have a settling influence on the boy.*

Rationalizing this, Julian stood, decisive.

****

Seb shoved Sary to the creek, hurtling a brush and soap after her. She ducked.

"Seb! Are you gone all over queer?" Her brother seemed fevered, gathering her clothes from where they lay drying on rocks and wadding them into her trunk. Sary grabbed them. "What are you doing? You're ripping—"

Seb halted, bright-eyed. "Got 'at right, sister dear." He laughed with hysteria, darting looks at the camp. "Don't know why I bother none. Soon won't matter. We'll both be wearin' silky under drawers!" He cackled inanely. "But reckon you need *somethin'* to cover your...*altogether,* for the time bein'." He sniggered.

Seb giggling? Sary eyed her brother's agitated state, edging away. Something sure wasn't right. All the way back, he'd been smiling, breaking into a guffaw now and then. Seb still tracked her, judging her as if she were a prize plow horse—or cow.

"Now. Go scrub yourself. You know"—Seb gestured, blushing—"all *over*-like. Everywhere."

"We're—leaving?" Her brother ignored her.

"An dab on some o' that cookin' vanilla. Like I don't know!" Seb smirked, scandalized. "I seen ya do it. Little dab 'hind your ear, makin' ya all sweet and dainty." He reached over to give Sary's cheeks a hard pinch. "Need color."

Sary slapped him off. "Seb!"

But then Seb, impatient, tweaked his own cheek just as hard. "Go on! I know all your filthy female tricks and womanly ways. Your mouth, too. Get some life in you! Nobody'd hanker after ya this way."

Sary watched him intently and pinched her cheeks red, eyeing Seb in the spotted mirror he held up critically. Behind her, he motioned, impatient, biting his own lips in illustration. Sary bit her bottom lip, shoving the mirror off. "There. Now what? What the Sam Hill are you up to, Sebastian?"

Seb stepped back, scanning her top to toe. He leapt forward and brushed a strand of hair in place, tugged at a wrinkle in her skirt, stood back again. "Reckon 'at'll hafta do," he allowed, forlorn.

"What!"

"You'll see." Seb seemed uneasy, and Sary dropped the mirror, her hand suddenly as numb as her head. The glass broke, unheeded.

"What have you done?" Sary breathed and turned on him. *"Sebastian!"*

****

Julian admired the pearl eardrops by the light of the moon, spattering them in a spasm of coughing and sprayed blood. He wiped them off and then wrapped them in a handkerchief before tucking the small bundle back into his breast pocket.

Chapter 10

Seb paced, hands behind his back, staring up the knoll trying to penetrate the dark and listening for a hoof beat, while Sary—a bedraggled ribbon knotted in her hair, gripped a plate, frozen as a knot on the log she was seated on.

"You'd sell me." She spoke in a flat, dead tone and dashed the plate to the ground.

Seb, still intent on the knoll, nibbled a hangnail. "Wanting you real bad, Sare," he muttered over his shoulder. "Could do worse." He whirled and gave a sharp nod, his fist curled. "A *lot* worse."

"You could!" Sary shouted. "You'd be lording it over the poker table and holding up the bar! I can see it now!" She began pacing.

"More'n just a good poke, Sary," Seb whined, backing from her. "He wants you *pure*-like. Just for him." He hadn't thought his sister would take on so. "Just for—"

Sary hurled the tin plate, banging Seb in the back of the head.

Seb threw up his arms to ward off more blows as Sary stormed about, pelting rocks as she went.

"Said you'd be a queen, Sary! Those exact words!"

"And what would that make you?" she demanded. "A court jester?"

The ground whirled beneath her feet—a sick

feeling swelled up her neck like a snake coiled in her stomach, and she was so enraged she could scarcely find breath to shriek. "You wouldn't be—*sleeping* with him! He's old, and yellow as lard! He stinks of death! Like something *died* and they forgot to bury it!"

A ghostly cough floats down from the knoll.

They both jerked, intent on the dark above.

"Old and yellow I may be, Sarabande Swinford." The voice was dry, inflectionless, yet hard. *"I'm waiting."*

Sary searched the night, but then Julian entered the fitful light, all peaks and hollows, his ivory vest and yellow teeth gleaming like dead fish in the dark.

Sary could hear the swish of his silvery coat and the creak of his saddle as he picked his way down. She faltered back. She'd been uneasily aware of a heavy perfume clogging the leaf-musked night for some time now...*so that was it. That crazy old man drenched with cologne.* Suddenly aware she mustn't hurt his feelings, she stuttered, "I'm honored, Mister D-Delacorte. Truly. A—a man of your...stature." Her mind raced. "But Seb didn't say—I'm under *mourning*," she said, desperate.

Seb gripped her arm. He dragged her, protesting, to Julian. Sary looked up at the gaunt man high up on the horse. The face was inscrutable and old as the mountains.

"Mourning here lasts till bedtime." The voice grated in the night, and Julian cantered down, leaned arthritically, crookedly, as if in pain, and reached for her, grasping her other arm, yanking her from Seb. "Take it up with kin," he barked harshly. "I bought you."

"You can't sell what you don't *own*," she couldn't

help snarling, glaring up at him more frightened than she'd ever been. Could her brother force such a thing? There was no real law here, beyond this man, Delacorte. Her clear green eyes were lost in the rheumy swamp of his. Long seconds passed. Sary felt the crackle of tension like lightning on a still night between the three of them.

Julian tightened something in his face. With effort, he dropped her arm and, without leaving her eyes, bawled at Seb, *"Where's—my—money!"* The words echoed about the camp, bouncing off the mountains.

Seb looked stricken. Uncertain, casting guilty glances at his sister, he withdrew Julian's wallet from his shirt.

Sary snatched it from him and heaved it at the horse's hooves.

Julian gazed down, then at Sary, her face pink as a rose, green eyes glittering defiance—hair wild and curling. He backed his horse without removing his inscrutable gaze from her face, until the light no longer held him and he was gone.

Seb scrambled for the money, waving it, running after the man long after the hoof beats faded. "Don't worry, Mr. Delacorte. I'll knock sense in her," he called. "I will!"

He stormed back to shake her, shouting, red-faced, "Now you done it! Now you *done* it! The Delacortes of the world won't come crawlin' back to the likes of us!"

Sary gave him a stony look. "What do they call men like you? There's a name."

Seb looked at her, spiteful. Finally, he spit, "Your jailer, sister-mine! I'll work you like a spavined mule."

Sary's eyes became slits. *And, you don't now?*

****

Sary was wakeful, as uneasy as before a brooding Indiana storm when air would turn green and still. She had moved her bedroll from the leanto and up close by the fire, fighting sleep. Her eyes drooped...*just for a minute...*

****

Seb was wakeful too, his mind churning for a way back. *Somethin' I shoulda, mighta said. Too quick. I didn't 'splain the right and proper benefits of such a union. After all, how long can the consumptive old hen's-fart last? Sary don't understand the ways of the world. Just a female. That's why they put Seb in charge, didn't they? By Gawd, she'll see the light! She won't deny old Seb the chance, neither. I'll yank her back to Big Bear in her bloomers and shift if need be...*

Seb drifted off with visions, not of sugarplums but of himself as lord of the saloon. In time, with old Julian dead in the grave and that crazy son of his put in his proper place, Seb envisioned himself dealing, smirking at greenhorns, drinking Julian's best whiskey, wearing fancy duds, and denying credit to those who...

He woke clearheaded and glum.

Between Delacorte's vainglory and Sary's pig-ignorance, the marriage union would *never* come to fulsome glory. He thrashed about, rummaging his poor belongings, accidentally brushing two odd, pear-shaped, green-glass bottles—thick and hefty as bombs. Seb chuckled, soothed by the cool, smooth glass, and drifted off. "Show'em," he murmured, half-asleep. "Show'em all..."

****

"What!" Sary gasped awake, startled by Seb's face

looming above her and blotting out the moon. A weak flame lit feverish eyes boring into hers, with flickering green glints, from something he held behind him. Seb thrust two corked, pear-shaped, green glass bottles at her face, bottles she'd never seen before. She scootched back instinctively.

"See this here?" Seb giggled. "Color of money!" Sary stared at him as he faded back, wrapping himself around the bottles. Sary strained the dark, bewildered and exhausted after the odd day, long after she heard him snore…

Chapter 11

It was barely dawn. Sary raced breathless up a nameless trail, feet thudding earth, never minding rocks, and fallen branches, calling, "Seb! *Sebastian!*" until she was hoarse.

Seb spun, quavering with emotion, and thrust out one of the hateful green bottles. "On your head now, sister-mine! No way am I crawling back, nothing to show but bare-assed knees in my britches!"

"But Seb! You don't know anything about—"

"*Don't know nothin'...*" he mimicked. "You hankerin' to do it?" Seb waved the bottles at her. "Pure gelig-nite! *Gold*-makin elixir to conjure me up a fortune! Gowan!" He jiggled them at her. "You wanna play the *man?*"

Sary eyed the shaken bottles, backpedaling. She'd heard about gelignite and its fearsome properties. It blew mountains to smithereens to make the railways. Lord knew what it did to puny humans. She gasped, hands on knees. "Blow yourself to Kingdom Come then. Go on! Do it! *Kill* yourself!" she cried. "I wish you would!" Sary raced back down the trail.

Seb will back down. Just trying to scare me into contrition—or forgiveness. Probably just go off in the hills and idle the day. Oh, what am I to do...?

If she'd raised her head, Sary would have seen the two men on horseback in the distance, picking their way around a shoulder of mountain, one massive in the saddle and the other slender, dark—and she would have, somehow, been forewarned...

Chapter 12

Jules sat his saddle in a leisurely manner, moseying his mount along as if secretly pleased with his private thoughts, gazing dreamily at hawks showing coppery wings against cobalt skies and cottontail clouds.

Silence bothered Ev'ret.

"Turned out ta be a nice day, huh, Boss. Boss? Hey! Where we goin'?"

Ev'ret contemplated, squinching up his eyes. "Goin' hunting. Huntin' maybe. I like huntin'. Don't like squirrel. But I like rabbit! 'N' bear paw. Bear paw's—"

Ev'ret screwed his face in thought. "Chewy. Yeah, chewy. Gets stuck in yer teeth. Even horse, or mule, if I *havta*. Ever eat mule? Mule's tangy, once you get past the—"

He pushed his lip out, narrowing his eyes at Jules. "Don't tell me *nothin'*. Don't never, never tell me—"

Jules glanced at him in irritation and waved a languid hand. "Those hills over there. A woman's hip. A sweet bosom…"

Ev'ret scowled and squinted where Jules waved. "Don't see nothin'. Sposed to be pertectin' you, Boss! How kin I pertect you, if ya don't never *tell* me nothin'?"

Jules smiled his peculiar smile and rode on.

****

Seb stopped cold. He looked behind him. *Wish Sary would have tagged along. Empty here.* An avalanche of ocher tailings and weathered silvery scaffold heralded the mine, along with wood winches and frayed grayed ropes sailing the wind and playing a lonely tune—plus a sign with letters faded in the harsh elements spelling ELIJAH K. BALDWIN LUCKY STRIKE MINE and, in fresher paint, JULIAN J. DELACORTE, ENTERPRISES.

****

Windowpanes of ice sailed by Sary as she bashed shirts on a rock with hands raw and red, in cadence to her heated words and thoughts, as if bashing Seb.

"Damnation, Seb!" *Bash!* "Lunatic!" *Wring— scrub.* "Get yourself killed for certain-sure!" A tiny guilty thought crept behind the door of her mind, whispering, *But then, you'll be free.*

Beside her, a mending basket lay pitched on a patch of snow, spilling out bright bits of ribbon and her silver scissors and a thimble.

****

Seb waded past rusty detritus, broken machinery nameless to him, a big, wheel-barrel-type thing, and grayed bits of rope, up to weathered, splintered supports and crossbeams sagging like the sky leaned heavy on them. Against the thin mountain air, the sign spanned the mine head.

Seb wiped his mouth, looking about as if seeking reassurance, or someone to stop him. He gingerly laid the gelignite aside and ripped up rotted planks inadequately covering a seemingly bottomless hole, peering tentatively down the musty shaft that dwindled to darkness. He ducked from the fusty air rushing out, rubbing his jaw as if still hoping *someone* might leap from the pines and tell him to hightail it on out.

He squatted on his haunches. *Nothing but ta do it!* Seb tested a boot on the first shaky rung but couldn't tell if it was his boot or the ladder shaking as he suspiciously eyed the rusty cleats sunk in rock. The first rung held. There. That wasn't so bad.

His head dropped past the rotting edge of the square shaft-head. He had the rope tied about his waist, the other end fixed to the mule's halter, tethered above. In truth, Seb still didn't look extra thrilled, facing clammy walls, his eyes closed as he descended clinging to the wood rails, half-crouching, his rear end sticking out into nothing but dead air.

He looked up, panicked at a sudden notion.

What if the ladder crumples, or peels off the wall? The wooden treads were worn by many feet, the bolt before him even now rattled loose and rusty...*The whole durn ladder quivers.*

No one'd blame me iffen I didn't do it. Hell, Sary wouldn't even know. Yet he hung on, unsure if the quaking was the ladder, the shaft, or his own self.

Of course, he could just rough himself up a bit and *say* he done did it. He stopped till his neck pulse slowed to a canter, then continued his quavery blind way down to the abyss. As he looked up, the sky was a bright blue square now, far above. Another world.

****

Jules and Ev'ret rode in, the clatter of their hooves masked by Sary's splashing.

****

Three feet from the shaft bottom, Seb warily dropped off the ladder, clutching his arms close. *Christ!*

It's dark down here, and blamed cold. He peered up again to the square of blue and then back to the dark. This far down, all he could see were the hands in front of his face. Panicking, he dug pockets for his Lucifers, striking one.

Instantly, a silent gale extinguished it; with the third precious match, his lantern flared. Adjusting the wick to conserve fuel, Seb timidly checked the gloom.

Dank. Littered with rusty miner detritus - a crushed lamp...a moldering cap...*Not good.*

Turning slowly, Seb spotted the black mouths like giant wormholes snaking off the central shaft. Hesitantly, one eye on the box of cheerful light filtering down, Seb sidled to one of the gaping maws and edged in. "Just scratch me a little arrow here," he cajoled. "Won't catch me sleeping at the switch..." Whistling comfort through dry lips, he shuffled on, led by his raised lantern, scratching arrows with hunks of rock on walls chipped by past picks, pacing further into the unknown. Seb realized with sudden sick insight he didn't know precisely just *what* he was looking for or what he was supposed to *do* as a newly minted miner.

Think to find a God-danged pot a gold just sittin' there? Well, yes, he did.

****

Horse's hooves entered the creek, masked by Sary's angry imaginary conversation with Sebastian and the splashing. Startled, Sary scanned the first hoof entering the stream, looked up and kept looking up, scrambling back an instant before Ev'ret and Jules rode her down.

What's wrong with them! She kept backing, treading on her skirt, hearing it rip, tripping, and almost going down.

Jules smiled. Ev'ret grinned.

Jumping up, Sary yanked her skirt. "Afternoon?" She managed a smile, but her lips tightened. The big one was the same barn door she'd run into in Big Bear—broad buffalo shoulders, a square face, and an eager, almost childlike innocence.

The other, well, she still scarcely knew what to make of him.

He smiled, but those dark eyes drifted and gleamed liquid, as if laughing at a delicious jest only he could hear.

The big man looked back expectantly at his boss. Jules still smiled his dreamy smile. That was just beginnin' to chafe Ev'ret some.

Sary edged off, calling, "Seb? There's—callers for you."

Ev'ret dismounted, showing his big square teeth.

"My brother—" Sary began, backing carefully. If she could just make it to the trees…

****

Seb flailed at the rock wall with a broken pick scavenged from a litter of discarded tools. Now and then, sweating in the clammy must, he flicked glances at the green wink of a bottle, then, uneasily watching timber braces, cocked his ear at the creaks and tortured groans—*wood on wood.* Flinched. *Did one move?* He eyed it, but in time he went back to hacking.

****

"Ain't here." Ev'ret grinned amiably at Sary. "We done watched." He stood close, too close. She couldn't see beyond him—his breath was on her face, full of peppermint and tobacco. She smelt heat, sweat, and sunbaked shirt. He reached and wound her hair around a thick forefinger. She jerked away with his fingers caught in the twist, pulling her.

"Din' we, Jules?" He stroked, or rather pawed, at her breast as if he'd never before seen one.

Sary swatted his hand. Subconsciously brushing the Derringer beneath her petticoats, she yelled, "Sebastian!" and ripped away, knowing he couldn't hear but hoping, futilely, while fearing he would hide if he were near.

Faster than he looked, Ev'ret grappled Sary, barely hanging on as she fought back, all elbows, knees, and fingernails. Wildly, she desperately searched Jules out. He'd aided her once. "Mister! Please…call him off!"

Ev'ret gestured to his boss as if to say, "After you?" As if not too sure how long he could hang on to this female, all sharp edges under her soft-as-kittycat looks.

Saddled, Jules, giggling, demurred, enjoying the show.

Sary broke free, leaving half her sleeve. *Where can I go? Where's Seb's shotgun?* Aware of the banging on her thigh, she was reminded again. *Yes, Handi's Derringer!*

The thought was jolted out of her as Ev'ret tackled her in a belly leap, landing short, dragging her clumsily to the ground. In the fall; gripping her about the knees, he snagged her skirts half off, and they both tumbled to the dirty snow. "Ooooph," Sary grunted. Her hip took the brunt.

Sary rolled, still fighting—*nails, hands, knees*— using Ev'ret's clumsiness against him, once more ripping free, only now she hobbled.

Altering grins with frowns, Ev'ret blundered after, wearing her down with his sheer size. Sary threw a last, exhausted, roundhouse punch. The big man hunched, spreading his arms wide and curved, and, taking a giant step under her swing, plastered her in a bear hug. Sary twisted within his bear-like arms and kneed him, hitting his tree-trunk thigh instead. "No. You. *Won't!*" She gritted, shoving against him with all she had.

It was like trying to shove a barn.

Ev'ret scowled, throwing appeals at Jules—"Now what, Boss?"—and spinning on Sary, remembering to be infuriated.

"You done took my candy!" he bellowed. "I done give you my peppermint, too."

****

Deep in the mine, Seb hefted a green bottle in palms slimy with sweat. The cool bottle slipped. Seb caught it before it hit rock. He slid, gasping and quaking, against the rough wall.

****

With a meaty hand the size of a ham hock, Ev'ret slammed Sary against a tree, pinning her by the neck, then unbuckled and slung his gun belt aside and fumbled pants buttons with his free hand.

Sary gagged, grimacing, and gripped him hard *down there*. She knew from Jonathan how a man could hurt "wicked bad" if hit in the wrong place. She shoved again at the mountain of a man.

Yet, Ev'ret, unperturbed, didn't flinch.

She looked dismayed—uncomprehending. One big paw still gripped her neck, the other now ripping at her blouse. Buttons flew, making little pinging sounds. Part of her was angry over those buttons. *One more job!* She wrenched free.

Jules frowned as Sary left most of her blouse in his erstwhile bodyguard's cabbage-sized fist, as Ev'ret, lurching, half-downed trousers binding his knees, clipped Sary from behind, felling her.

Jules yawned, adjusting his cape.

Ev'ret hauled Sary by her hair and the torn sleeve to the creek—and Jules. There, he sat on her, gasping hard. Sary couldn't breathe—her face had landed half under water. Coughing, gasping, she managed to crick her neck up and suck in air, only to be rolled under again. Futilely she clawed and grabbed at his clothing. The big man didn't even know it. Face under water, on her last breath, Sary groped for the little Derringer tangled somewhere in her petticoats.

Can't—reach it!

She stretched her arm blindly back and overhead, bashing the huge man with rocks, a mining pan, and, with her last breath, her sewing basket. Bright thread, ribbons, shining thimbles, and the scissors were flung across the snow.

Jules twisted, greedily following the bright treasure of color and sheen flying through the air and landing on a patch of white. Then he glanced back at Sary and Ev'ret, odd emotion flickering across his face as they rolled in and out of the creek, getting muddier and more undone every second, their wrestling spattering him.

Frowning, Jules drew a pristine monogrammed handkerchief and daubed prissily at the mud landing on his breeches as Sary, bashing Ev'ret about the head and shoulders, beseeched him, "Call off your *dog!*"

Jules winced at her voice, more fixated on Sary's ribbons and scissors glittering in the weak sun than on the bizarre action beneath him. Snagging a ribbon with his crop—a red one—he focused instead on weaving it in and out of his jacket buttonholes, while Ev'ret, bleeding from the head, sputtering from the first bath he'd suffered in years, fell atop Sary, again in a meaty heap.

Sary's head snapped. Groggy, once again Sary went for Handi's pistol, but she couldn't wedge her hand far enough, with Ev'ret pressing her fast to the creek bed.

Ev'ret once more offered a barely subdued, muddy, brawling, angry, shrieking Sary to Jules, with bravado. "Well, Boss! Are ya, or ain't ya?" was his querelous demand.

****

Seb pinched his eyes shut tight.

Trembling, he hesitated, then timidly lobbed the green bottle around a leg of the tunnel, ducking, with his fists clenched over his head, whimpering a silent plea. *Oh, Lordy—!*

He waited agonized seconds, lifting his head as worlds imploded with awesome heat, light, and concussive power, enveloping Seb in a stinging dark shower of earth, rock, and wicked spears of splintery wood.

Glass shattered in Seb's ears. Maybe he imagined it.

****

Jules, eyes flashing purple and wet, watched the scene—a drenched Sary, with mud-stringed hair dripping in her face and down over a filthy wet chemise, and Ev'ret's mulish, hurt face. Jules sneered and made a bored "Let's get on with it" gesture.

Sary's hands finally groped chill metal—her small sewing scissors were sunk deep in the snow next to the creek. Without thought, she hopelessly arced them swiftly overhead. *Like sticking an elephant with a needle.*

Ev'ret blinked, yanked them irritably from his meaty back, flung them off, and ripped Sary's skirts up in a frenzy of outrage, hurt, and lust. Jules at last showed concern, drawing a long-barreled blue-black Colt he dangled from one pale hand as his horse danced a few steps back.

Down at the creek, Ev'ret bawled at Sary, "You done took my candy!"

Sary focused on the red perspiring face above her, and her hand felt the slippery mother-of-pearl handle.

"Peppermint's my best-est kind!"

****

A muffled explosion coincided with a horrendous explosion from the direction of the mine tunnel. Sary's gun hand still jammed between them, Ev'ret sucked air, jolting back in a painful jackknife arc. He twitched once before his body slumped onto Sary like a dead horse, weighting her head beneath the creek's surface one last time. She gagged as the frigid, muddy water gushed up her nose. *I'm dying...*

Crushed by the inert heftiness, Sary still managed to crane her face half out of the icy stream, aware of tobacco-scent and still-living sweat and sunbleached shirt, on what she grasped was dead weight. Then Ev'ret's heartbeat, thudding against her breast, stilled, mid-beat. His shirt blossomed with scarlet flowers that bloomed ever wider, soaking what was left of her blouse with loathsome heat.

She panicked. She forgot all about the other man, the one who had helped her in the store. She shoved, wriggled her fists beneath his wide chest, and thrust up. He wouldn't budge.

Jules, rubbing his pale forehead, looked on, dazed, with ribbons half woven through his waistcoat buttonholes.

****

Deep down an obsidian tunnel, an overhead beam splitting its rotten heart groaned a death rattle, letting loose a thunderous hail of earth, clay, rock, and vicious shards of wood as a relay of rotted timbers caved, releasing tons of crushing debris.

In that split second before oblivion blanketed him in torrents of suffocating earth, Seb looked up in terror as a beam spike plummeted, nailing him to the tunnel floor.

****

Jules flinched on his skittish horse, giggling and frowning in turn, watching Sary struggle with Ev'ret's body. He backed his mount when the female clawed her way out from under his bodyguard—caretaker—court jester—slave. To him it was with comical effort that the female dragged her legs out.

Jules's pants showed a sign of fear as Ev'ret toppled back into the creek and lay still as a lump of dog meat. He chewed his nail and stonily studied Ev'ret, waiting for him to sputter and curse and rise from the dead. He waited. Water still rushed over blind eyes.

Then he swiveled his hot mad gaze to Sary as she hauled up.

Waving Handi's Derringer, hurting and bloodied,

she shrieked like a mad woman, advancing on him. "Git! Take this—this *thing* with you!"

She watched his insane face as he hacked at his cape, snagged on the pommel, then dropped the knife shakily to aim his Colt, steadily enough, two-handed, right at her. He couldn't recall whatever attracted him to this filthy thing. She was mucky, wild-eyed, shivering uncontrollably, hair hanging in muddy strings.

Sary saw the end of the Colt, a black hole to eternity. She backed till she hit a tree. She heard the click of the pistol in the still mountain air. Squinting her eyes, she lifted the Derringer, pressed the tiny trigger, and fired wildly in his direction. *Oh, no, oh, no, oh, no...*

Shock reigned as Jules clutched his neck and gawped, horrified, at blood pumping like a fountain through his drenched fingers—a particularly messy wound. He gaped at Sary, and as the black wager-horse shied, Jules tumbled to the ground, still wrapped in the cape. The horse cantered off.

Sary staggered over, dropped beside Jules, and pressed the horrific wound. Blood pumped through her fingers too, but soon slackened to a dribble. She pressed harder, aware of his bruised eyes and white face looking up at her. *Please, please, please...*

Jules finally spasmed, gargling something that sounded like, "Beholden..."

Murmuring inarticulate prayer, Sary could only give comfort with her eyes, until finally Jules bled out.

****

Sary hugged her knees, rocking until the sun slanted low, yet her eyes were dry and distant. Aches, hurts, and a raw ragged feeling she hadn't been conscious of till now descended like a barbarian army invading her body.

A sudden shiver coursed through her. She flinched as her dull gaze traveled the muddy wallow and trampled bloody snow.

She started at the sight of the two bodies—one large and lumpy, the other slight, all in black, bloody and sprawled—as if they were apparitions. She crawled a little closer, wary, focusing. *It was real, then.*

Sary wearily hitched herself up. Only the pain between her legs and the scrapes and bruises seemed real. Her aches and the battle had solidified her muscles and bone and mind. Still she must *do* something—*Some urgent chore.* The thought came vaguely, with irritation. *So cold, so very cold.* Her flesh was one big shuddering goose bump, and her teeth chattered like musical spoons.

Seb will be back soon. The thought galvanized her. *She could just hear him, now, somehow blaming her.* Suddenly, she found she had reached the bodies. Sary poked Ev'ret. Dead weight. Numbly she inched and tugged Ev'ret from the creek. At first, he wouldn't budge, until she rocked the body like a huge log. Looking away, she draped his trousers over his nakedness and then looked to Jules, but suddenly she could wait no longer.

Rolling in the creek, ignoring the body on the bank, Sary let water baptize her fresh and wash Ev'ret away. She scrubbed herself raw, dug sand and gravel into her flesh, ripping her skin, relishing the pure cold cauterizing hurt with her hot tears blending with the frigid water.

Shuddering, Sary limped to camp, crammed herself

into dry clothes, blew the dead fire to life, and tossed in kindling that should have lasted a week, until it roared to the sky. Still she shuddered, mind empty as the stars beyond the coldest, deadest, farthest moon.

"I'm a murderess," she finally whispered. "I killed them. Oh, God. What have I done? Seb will be back soon. Sebastian! Where are you? I need you."

Her eyes lit on Ev'ret's saddlebags. She crawled over and timorously searched, at one point looking wonderingly from a sepia tintype of a lumpy girl to Ev'ret's hard-favored face.

"You had—a sweetheart?" She shook her head, and jammed the tintype back. Coins fell into her hand, and she wavered. "No. Stealing's stealing, pure and simple."

So is murder, her mind crabbed. *It wasn't murder—it wasn't!*

Slipping the coins back, her hands dragged out a sticky mass of hard candy. "Unghhh!" She tossed it vehemently into the creek.

Next, Sary found the round shape of an apple. "Oh, Lordy," she breathed, and shamefully devoured it on the spot, feeling her strength renew with each bite. She found two jugs of whiskey and set them aside, and a dirty comb. "Euuuw!" She dropped it, and then thumbed a child's picture book about a pony, murmuring, "How odd." Disturbed somehow, suspicioning it was Ev'ret's; she laid it aside, too. Digging further, she withdrew a frayed envelope, the name on it writ in pencil: "Everett Elliot Eckhardt…"

She laid that aside and slowly crawled to Jules, not seeing his stark white monogrammed handkerchief fallen against a patch of snow. She studied his fallen-angel face.

A chorus of ululating coyotes jerked her out of her fugue, and she quickly shuttled ammo, tobacco, whiskey, and guns, all except the blue-black Colt, back to camp. Then she slapped Ev'ret's horse on the rump, yelling, "Hiiiiiyah! Go free!"

Wistfully, she watched it canter off. "Go free…"

It was then Sary noticed the white blotch of the elegant handkerchief, plucking it up and tucking it absently into her waistband. Her mind reluctantly on the two bodies, she turned, unwilling, to Ev'ret and Jules. *Yes, still there.*

"*Have* to do this. I *must.*"

Without thought, Sary grabbed Ev'ret's boots, hauling him by inches and jerks away from the creek, then came back for Jules and dragged him beneath the arms to a spot above camp, where the soil was loose and pebbly, and hacked out a wide shallow grave. Stooping, she rolled the two bodies in before she could ponder the situation further.

Ev'ret's body fell at a slant, half on Jules. She tugged, arranging both of them face up, drawing stiffening limbs to a gesture of repose before flinching a look heavenward. "Guess it looks right."

Sary tucked Jules's watch into his hands and the Colt into his waistcoat and shoved the letter and tintype in Ev'ret's shirt. Sary heaped their faces with leaves. Then, with motions flagging, she scraped thin earth and rock over the bodies and strewed the slight mounds with more brush, needles and dead leaves.

Straining, Sary lastly rocked two larger stones over the site.

From a distance, it looked like any other wilderness

spot. "There. Have to do, for now. Seb will never know. *He will never have anything over me, to shame me for...* Sary dropped by the fire, head in her hands.

****

The sun slanted low. Dusk. Sary jumped up to again check the path her brother last took.

"Seb?"

Her voice seemed swallowed by dark.

Sary boiled acorn coffee. Still no Seb.

Chapter 13

Sary wakened. Why this unease? It came back to her with a rush. Still night. Only embers left. Coffee boiled dry. She heard a steady *lap-lap* and stared into the incurious dead eyes of a bobcat lapping blood. She shouted, chasing it with a fire-stick with all her anxiety behind it.

Returning, her eyes darted to Seb's empty bedroll. Sary screamed, "Seb? Sebastian!"

****

As Sary pelted the trail with a bobbing lantern, shadows made the black conifers dance and jerk in all directions. She sensed unseen eyes, followed by claws, and teeth. It didn't seem this long this morning— yesterday morning. Had she taken the wrong turn?

She tumbled, hitching from lack of breath, but the sketchy path opened onto a clearing with heaps of silvered timber and rusting ghosts of machines surrounding a black hole in a wooden square. Tall arched sentinels, as for an ancient temple, backed up to a slope of mountain. This would be where he would come.

There was a sign, too, high overhead, but she couldn't make it out as she picked her way to the square of warped wood, surrounded by a platform that creaked and groaned when she walked on it, all made important by the pitched scaffolding *skreeing* in the wind, with the sign over it. She still couldn't read it—the moon scudded behind clouds, playing games with her sight. She knelt, bracing herself over the evil void.

"Seb!" *He can't be down there, surely! Oh, please don't be.*

Sary squinted, scanning the dark, her lantern flickering. She lifted it high for a complete turn.

"Seb? Where are you? Dammit!"

Surrounding ranks of fir swallow her voice. "Sebastian Swinford? You come out here!"

She listened. Not a whisper. No Seb strolling with a sportive grin through the trees.

She strained her eyes back down the abyss and once more at the waiting night, the secretive whispering pine with its unexplored crackles and rustling brush. Finally, in the growing dawn, she spied the blotch of faded red.

Seb's bandanna, the one he wore about his neck, grubby and pink, snagged on a ladder dwindling down.

****

The lantern banged, tinny, echoing, as it struck wood rungs bolted to a wall. Holding it below her, hanging on, Sary could see only a foot down the rocky black throat that hungrily gulped all her light.

Still she descended, testing the ladder one careful foot at a time. Toeing each unseen tread, she mis-stepped into air and the lantern's wire handles slipped in her fingers. She almost dropped it and lost her grasp of the ladder in the bargain, waiting while an updraft billowed her skirts and pantaloons with a cold breath.

The level of kerosene sloshed. Flame stuttered. Sary watched it, tense until it flared again. Must save fuel, though. Blowing it out, Sary bent her head over the rungs murmuring, "Help me, Heavenly Father, as I descend this pit, which surely must be close to Hell." She felt foolish, and dramatic, all the same. She called again. "Seb? Are you down there?"

One foot after the other, down, down. She peered into blackness pressing her face. Why she kept going, she couldn't answer. Her toes often wavered in nothingness before they grabbed thin rungs. How much farther? She made a sound, and it bounced off the rock. Her heart stilled. *Are the rungs whole? Will the ladder loosen from its anchors?* She gave a careful shake. The ladder rippled. Oh, why hadn't she thought this out, gone down in full light?

She cricked her neck back.

A dim light square marked the surface impossibly far above her. As long as she could still see that...

She peered below her. Black velvet swallowed her toes. The air grew thicker. Still she placed one foot after another, each step reluctant, as if she yearned to ascend instead, and waited for unseen things to rush up to her with the updraft of her skirts.

"Seb?" Her voice was weak, hollow, scaring her. "Seb!" She croaked louder. "*Sebastian!* God damn it to Hell!"

Again Sary strained to see *anything* in the mine's deeps. "Oh, Brother, *please* answer."

Can't go on. I can't. What am I doing? Seb can't be down here.

She began to doubt her sanity and laid her cheek against the back of her hand, swiping tears on her shoulder, and once more felt for rungs.

Keep going. Keep going. There. Toe touching wood. The rung's whole. Her world now was comprised of splintery wood, knuckles scraping unseen rock, clammy wind sailing up skirts, her face brushed by sly cold fingers as she imagined bats and unseen things. She yearned to swat, but held on instead. *Feet slipping—another step down—how far to bottom? How will I ever have the strength to get back up this ladder?*

She screamed, her screams sailing up the shaft, as a rung cleaved in two and her foot plunged. Her knee banged the wall. Dangling, she glimpsed something below by a thin shaft of moon, between swaying skirts and the toes of her boots. *A scrap of rusty machinery, a wheel...*

Abruptly, her foot thunked on earth, and Sary splashed to ebony bottom and relit her lantern. Instantly the wick guttered. Shakily fumbling precious matches, she struck another—a thin light flared orange—and she opened her eyes a lash at a time, afraid of what she would see, circling much as Seb had done. She was at a cavernous junction, a sort of gathering point where crooked, rusting tracks converged. All about lay broken picks, barrows with wheels askew, dashed lanterns, and smashed headlamps, with black cavities like snake holes boring into the earth. The rails led off in all directions. She jumped as the match burnt her fingers, resisted the urge to shake it out, and touched the wick with it instead. She circled, holding the lantern high, studying the tunnel mouths.

Edging to one, with one eye on the shaft, Sary tentatively called, "Sebastian?"

Must be insane. Seb isn't down here!

Yet something compelled her to step further into the airy ink brushing her face, coughing in dust filtering to meet her, and she realized it was that faint powder drifting from the tunnel that made her choose *this* one.

Inching the rough walls, her fingers skittered into a void. She waved them in the dark—they brushed *nothing.* A bend. She must round a bend now. She looked back, no longer making out the junction. Holding the light close, she made out an arrow pointing back the way she came scratched on the rock. *"Seb."*

She picked up her pace, stumbling blind.

Then, by the lantern glow, Sary spotted a hand—Seb's arm in the faded green-plaid flannel he wore, day in and day out, poked from wood and dirt clogging the passage almost to the ceiling. *Her darn on the cuff.* It could be no other.

Sary threw herself at it, gouging, clawing the heap. Rubble sifted, with creaks and groans, to cover her hair, replacing the litter almost as swiftly as she heaved. Sary tugged at Seb's unyielding arm, ignoring the glittering garnet pool seeping from beneath the dirt.

Head to the ground, Sary placed the lantern close and peered into an earth pocket made of beams, spying an ear and thatch of dusty hair. "Oh, Seb! You damnable fool!" She laughed giddily and, grabbing a broken pick, maniacally hacked away at the mound. Throwing off the last bit of debris, she reached his face and on hands and knees brushed away dirt so Seb could breathe.

Odd.

Something hard and rusting poked through the earth still partly covering his face. Gently brushing more dirt, she uncovered the beam spike nailing Seb to the ground.

Her heart stilled at the gruesome, improbable sight. "Oh, Sebastian, what have you done? What have you…"

Frantically, she clawed, uncovering his face amid a shower of earth.

"…*done?*" she whispered.

****

She wriggled the spike from his shoulder above his heart, palming the dreadful wound as if healing or hiding it, unaware earth still showered her head as she patted him and smoothed his hair, unaware she crooned an old lullaby…

"Sleep, my child, and peace attend thee,
all through the night.
Guardian angels God will send thee,
all through…the…the…"

She broke down. *"Through the night,"* was all she could manage further.

****

Behind her, a bronze swath gleamed on the wall of the mine face, reflecting the lantern light.

Sary looked up in wonder.

In the lamplight's flicker, her hands glowed, awash with yellow light. She turned and crawled to a jagged ribbon of a wide, glittering gold vein running through the dull rock face, tracing her raw fingers over the gleaming swath; barely daring to breath for fear it would take its rich light with it…

"Seb! Oh, Seb-as-tian. You did it!"

The lantern sputtered. Gold faded to black.

Sary shakily whispered in the false night, "Don't worry, Seb. You'll be all right. I won't leave you in…in the dark…"

Chapter 14

"Ned! Consarn you, fool mule! Here, Neddie! Ned! Come here!" she cried. Ned whickered, trotting amiably enough up to Sary. "Thank God, for once..." Sary didn't finish, too bone-weary to think. Barely standing, she knotted the rope to its hame and dropped back down the shaft with the other end secured about her waist, much as Seb had done, before she could think on it.

At bottom, she kept lighting matches, groping Seb's tunnel. The lantern was just ahead. She couldn't stand to be in the dark any longer, watching the slender Lucifer char to her fingertips. Black pressed her face as though it were another being, with weight and chill breath, just as she caught a glimpse of plaid. She lit the lantern, holding her breath. It sputtered as she groped for Seb's cold wrist...his shirt...and by feel, whispering reassurance, quickly knotted the rope under his arms. "Shhh, shhhh...got you now, Brother."

Sary hated to leave him at the mouth of the tunnel, where the sun still gilded the shaft. She watched her hands race up rungs, following the rope to blessed light. *What's this?* The ladder shuddered, then swayed sickeningly out into the void, taking her with it, as if she would never stop arching back. Reaching the end of the arc, inch by inch Sary swung it back, until she smacked the rock face, knocking her breath out.

Pressing her body and the ladder to the shaft, Sary finally breached the top. Gratefully she patted Ned's velvet nose. "Sweet Neddy," she urged. "Now, pull!"

Ned planted his feet and heehawed.

"Ned!" She yanked the mule's hame. "Come!" She grabbed a few acorns.

At last, Ned lurched out of the trees, trotting after Sary.

She watched the rope stretch taut, *zing* and *twang,* scraping splintered wood as she led Neddie away from the mine and poor Seb was bumped and dragged the whole way up the shaft until Sary hobbled the mule and she hauled Seb, as gently as she was able, over the lip.

****

At camp, Seb thudded to the ground from Ned's back before she could untie him. A thunk followed. Sary sank beside him and crawled to the nugget, then stared over at her brother's broken body. "Were you going to tell me, Seb?"

Later, Sary slept where she fell, tightly gripping the jagged lump of gold.

Chapter 15

Sary laid the last stone, scratching a faint cross. She bent her head and haltingly began, "Lord, here lies Sebastian Hercules Swinford. A fancy name for a—a good man."

Sary stumbled on. "No one could live up to that name, Lord." She looked up. "But he tried." Her gaze veered to the other graves and away.

"Don't have proper acquaintance of these two, but I guess you do."

She thought to say more, and failed. "Take him, Lord. I reckon you'll do what you will with the others."

Folding her hands, Sary dropped her head, this time more from exhaustion. She must finish this properly.

"The Lord is my Shepherd," she began. *"I shall not want. He maketh me to lie down in green pastures, he leadeth me beside the still waters, he restoreth my soul. Yea, though I walk through the valley of the shadow of death I shall fear no evil, for Thou..."*

She faltered and patted the grave.

"Fare thee well, Brother. Give my love to Jonathan."

Chapter 16

She must eat in the meantime—survive—
somehow. She dared not show the nugget. It might as
well be another rock. She would keep it, but she
surmised well what would happen. Oh, she could ride
her poor horse to Big Bear, sell the mule, or—she
glanced at Ned—set him free to frolic with the wild
mules the failed miners and panners had let loose. What
then? Hope for the fine folks of Big Bear to warm their
hearts? Be a Handi girl?

Never Julian!

She dared the notion to creep in…of cloying
connubial contact in Julian's bed, or worse—the horny
rasping grasp of those veined, knotted, loose-fleshed
hands roaming in the dark, clasping her to him on bitter
nights, the yellowed knotted fingers somehow longer
than they should be, as if his hands and wrists had too
many joints. Living out her days with a spitting,
hacking scarecrow whose breath wafted corruption until
her very flesh stunk of it…

She wryly studied her dress and hands and dirty
feet. Best not think too highly of her own self. She
allowed other notions to slither out for examination—
Wash plates thick with bacon and congealed ham fat in
cold greasy water at the drab boarding house? Scrub a
panner's grimy clothes in water so black one could
make indigo? Marry a rancher?

Why not? Better a helpmeet as a rancher's wife, scratching soil, than starving… All the while, she knew, bitterly, the long arm of Julian Delacorte would make certain no rancher or tinker-tailor, down to the grizzliest panner, *ever* came near her. She could teach. She'd had some learning before Jonathan, clear to grade eight. Yet she intuited the town would never allow their children to come to her.

What else is true? I have no wherewithal.

No money, no provisions, her precious quilts shrouding the dead, the ax dull, and winter stalking like the white ghost of a starving bear.

Memory of the Derringer's explosion came unbidden, along with that of slick fingers fumbling with the tiny, oh-so-lethal hammer of the elegant toy, the hot sensation drenching her clothes to the skin, clothes now washed pale and dried with an overall stain not unlike tea.

She laughed bitterly. Would the world suppose her clothes stained of innocent, *civilized* tea? Her head was addle-pated from shock and fatigue—and most of all hunger.

Where innocence fled, a plan entered in. The weight and heat of the nugget burned.

Sary leapt up and thrust her precious dress in the fire, poking at it with a stick until the fire burnt low and only ashes remained. A vague idea formed of what she was destined to do, but she scarcely wanted to examine those terrifying thoughts.

Dregs of supplies and the few items saved from Jules's and Ev'ret's saddlebags surrounded Sary. She studied her raw hands and cracked, dirty nails, smoothed her mud-caked petticoat, then lifted her face and gazed with yearning to the far hills.

Her stomach rumbled. Sary absently dragged out the whiskey jug, uncorked it, and sniffed. Making a face, she wiped the rim. Her tentative sip was followed by a shudder. *"Uuuuhgghhhh!* Oh! *Foul!"* She breathed deep and sipped more. Underlying the bitter was a wild sweetness. It fired her belly better than any copper warming pan, and she studied the jug affectionately. "So that's what all the hooraw's about. Well, forevermore!" Suddenly stars never looked lovelier, and she imagined a southerly breeze played across her face.

Sary rapidly dug out the flimsy papers and tobacco sack, clumsily rolled a cigarette, gingerly puffed. Tears tracked Sary's dirty cheeks as she dragged in harsh smoke; picking tobacco off her tongue, she puffed till the paper flared. She immediately wanted to roll another and was alarmed at her sudden need. *Save the rest, till hunger bites again.*

Sary swayed up, steadied, and looked past Big Bear Mountain, all the way to...*the gilded hills of Rome, or the wet acid greens of Cornwall...or Provence's empurpled fields waving lavender perfume in place of corn, or wheat...*

As she fondled the nugget, a bemused grin spread Sary's face, squinting at the layered peaks made gauzy in moonlight as if she spied a shining path.

She gripped the nugget tight, whispering, *"Velvet and jasmine and long skinny boats..."*

Chapter 17

Wham! Wham! Wham! Sary hammered fresh rungs in the shaky ladder, rungs whittled by firelight with a vengeance. She sucked at her thumb. A welt engorged as she watched—another injury joined the confusion of bruises, cuts, and gouges as she rammed splinters of wood into rusty bolt holes.

"There!"

At bottom, Sary paced "Seb's" tunnel, avoiding the mound of earth where he'd died, leaving it as a poor memorial; she set to checking the still-standing timbers, shoring the surviving uprights, straining her back and pulling her arms nearly out of their sockets.

The shaky ceiling was still a problem. A black dome of gouged earth, stable for the while, loomed above her like a black threatening sky.

Saving the best for last, Sary feasted on the golden swath belting the tunnel, running hands along it.

****

Day after day, and many nights, no matter the weather, Sary trudged through snapping bedsheets of rain, her hair plastered in dripping strings, or later over a dense snow pack, with ice spicules spearing her face, or braving the heat-shimmering winds of false spring, thick with pollen, always to the mine, hacking at the belt of pure ore, a woman obsessed.

On off-days, and those there were, she practiced

loading Ev'ret's Winchester, an ancient carbine, and Seb's shotgun, clumsily fitting shells to breeches, dropping them, pinching her fingers. Finally, she hefted the Winchester, fighting the stiff trigger. The gun smacked and spat fire, knocking her end over teakettle.

When Sary next fired the Winchester, she stayed planted, hitting the mining pan fifty feet off. Satisfied, she cleaned and oiled the weapons but kept Seb's shotgun, wrapping the rest in oilcloth and burying them close by the graves. It seemed appropriate.

****

Sary lay prone on snow patches, for winter's snowcap still hugged the rocky scalps of Big Bear's inaccessible peaks, and the wind soughed a bitter breath down her neck. She peered through a thicket like an animal, scarce breathing.

The scrawny creature twitched transparent ears as it approached her washing pan propped on a stick. The stick was tied to a string—and the string to a sprig of acorns smeared in fat. It took its prize as she watched, and in doing so, the hare yanked the stick. The tub *whumped* down, leaving the hare in what must seem premature dusk.

Sary hung the hare by its hind legs, making swift cuts at the neck and paws, then peeling the fur like a small coat and scraping its hide like Jonathon had when the men went hunting, back then. The pelt turned brittle as old shoe leather and was never used.

Grimly she checked for black blotches. Jonathan had said those meant fever sickness. The rabbit seemed healthy—pink...and scant.

****

That night Sary hunched, gnawing bones, with

grease running down her chin, eyeing the remains clinging to the spit. She grinned.

"Crazy, but not hungry!"

But she was. Throwing the tipped basin aside, the next dawn, Sary watched it roll downhill. Another stolen precious bit of bait. Sighing, she clung to roots as she climbed down to fetch it. As time went on, she wept, gnawed roots, boiled acorns for coffee and ground them for flatbread or gruel. She caught a glimpse of her face in the pail of water. It was pale from the mine, and thin, with huge eyes staring back at her. If Jonathan were alive, would he even know her? Would she ever know love again?

Odd, though—as her hands smoothed her belly, it seemed to have grown more rounded, while her face drew close and the scrap of rabbit saved back made her ill.

****

Julian awoke. He hung on. His couch danced across the floor. Objects crashed.

****

Deep in the mine, the earth rumbled. Sary braced, eyeing the timbers as they groaned, jumping in place. Closing her eyes, she thought of Seb and his arm sticking out from the mound of dirt. Sary pelted through the tunnel. Jolted to her knees, she crawled...and grabbed the quivering, juddering ladder and climbed, climbed, ignoring trembler after trembler, scrambling out topside. Ned heehawed and pulled at his rope, while she waited, eyeing the shaft, and once more descended as soon as all was still.

Later, after stuffing a growing heap of nuggets into Ev'ret's saddlebags, Sary gouged another safe-hole near the graves and slid a stone over it.

****

The creek, turgid with snowmelt, made shards of a weak spring sun as Sary gnawed a half-raw fish over a smoky fire.

Later, she sipped handfuls of water and gripped her belly with a look of utter horror while the skies opened to shed rain like tears. With water streaming her face, Sary goaded the thin horse to a gallop. Where? Anywhere would do, as long as the jouncing would change what was happening inside her. But eventually she was back where she had started, and with no alteration to her condition despite the rough riding.

In her slamped-down dress, she saw her belly plainly outlined. The horse bucked and drooped, until finally Sary lay on its mane, groaning. "We're both hungry, poor thing," as the sky crashed down.

Sary huddled, drenched, in the lean-to. Thunder nailed the sky and lightning sawed the mountain open, matching the tumult in her head.

****

Handi eyed Julian as he lifted sumptuous drapes in her cozy parlor. He flinched from the lightning splitting the air, bleaching his face.

"Jules likes his creature comforts. Hates cold!" Julian declared for the tenth time to torrents slashing panes like thin swords. "Cold as a whore's bejesus out there."

"So," Handi said, "do something. Anything. Respect's worth more than gold. Fool's gold, maybe, but you keep digging to keep your claim in."

"Fancy concept for you, Handi."

"Wasn't much valued for subtlety."

Handi lit lamps, revealing their ravaged features.

As Julian left, she whispered, "Get my boy back, Julie."

Julian briefly touched her shoulder.

****

A dying sun painted Julian's face bloody hues as he sat astride his horse at the edge of Big Bear. Night after night he sat saddled, eyes straining into the fading day.

Chapter 18

Soiled doves wandered in and out of Handi's kitchen as Julian leaned close in earnest confab, over a skillet of peach cobbler, with a potbellied man wearing a star.

The buttery morning contrasted cruelly with Julian's wan-as-ashes face and repressed strain as Sheriff Will dandled Pearl in corset and knickers.

All three ignored a weathered Indian hag, hung with fetishes, dozing by the stove, her shift peppered with burn holes from a clay pipe.

The girl finger-gouged the pastry. To her, the men might as well have been furniture as they forked cobbler straight from the pan.

Julian soured his mouth. "You *need to* be here?" He jerked his head. "Pearl, out."

Sheriff forked a bite, dandled the girl, wiped his mouth, and looked out the window before finally directing his gaze at Julian.

Julian shrugged, almost putting his face to the table, and with barbwire tension hissed, "My boy's *missing*."

Will nodded, as though to say, *So?* Pearl remained stoic.

"Three months now." Julian looked away.

The sheriff forked cobbler. "Figured Ratchet's top hound in your kennel." He licked the fork and squeezed

Pearl.

"Ratchet. *Ratchet!*" Julian snorted. "Ever see Ratchet break a horse? Uses bob wire for snaffles. My Jules is already a mite"—he looked at Pearl—"frisky."

"Un-hunh. Jules's in 'Frisco or the moon by now. Ain't the first time." The sheriff turned to Pearl. "He'll miss this peach pie, won't he, sweetie?"

She shrugged, shoveling it in.

Julian knocked Will's hand aside from helping her.

"I tell you, I gotta feeling, Will! Dammit!"

"Havin' his own peculiar hootenanny. Down to Belleville. Shoot! Drunk, in jail! That'd be the making of—"

Will halted at Julian's glare.

"Different, Will. Want you to see to it. Sweet on that plowboy's sister—Sary something, think her name was."

"Aim to be perlite, Julian. Don't mean no offense-like. Is your leg broke?"

"Victorville's brought in faro. A whole parcel of fresh meat without a mark or pox on 'em."

Will glanced up with sudden interest.

"Heard that."

"Got to keep customers sweet as aces." *Beseeching.* "You *know* that, Will. All this is Jules's. Someday—"

Julian hacked and spat, breathless, narrowing his eyes. "Why I pay for that hunka tin you got on your shirt front…"

Sheriff watched Julian struggle for breath, hitched his shoulders, and sighed, dumping Pearl.

"Sary, hunh? Heard some scuttlewag they mighta stumbled on some pinchbeck?"

"Pinchbeck, fool's gold. Greenhorns piss up more than creeks! See to it—and keep it in your vest."

"Got that right."

As he straightened his hat, Sheriff Will muttered, "Too dang embarrassed. Wet nurse. Might as well have teats."

****

Handi poured, downing two whiskies, passing tumblers to Julian and the sheriff.

The sheriff awkwardly twiddled his hat in the parlor's overripe elegance. "Camp's just okay. Poorly. Woman's jumpy as a branded calf. No sign of her man. Seb, is it?"

He downed his glass, saving the best. "Seen the horse. Big black runnin' with one of them old miner's mules."

Handi's hand shook as she poured again.

****

A hypodermic needle and a stained velvet case lay open beside Julian as he stared fixedly at a rubber tourniquet tied about his arm after he slipped the needle under. Uttering a slow raspy groan, he slumped, unwrapped his raddled arm, and brooded over Jules's tintype.

In time, he dropped it, bellowing, "Rat-chet!"

****

Sary, unkempt, muttering, wrapped in shawls, fondled gold gleaming dull by a fire lending her thin features a look of the witch—all flickering peaks, depressions, eyes red and feral and rimmed with purple. At the sound of thudding hooves, Sary hastily covered the saddlebags as Julian and Ratchet galloped in to a rock-spitting stop.

Julian barked before his mount skidded to a halt. "Happen across my boy and a big ugly buff of a man a while back?"

"Haven't anything but burnt acorn. You're welcome," she whispered.

Julian swatted Sary's offered pot.

Sary picked it up, hiding her face and shielding her body.

"Want nothing of your hands!" Julian rode over the camp, trampling the fire pit and her meal of boiled rabbit and fish bones, scoping the site, extending to the graves—he stopped. Sary quit breathing. He moved on as Sary shifted her skirts over the saddlebags, while Julian poked her poor lean-to.

Making a face, he inspected the scattered skillets, near empty hogsheads, the whole barebones mess, sneering, "Done well for yourself."

Ratchet lifted ragged under-drawers drying on rocks, dropping them with distaste.

"Only women's gewgaws."

"Where's that brother?" Julian turned eyes on her cold as marble tombstones.

"Hunting."

"Hunt a lot, does he?" Julian's gaze raked the gravesites and the hills. "Haven't seen the big spender in town of late."

****

From the knoll ridge, Julian and Ratchet watched Sary salvage a few crumbs from the dirt, eating as she went, before she hastened off though the trees.

****

Later the two crouched beneath a cedar at the edge of the clearing around the mine head. Julian choked a cough as Ratchet waved the sweet-spicy fronds aside.

"May I rot in Hell," Ratchet breathed. "Either the bitch's got sand, or she's loco."

Julian brushed branches in time to see Sary drop down the shaft, barely detecting a whisper of cloth against rock or slapping hands and feet scraping rungs.

Ratchet backed as if the mine smelled punk.

"Your brother had a jest played on him." Julian raised his voice yelling down. "I *said*, your brother's a *simpleton*!"

Sary jerked, stunned to see Julian's haggard face above her.

"Every last sorry son of a bitch in Big Bear'd plane this mountain to sea level with a teaspoon, if a whiskey tot of gold's left in her!" Julian continued.

Ratchet snorted and flipped a rock, tossing it dismissively, commenting, "Lucky's clapped out like a China whore."

Sary looked down, then huddled against the ladder as Ratchet wrenched it. Rubble bounced off her head. Sary flinched. The ladder bucked.

"Something to relate, Swinford?" Julian called.

"Please! I never *formally* met him—your son."

"Name's Jules. Jules Alexander Delacorte. Say it! *Jules!*"

Above, Julian nodded, grim, and Ratchet jerked a bracket from rusty bolts. Sary jammed a rung and started up, panicked the whole ladder would come loose.

"What with all the keep-out signs, Sary Swinford…" Julian coughed, then resumed, "Townsfolk know enough. Nobody much comes up here."

"Jules! Jules Alexan—?"

Footsteps crunched off.

Sary drooped over the rung and finished, "—xander Delacorte."

She tested the ladder. Her hands slipped, and she half-slid, half-tumbled to the rocky bottom. Far off, poor Neddie heehawed.

Sary shouted up. "Don't hurt Ned! Don't you dare hurt Neddie!" She was answered by laughter.

Chapter 19

Where was she? *Clammy earth. Rocks for a bed.*
Sary moved a dead arm out from under. "Ow!" Her
entire self was stiff, cold as an effigy. *The one missing
an arm,* she thought wryly. Aching hip to shoulder, she
slowly unbent.

That's okay. She had spent the night in the mine
before. Looking up at a muzzy sky, she thought, They'll
tire of this fox-and-geese game. But she was so hungry!

****

On day four, after three endless nights, Julian and
Ratchet dealt cards, dully quarreled, roasted hares, and
drank. They had long ago run dry of items of mutual
interest.

Julian seemed to thrive outdoors rather than
succumbing to the occasional fog and drizzle—his
cheeks had reddened, giving him the ruddiness of
health as he hacked the corruption of smoke-smogged
saloons from his lungs.

Below, Sary's nose twitched. Ratchet waved a
haunch over the shaft. Awakening with bones
clattering, bouncing off her head, she had dreamt of
food—*oatmeal swamped in cream and sorghum,
crumbly corn bread steaming with fresh-churned slabs
of melted butter, sausage seasoned hot with sage and
pepper. Thick hams browned and bubbling in the big
iron skillet...*

She wouldn't eat Ratchet's leavings. The thought revolted her as Ratchet's voice heckled, hollering down to her, "Dang! This jackrabbit's juicier than the last one! Big varmint, ain't it? Don't reckon I can stuff any more in. A downright sin. Just go to waste."

She heard Julian cough a laugh.

Sary paced, clenching her fists as Ratchet continued, "All crusty brown…"

She heard another rattle and stumbled over rabbit bones… *Good, there's a shred of meat.* She didn't heed Ratchet's chuckles. *Laugh away. You can't stay up there forever…but what if they destroy the ladder?* Her heart skipped mid-beat, and she rushed to test it— wobbly, but there.

****

Sary warmed her face in a thin blade of sun slicing the shaft, closing her eyes. She looked forward to it at this time of day, every day, as an event, with a chill sense of alarm. *How long will I be down here?* She'd long ago lost any real hunger and now sensed only a dull ghost of need and a terrifying feebleness.

To nail her coffin, Julian dribbled a canteenful of water down onto her like rain. A few drops splashed her head, the remainder lost in a fine mist.

She croaked up, "Mine's full of water, Delacorte!"

"Mine water's poison. Lead, arsenic, gypsum, chromium, mercury, and I don't know what all. Wouldn't be thinkin' on drinking it, Swinford. When it rains, whole mine floods. Rainy season comin' up." He gargled laughter.

"Least I'll be clean!"

****

By the sixth day, Sary was staggering, shaking

with cold in the dark wet tunnels. Rain trickled down the walls, wetting the floor, as squalls passed over her open tomb. She drank seepage. Seepage turned to a deluge—water poured into her boots. She hiked her skirts and checked the surge that swept out of the tunnels. Wading to the shaft, Sary hung on the ladder, near defeat.

Soon the water was waist-high, tugging her off, away from the ladder. Sary swam back, hands slipping, plunging beneath inky chill. The things bumping past her foretold a happening yet to come, one she could not dream of, as she bobbed, gasping, to the surface.

"Delacorte?" she croaked through chattering teeth. *He can't hear me! Are they there?* "I'm ready." She rasped as loudly as she could. She didn't know whether it was black water or tears running down her cheeks, and was only vaguely aware that Julian held the ladder while Ratchet climbed halfway down to drop a rope for her to cling to as he hauled her up.

****

The two men slapped and tossed Sary in her near-lifeless state back and forth between them, until Julian stayed Ratchet. "Hold on! She's gotta talk!" He gestured to the shaft. Ratchet nodded and yanked Sary back over the hole, flipping her head down.

"No!" Sary clawed to right herself.

"No Grimm's fanciful tales then," Julian warned.

"I'll tell. I promise! I'll show you." Ratchet upended her as Julian looked at her with curiosity. "What in pluperfect Hades you diggin' for? China? No *gold* down there."

She grimaced and dropped an egg-sized nugget from her fist, toeing it under pine needles as they dragged her off.

****

Sary guzzled cold acorn coffee straight from the pot, scanning the untouched graves.

Julian tossed her half a hard biscuit and jerked her around to face him and his cold mucous-gray eyes. "Time!"

Sary gobbled the food and spoke meekly enough through a full mouth. "Brother was hot as coals 'fore he went, Mister Delacorte. Seb went *awful* hard." She averted her eyes again. "Cankers. Bloody flux. Raving one minute, sweating and shivering the next, and when the deliriums took leave, Seb had these big bruises like silver eagles all over—"

Julian screwed his face. "Jules!"

"Wouldn't recollect him if he were standing on my toe. You asked where Brother was. That I can swear to."

She tugged a speechless Delacorte to the gravesites and urged shyly, "Dig him up if you like."

Julian stared at her, apoplectic, but Sary hung on while Ratchet choked with laughter.

"He'd be honored." Her words were earnest. "*Truly.* Brother didn't have any mourners."

Julian backed in frantic haste, swiping his hands on his fine coat, twisting his mouth.

"Get off me! Jules wouldn't have congress with the likes of you. Filth! Diseased filth! Look at you! My Jules? Hankering after you? I must have been mad!"

"No. I am," Sary breathed.

As they mounted, Ratchet eyed Sary's stomach. She tucked her shawl closer. As they rode out, Ratchet threw Sary another glance.

"Gettin' fat."

Julian looked at him and then at Sary, puzzled. "Don't see how. Let her rot."

She waited until their horses had thudded off, gobbled moldy wet cornbread, and then paced, head down, weary, back to the mine.

There she knelt, tossed in a rock that splashed far below, and waited.

****

The pick bit deep and stuck. Sary wrenched it out. *Hack, thud, scrape—screee,* skittering on the rock face, the sound muffled, yet her ears would ring long after she finally ascended to sun or moonlight. The impact jarred her whole body. The handle slid and blisters hardened to pads of callous. Sary sagged over the pickaxe to stare into the gloaming beyond the circle of oil lamp—she used fat from the occasional rabbit now. With a grunt she heaved the pick out to raise it again—a machine, halting, rusty, but still an unfeeling machine numbed to chill and gloom as she worked up a clammy sweat. At times she awoke where she fell, disoriented, the lamp out.

If she weren't still young, she would never have been able to endure, certainly not with the burden of her ever-growing tummy. She scarcely thought on it. Her gowns became filthy rags soaked with minerals and earth and dried so many times they were armor and insulation, until at last she donned some of Seb's old trousers, scarce snapping about her middle. Her hair was colorless, dry and thick with grit. But at least the mine held no terrors now, as a steady dribble of gold chunks and flakes littered the earth. The pick slipped on a down-stroke from her numbed fingers, dropping with a ringing clang. She stepped back a pace and again hefted it.

Periodically she stooped to sweep up the bronze pebbles, filling empty flour sacks, finding it more difficult as the days and weeks went by for, despite her privation, her belly kept growing. She feared her time would come soon.

One hand on her back, Sary dragged sacks to the shaft. For a while she affixed them to her waist to haul them up the ladder with her, until her waist grew too big. Then, experimenting with the mine's rusted pulleys, she hauled the ore in buckets to the surface, climbing the ladder after it in slow stages.

At times, she slept on the ground, where she would be wakened by Ned, with his foraging for acorns at dawn, to start all over. She didn't know what to do with the ore, or what her plans were, yet was terrified Delacorte would bring back vengeful townspeople.

There was no telling when or if the men would return.

****

On a rare night of rest, Sary scribbled in her Bible by the thin comfort of a fire that lent her pinched face a peach glow of health, muttering as she wrote, chewing her pencil.

"Don't know why I stay." She pressed the stub. "Harder each day. Into the Devil's bargain, Lord, I've inherited Brother's disease of greed and want."

She bent low, gouging the paper. "Like descending into Hell. I keep going down that mine like a fever. My blood tastes of metal."

Sary stared at demons in the light. "Lord help me…" She took a sip of whiskey, sloshing the jug to judge the remains, then corked it and stroked her tummy.

"And there's this baby, this—God-blasted *child!* Will I love it? Please, Lord, help me not hate and despise it."

****

Night-horses thudded across plains in her sleep— *descending the mine, over and over. At bottom, Julian holds a beam spike, beckoning. She runs on legs that melt, into Julian raising the spike…*

****

Sary awoke groggy the next dawn, raising her head from a rock pillow, arching her back. Tucking her shawl around her, she scratched together a fire, profligately tossing on it a largish log she'd saved back, and set crushed acorn to boil. She started, at a loss, as rocks gouged the earth by her fire pit. The very sky seemed to pelt stones of all sizes. Missiles thudded all about her, pocking the ground like hard rain while, on the knoll, town kids were yelling unseen, Ellie and young Cora Doheny and a lanky fourteen-year-old among them, lobbing pinecones and stones.

"Yah! Over here!"

The fourteen-year-old cupped his hands and shouted down. "Pa sez you're unhinged as a broke gate!"

Another boy. "Chase us! Bet you can't catch *me-ee!*"

Then five-year-old Cora piped, "Yer a fief, ana fat wady!" And tossed a small cone.

Sary's eyes grew huge, ignoring them as children of all ages spilled over the knoll, scooping barbed pine cones big as their heads, lobbing them as their legs blurred faster with momentum.

One of the children gnawed on what looked like—bread!

She clambered to meet them. "Fly on home now. Your mas wouldn't like you bein' here!"

They stopped, and some shrieked and scattered. She must look like a scarifying witch formed of mud. One dropped his bread, and Sary snatched it from the dirt. The bread had a round of sausage sticking to it. Smoothing her belly, Sary's crooked grin dissolved as she relished the spicy goodness, the peppery bite—the grease! "Fly away on home now, babies," she mumbled.

Yet the sustenance also gave new sight. She eyed the campsite as *they* saw it. The sad torn tarpaulin and heaped stone around her shelter, empty bags and battered tins. Long ago she had burnt the wagon for warmth.

She indeed must look like a witch, in a witch's lair, a witch who needed to conjure food fast.

****

Brushed and cleaned up the best she could, Sary rode through Big Bear on her thin horse, ramrod straight, bundled in her thickest shawl, looking neither right nor left, yet seeing everything.

Folks peered through windows, traveling one to the next.

She slanted a look at Handi's—*a twitch of curtain*...

****

The proprietor looked up, grin still in place at the bell, drooping like his mustache as he assessed Sary.

"No more free grub, *hear?*" He jerked a look to

Delacorte's saloon. "Told you—your kind ain't welcome."

"But I have—"

"Don't care none, do I—you could have a pocketfula gold, and I said—"

"No." Sary tried a shaky laugh. "No gold." And, as she retreated, her gaze leaped unwilling over sorghum, salt pork, pickles, crackers.

She walked on stiff legs to Doheny's Mercantile, next to Delacorte's Saloon, and showed something to Aaron.

He shook his head—No. Grace almost took the small cameo wrapped in a scrap, while Ellie and Cora stood mute.

"Anything?" Sary fixed them with her eyes.

The Dohenys stood, arms crossed. Aaron flicked concerned glances at the door.

Once outside, Sary gazed with longing at McAdam's Hostelry. Between drapes, Handi squinted at the hazy figure. She knew who it was, all right, and felt a tiny warmth that quickly hardened to lead where her heart was. She couldn't make out details, but the gal looked rough. Well, she'd warned her, hadn't she? She wasn't sure she *would* take her on now. She dropped the drapes.

Behind Sary, bare feet swiftly pattered the muddy planks as Pearl ran up, sobbing. She walloped Sary in the face and dashed off.

Sary, stunned, wiped her cheek with Jules's monogrammed handkerchief, then tucked it back at her waist—and didn't notice that the handkerchief dropped into the muck.

****

She would have had to be a seer to conjecture that Little May—a chunky Spanish girl and one of Handi's soiled doves, plucked it up from the mud a few seconds later and hence set a wind in motion that would blow Sary's life awry sharper than could any cutting mountain gale.

Chapter 20

Grace, her daughters Ellie and Cora, and three other women glanced up as Sary rode out, head held high. They smiled knowingly, silver needles flashing over a quilting frame. Grace could scarcely wait for the right moment to drop her account on their ears of how bedraggled the uppity flatlander had looked earlier and how *hiz honor* Delacorte warned Aaron not to have no truck with her. Why, she didn't rightly ken.

A sweet-faced old woman with her nose bent to the quilt squinted, murmuring, "Hear poor mite's crazy as a bedbug."

A woman with eyes like a bird, stabbed her needle in pecky stitches. "Wicked! I say! I heered she runs buck-naked in the snow."

The pretty young matron, whose parlor it was, smiled gently at Ellie. "Must get awfully cold then." Ellie giggled, and then Grace nailed the group with eyes hard and shiny as her thimble. "Heard she slept with her brother."

"Grace!" The young matron nodded to the children.

"Not *deef!* Unnatural congress with her brother!"

The old woman muttered, "A closed mouth maketh a wise heart...*Gracie.*"

"You can well scoff. But it ain't natural..."

Then Cora piped up in a yelp, "She's real *fat!*"

123

The women dropped their needles. The sweet old woman asked, "Little Cora? How do you know these things?"

Ellie butted in, pooching her flat tummy out, mimicking pregnancy. "We go spy on her!"

Little Cora shrilled, "An' she jumps in the water wiv-out *any* clothes on, an she talks to the *ay-er.*"

The bright-eyed woman stabbed her with shiny needle eyes. "What else did you see, Cora?"

Cora hung her head.

Grace prodded her daughter. "Don't stop now, Cory Anne!"

Ellie pinched her sister and took up the tale. "She goes down that mine-hole you tole us to stay way from, Mama!"

The women looked at each other.

Ellie continued, "And she got a whole sack a gold!"

The women abandoned needles in the quilt and looked out for a sighting of Sary, spinning back to Ellie with avid eyes.

****

Lamps were lit in Doheny's Mercantile as townsfolk, panners, ranchers, and shop owners trickled in with food and jars of whiskey and beer. Someone messed with a harmonium, until a rancher rapped a jelly jar filled with spoons, braying, "Shush down now—ain't a cotillion."

The ginger-bearded ironmonger barked, "If her brother stumbled onta somethin' big, why're we sittin' here beatin' a cold anvil?"

Grace shrilled, "The Lucky's ours more'n anyone's."

Ginger-beard contributed, "Ain't seen the plowboy."

And a bright-eyed woman drew the conclusion, "Murdered him! What kind of sister'd do that for Satan's lucre?"

"Don't like the way she dresses—or *don't* dress—around my boy." The bright-eyed woman harrumphed at her lanky fourteen-year-old.

Ginger-beard grumbled, "Why ya think he goes up there?"

The bright-eyed woman snapped a cookie, breaking it. "How we gonna do the serpent in? Hang her? We gonna hang her? Let dogs lap her blood like Jezebel—or Mess-a-*lina!*"

Grace nodded, thunking Aaron sharply on the arm.

Men sighed, embarrassed, and spoke low, while women set out food and avidly listened.

****

Sary knelt awkwardly by the creek, dippering ice water even though blessed summer approached. She'd boil some bones, again mixed with spring greens and acorns beat to mush. It numbed hunger somewhat. She snapped her head at a distant but approaching commotion, like the feral woodland creature she had become, alert, on guard.

"Not town kids again. But"—she smiled—"they'll have food! Pockets stuffed with maybe nuts and raisins and apples…"

Sary crouched, bewildered.

In place of youngsters, she eyes a mob rushing down, spilling through her camp—a ginger-bearded man picked up a burning stick and fired her poor lean-to, and ordinary women ventured behind the men to stroll like inspectors though her camp, her home, making faces and soon cavorting about the fire.

"Where ya hidin', Sary?" they hailed. "Wouldn't show my face, neither!"

Bitter at their antics, she nevertheless grinned. She needed to blend in with her drabness, let them think she wasn't there. *Let them have their fun. Nothing worth saving. The gold's well hidden.*

Her smile froze as a fat woman yanked Sary's wedding dress from her little humpback trunk with the roses painted inside and pawed deeper like a dog, tossing what looked like rags into the dirt.

Then Grace pointed at the fat woman and pelted over, screeching, "She's found gold!"

The mob, frustrated and eager for mischief, shoved the fat woman aside, upending Sary's trunk of its poor keepsakes, tossing it aside. Then she watched them circle, agitated, through the pines, guns thrust out as they edged closer to the graves. The women still clawed over her wedding dress, even while the fat woman tried to struggle it over her bosom, ripping off bits of the lace Sary had tatted herself.

Sary jerked around at a cracking sound.

The panner, the man she and Sebastian had come across that first day so long ago, had just smashed their chute against a tree. She jerked back at the sound of gunfire and Ned screaming, and watched, stunned, as another brave townsman target-practiced on Ned the mule. She had never heard a mule scream before. Ned was down. Sary shut her ears and eyes as she groped for Seb's shotgun. She opened them to see the man with ginger hair walk over, shove the shooter aside, and put a bullet though poor Ned's brain.

Ginger-beard turned wild-eyed as buckshot zinged the rocks in a fuselage out of nowhere, spitting granite left and right. More pellets gouged the earth, this time around his feet.

"Who's there?" He hopped aside awkwardly, flattening, looking everywhere. "Hell's fire! Why didn't we hog-tie her first?"

"Did *you* see her? Didn't know the bitch had Custer's army, did we?" the panner snarled. He backed to a horse, eyeballing the firs. Women shrieked and scattered, red-faced and cursing in their fashion, as Sary jacked and aimed. Buckshot now peppered around Grace's toes. She shrieked and ran for Aaron. Aaron tugged a furious, beet-red Grace, speechless for once, off out of range, where Grace tossed him aside and shook her fist at the trees. "Can't hide it forever, Swinford! We'll find it! You got gold, and we'll ferret it out, last thing we do! Thief! *Harlot!* Hear me?" she screeched, "That gold's ours!"

"Gracie! Come. You'll get shot. *Sweetheart.*" Aaron looked hopeful, but then the bright-eyed woman yelled, exasperated, at the men, "Jaspers! Come back here!"

When they kept saddling up and galloping out, she too shouted back at Sary, "Don't sleep, whore a Babylon! Dogs will lick your spilled blood!"

Ginger-Beard dragged her off. "Save it till Sunday, Martha."

The fat woman tried to stuff all the things back into the trunk and carry it under her arm, but then she dropped it and fled with the rest.

****

Sary wandered aimlessly about the desecrated

camp. Her wedding dress was lost forever. Her fate seemed to be one of listening to fading hoof beats. Sary backed, tumbling over a stump, as a brown bear reared, stretching wide jaws filled with yellowed, curved tusks dripping saliva. It gave a garbled roar, affixing her with small brown eyes, then shuffled, pigeon-toed and snuffling through its nose, to drag off Ned.

Later, Sary studied Ned's carcass. The bear was gorged and no doubt, she hoped, sleeping. She had no more shells in her pocket or she would have killed it for food. Eat or be eaten. She squatted with a cleaver, hacking Ned's meat from bone. Gagging, Sary tore strings of raw meat off with her teeth. She rested, trying to keep the rubbery, gamey stuff down, and finally tossed the gnawed bones into a stew pot, numbly watching it foam and boil. Late snowflakes melted on the surface. She shivered and waited for the bones to soften.

****

Handi nibbled fruitcake and poked about her foggy kitchen, stoking the cherry-bright stove hotter still. Laundry steamed on lines crisscrossing the room— chemises, underpants, petticoats, and pillowslips. Behind her, the Indian hag tossed herbs into washtubs fronting the stove.

Handi's mostly naked gaggle of girls were in high good humor this night as they lined up, naked to the waist, for the hag's clinical inspection, pantaloons down, petticoats hiked.

As the hag fingered the last dove, Handi clapped hands. "Time, my soiled little doves! Time to wash your funsies and your fancies." She hummed. It was her favorite time. All her girls together, having fun in a sisterhood and being the age they were—*mostly,* she amended, eyeing Sobriety Sally's gray strands. *Have to darken them up some, with strong black tea…but she's a heller in bed.*

Girls goosed about, squealing, stepping in tubs as Handi wandered to a drying line, smile still fixed in a withered line of carmine. She spied the monogrammed hanky, admiring it in the rosy light.

The smile turned to a crimson downward slash. Handi, as white-faced as the fine linen hanky on the line, yanked it off, mouthing the initials.

"J-A-D," she breathed. *"Jules Alexander."* Crushing the hanky to her breast, she whirled, stabbing them with her voice. *"Who. Stole. This?* Where did this come from?"

Girls halted in soaping each other, wide-eyed and sulky. Little May glowered, ducking. Handi slapped her, dragged her from the tub, and yanked the wet naked fat girl, soap in her eyes, kicking and yowling down the middle of Big Bear, through the saloon and hence to Julian's office. Slamming the door on a curious crowd, Handi forced Little May to her knees, thrusting the handkerchief at Julian.

"Little May didn't have this before!"

The fat girl covered herself. "Didn't snitch it! Found it! I didn't! That daft bitch!" And broke into coarse bawling.

Julian buckled on a gun, knocking Little May over as he rushed out. "Put something on!" he yelled back.

****

Sary patted Seb's grave, took a nip from the jug and waved it, drunkenly singing. "This is it, Seb!" she bawled. "Las' a your gold! Ever little scrap." And she

129

spun a clumsy dance step, nearly falling. "Gonna be rich as tha' king, Sebastian! *Everythin'* gold an' velvet, silk an' lace an'…an'…an'…"

She caught sight of her own ragged skirt, fringed in dried mud, averted her eyes, and continued bellowing to the moon.

"Gonna smell like *jasmine!* Ya hear? Roses! And lily of the valley! *Hear that, Seb?* And all you women, and the whole damned town—Gonna eat till I'm sick of liftin' a *spoon! I'LL SMELL LIKE A HARLOT!*"

Sary collapsed, giggling.

Dropping the shawl, she lurched into a dance led by her belly, warbling off-key, *"I'm only a bird in a gilded cage. Oh, what a…sight to seeeeeee…"* And so she didn't hear Julian falling off his saddle, watching her stumble through another chorus…

"Oh, what a life I've led…" Sary sang.

Julian could hardly believe what he saw. In his befuddlement, Julian might have said Sary was a vision of all that was *holy*—if he were a religious man—an icon, her full figure backlit by fire. He clutched Jules's handkerchief and called down shakily, "Truly? Seb was your brother?"

Sary slurred, "My brother?" She looked into the dark, suddenly sober. *"Delacorte?"*

Julian stumbled to the ground, half hands-up, half rushing to his reward. "Said you didn't know him, by God!"

Julian swept her bursting figure as Sary stood rooted. "And you've got—"

His eyes were all the stars in heaven.

"Jules's—*my boy's* brat's in there!" He dropped to his knees like a supplicant seeing the Virgin Mary. "I knew my boy was foolin' around with you. I knew it in my bones!"

Sary had a splinter-flash vision of Ev'ret on top of her and Jules sitting atop his horse, before flinching as Delacorte jumped up and wildly eyed the camp. He strode about, yelling, "Jules!"

Sary's eyes darted to the graves and back, reliving that day. *Seb. The shot fired. The blood. Her weariness to the bone.*

"He'll be back." Julian paced, circling the trees. "Jules left *that* with you!" He stabbed at Sary's belly. "You come with me now." He called feverishly into the night, "He'll be back, foolish boy!" Julian snatched at her. "Come on! You can't stay here."

"If I could ease your torment, I would. Don't mean I'm going *anywhere* with you!"

He grabbed at her. She snatched Seb's shotgun. "I'll blow this baby to Kingdom Come and myself with it. I will!" she warned.

Julian backed, palms up, crooning. "Overwrought. *Delicate.* Like a woman *should* be. You're in the family way. You—"

He moved to her.

Sary jerked the shotgun.

Julian retreated, infuriated. "Agreed. Agreed!" Julian snarled. "Never notioned violets wilting on a fainting couch, all corseted, were worth warm spit anyways!"

He struggled to mount. "See, I'm going." He stared hungrily. "Be well!" Julian croaked back from the dark. *"He'll want for nothing! You'll see. Jules's brat will be healthy—strong!"*

Sary didn't wait until more hoof beats thudded into

the night. Hobbling to the graves, she dug out the saddlebags and dragged them to the horse. On the second trip, Sary doubled, moaning, to the ground and, in time, reburied her gold.

****

She awoke, shotgun by her side, curiously rested, her burden at ease. She rubbed her belly—the child she still couldn't quite believe in was still stirring. There was an icy blue sky and sun with the kiss of spring on her thin cheek. Little did she guess the drama soon to descend from the knoll ridge was not Delacorte, or townspeople, but in the shape of kids—Ellie, little Cora...

Sary roused, gathering brush, building a fire, mind racing like a squirrel up and down a tall tree, leaping branch to branch for a way to escape Delacorte and his suspicions. On the knoll, the fourteen-year-old boy avidly observed every motion, hissing to the others. "Let's go get her. A *har-lot,* Pa said. Almost made a sieve outta him the other day!"

Little Cora ran ahead, windmilling down on scrawny little legs. "Let's go get her!"

"Cora! Stay here. Cora-Anne!" Ellie's commands were lost among the town kids' screaming, lobbing stones, pinecones, clods of dirt. Below, a sudden whinny as a rock struck Sary's horse.

It bucked and fought its rope.

To Sary, everything erupted about her.

Boiling water fell into the fire like an explosion.

Steam hissed like a snake, billowed, and formed thick, moist, shifting curtains.

Tinder-dry pinecones exploded all around Sary like sharp bits of shrapnel. The barrage of explosive *pops* continued, detonating like gunfire, spitting hot cinders, striking her hard as bullets.

Squinting through smoke and steam, Sary dimly viewed darting images. Her horse screamed as burning missiles pocked its flanks. Then, breaking loose, hooves slashing, it pranced through the coals.

Sary whirled in confusion and fright, firing at the air, ducking from the hooves, backing, flinching as pine barbs sizzled on her hair and skittered down her face.

Explosions burst all around her. Bullets that stung but didn't draw blood.

"Stop! Stop shooting at me! Why are you—?"

Sary hobbled, one arm over her head, the other on her belly, twisting, turning, and still the cones came, bursting, flinging their hot sharp barbs. She spun clumsily and reloaded blind, firing into the air as emerging figures became more distinct. Flashes of color now, with misty howling faces. She laid down the gun.

Cora came running, hysterical, legs pinwheeling out of control, down the hill and tripped, striking her head on a boulder, and lay there—inert.

"Cory! Get on up!" Ellie urged. "Mommy's gonna be mad on you!"

At the sound of scared young voices, Sary dropped her gun like it burned and waddled clumsily, holding her tummy, up the rise.

"Ya kilt Cora!" Ellie cried. The fourteen-year-old scooped little Cora up, shrieking, "Our Pas'll come after you, and fix you good, now!"

"Wait!" Sary sprawled in the dirt. "Let me see her!"

When she tried to rise, she doubled over, gasping in pain and shock. "Oh, God!" She looked fearfully back to camp. "They'll come descending like the seven plagues of Egypt." Hitching up as fast as she was able, Sary lurched after her skittish horse as the children wailed into the distance.

****

Behind Handi's outhouse, Julian gripped the Indian hag's withered arms and looked up in irritation at the disturbance, even more irritated as a dove trotted out of Handi's kitchen, glanced sourly at the two of them, and slammed the outhouse door.

"Piss and get out!" Julian bawled.

The dove exited, dragging down her skirts. "Hmmmmmph!"

The hag jerked Julian back, watching his mouth as he spoke. Half listening to the ruckus out front, Julian absently handed her whiskey and a rifle, refocusing on her creased face. "Do for Sarabande Swinford like you do for Handi," he hissed. "Only it lives. You hear? It *lives!*"

The wailing of the children became louder, closer. Both glanced to the street, but the hag tugged him back, eyeing his pinkie ring. Julian wrested it off and threw it at her.

Out on the main street, Grace took dead Cora into her arms, crying, "Mister *Doheny!*"

****

That night, Cora was laid out on Doheny's dry goods counter. Grace wiped her limbs and face, combed Cora's lank blond hair, kissed the gash on her forehead, and drew a quilt to Cora's hands, tucking a few dusty mountain weeds betwixt the small fingers.

Ratchet hovered, greedy for Aaron and Grace's pain. "Ain't fambly rakehell for nothin', Aary. Use me."

Aaron looked up, pink-eyed and weeping, as Ratchet drew out the pain. "Little Cory's too *yo-ung.*" Ratchet threw the quilt back. "Poor little mite. Just look at her." Grace flinched as Ratchet stroked Cora's waxen cheek.

"Julian. Julian takes care of us," Aaron sobbed.

"Little Cory's yours, Aary." Ratchet leered.

Aaron looked off from Ratchet's rapacious face. He stiffened.

"I'll do it. Me. I'm Cory's pa. Someday." He lifted a pale curl, looking up at Ratchet with wet eyes. "Help me."

****

Julian, lavishing more gingerbread to a small side porch of the ever-expanding drawing of a Victorian house, frowned at riders thundering past, tossing his pencil as he rose. "Fuckin' tent show out there!"

From the saloon porch, Julian watched the last rider gallop out. At a flashing glimpse of Ratchet's face, sudden alarm gripped him.

Ratchet was chafing his hands with grim glee as riders passed the saloon, ropes looped about pommels and a jug of kerosene in one's hand as they galloped away from Grace and Aaron's store.

****

Sary waited, crouched behind one of the huge boulders with Seb's shotgun cocked. The ground quaked beneath her feet before the lynch mob thundered in, sighting on the first, then the others as most dismounted and spread warily about camp.

She tracked a man with a slouch hat stepping past her boulder. "Over that copse last time," he said. "Step lively!" He twirled as Sary showed herself, her belly thrust to counterbalance the gun, shouting over his head to tell all of them, "Wasn't my intention that sweet child got hurt. No intention you saying it was!"

Sary hadn't noticed Grace, but now the woman raged forward, hands curled into claws and screeching, "*Hurt!* Ya killed her! Kilt my baby!" as Ginger-Beard circled behind.

"No!" Sary cried. "Job would've been sore tormented and found wanting!"

Behind her, Ginger-Beard's boots scraped rock. "Job, is it!" Ginger-Beard hissed, his face mottled and red as his beard. "We'll torment you to fuckin' perdition!" Sary backed against the boulder, bumping the stock. Her gun exploded. Ginger-Beard fell ugly and died ugly.

Aaron peered around, saw him, and threw up. "Oh Lordy," he gasped, before calling out, "Gracie!"

Sary eyed the stunned, infuriated mob robbed of their easy prey, scanned the rope and kerosene. She reloaded, but there were just too many of them. One dragged her out. One splashed Sary with kerosene. The harsh oily stench clogged her nose. Fortunately, it only landed on her arm, but her skirts sparked and caught as the mob yanked her through the fire pit to a cedar with one branch hanging low like a twisted beckoning arm.

Grace pushed through, still screeching. "Knot the rope! Aary! Knot it! Knot the damn rope!"

"Already done." A short man with glasses shoved Aaron aside. "Already done, Gracie."

But she yanked it away and threw the rope at Aaron. Aaron gently tossed it at a branch, taking several tries. Grace snatched the noose from her husband and threw it vehemently over in one go, then grabbed Sary and looped it around her neck while the mob held her thrashing legs.

"Like your new necklace, dearie? You and your unnatural whore's son can wear it proud in Hades," she gloated, backing as Sary's skirts began to smolder. She cackled. "Maybe Hades can't wait!"

"Stand back!" A rancher shoved Grace off-balance, hitching Sary, kicking and clawing at her neck, onto his shoulder. He too jumped aside from her charring skirt while she desperately toed a tree bole, striving to boost herself and give her neck ease.

A woman moaned in the crowd, turning from the inevitable *thunk* of rope and crack of Sary's neck, the expected odor of fire, bracing for Sary's terrible screams—but the *thunk* didn't come, and the woman peered out, slightly disappointed, to see Grace dash Sary's foot from the toehold, snarling, "No, you don't!"

Sary slipped. If she weren't strangling, she'd choke from smoke. Stretching for a branch overhead, just in fingertip reach, she gripped it and kicked Grace square in the chin before the limb snapped and her toe found the tree bole again. Her smoldering damp petticoat steamed as Grace yanked Sary's ankles, avoiding most of the next blows Sary aimed. However, the mob seemed to have a mixed reaction, undecided between Sary's efforts and Grace's terrifying force.

Suddenly Julian exploded into their midst. Reined short, his mount reared and the man with the glasses was felled with a horseshoe indentation. Julian circled, raking them furiously, lashing reins, bellowing, "Thought I wouldn't hear? Sneak in like cowards and do your *filth*!" He turned purple but continued slashing and screaming at the stunned mob. "You'd murder my boy's *boy!*" He gasped, breathless, as Sary dangled and struggled to place her foot on the tree knot. Grace jumped back with evil still on her face.

The rotted bole snapped. So consumed by her concentration on that small toehold and the barbs of hemp biting her neck, Sary had never thought she'd really *die,* but she braced now for the inexorable jerk, thunk, and irrevocable tautening of rope— Would she hear it squeak as she twisted at the end for the delight of the haters…be a lesson and spook-tale for the young?

She couldn't breathe anyway, with smoke skirls now flying away in charred calico, for her dress has caught. Her petticoats, damp, smoldered rather than burned. She thought all this in the split second she plummeted, clawing the noose.

Julian, choking in the same smoke, cantered up. Sary detected the dark blur of a sleeve as he slashed the rope and her body thudded heavily to the ground. She beat at her charred skirts, coughing raggedly, her throat constricted by the noose.

Meanwhile, Julian wheeled his horse, firing indiscriminately at the skulking mob and roaring, "Puling scum! Never come to my stores, drink in my bars, or be welcome in my house!" Behind him, Grace still strove to yank Sary back to the tree.

Aaron timidly offered, "Shot our kids, Julian— Mister, ah…Delacorte."

"And the whole world's weeping!" Julian snarled.

"John?" whines a wife. "Need somewheres ta buy provisions. Somewheres ta go."

Julian knocked Grace aside. "Loosen it!"

Grace bared teeth but savagely yanked the rope off

138

over Sary's head with extra harshness, kicking Sary's ribs before Julian jerked her away. He glowered at Sary, reaching down, his face purpling with effort. "Now will you come?"

Sary rubbed her neck and twisted her mouth. "With *them*?"

The mob sniggered as Julian circled, impotent.

He cantered over and snatched Sary's horse. "Stay in your own Hell then!"

"Best go, Gracie," Aaron said. "Heard Mister Delacorte. Cory's gone."

He held out his hand. Grace accepted it.

The rest trailed after.

****

A rooster crowed.

Her throat was raw, swollen. Why?

Sary fumbled at her neck. It all came back…a rope like rusty braid, skirts burning, acrid. She jumped from her cot whooping and squinting at an apparition and sat down hard: Handi, in ruby velvet, frothy pink petticoat, and a glitter of gold and amethyst, smoking, skirt spread around Sary's three-legged stool on the dirt.

Sary squinted again.

Another apparition loomed, hung with fetishes, wrinkled as a wadded rag left to dry, in stained, cinder-pocked chamois muttering *Serrano*—Indian talk.

The hag prodded Sary with bony, dirty fingers.

"*Boy!*" The hag's eyes widened from flinty pebbles to polished agates in the parched earth of her face, addressing Handi in English. "Big!"

The rooster squawked mid-crow as she swung it. The snap was a crack shot. Blood spurted in a tin mug. She rummaged in her sling bag for eggs, cracked two in the blood, stirred in chilies and dried herbs with a dirty finger, and grabbed Sary's chin.

Sary guzzled it, holding out for more, wiping her bloody chin.

The Hag's grin showed two teeth, one on top, one on the bottom. She squeezed the rooster's neck over the cup.

Handi tossed a last look and patted a cow on passing, a cow hitched to a travois and prodded by a sullen Indian. As the youth hacked saplings, the hag bossed him without mercy.

****

Stars scintillated, stuck like sequins against the bosom of earth's black velvety shawl, Sary thought dreamily. The hag had given her something. A fire blazed. Sary gulped warm milk. The leanto had been transformed into a woven sapling-mud hut. Sary never saw the young stripling Indian again.

Still gabbling in *Serrano*, the hag held a tiny chamois shirt and fist-sized moccasins to her own scrawny chest.

Sary supposed she was grinning, but it was difficult to tell.

Souring her face, the hag withdrew delicate infant finery from behind her back. "Handi. No good!" She spat. "Like smoke!"

Sary giggled as the hag's face showed through the thin garments Handi had sent.

Sary stirred in the night. Tiny beaded moccasins lay by her pillow, while the hag sat nearby in the dark.

****

Handi wandered through a jungle of a nursery, carrying a kerosene lamp, revealing ghost shapes that sprang to life before her haggard, yearning face—a claustrophobic evil of furniture and toys—a gaudy hobbyhorse with large plume tail and glittery eyes, an ugly cradle suffocating in yards of tulle and rosettes. Handi touched things, stroked them, and opened a chiffarobe to even more overweening baby finery.

****

Sary sweated, biting her lip, holding the Derringer under the hag's jaw. Yanked from her grateful dreamlike state, Sary now saw the hag for what she really was, Delacorte's jailer and spy, for all her worth and comfort.

Then Ev'ret and Sary's boy was *there*, robustly squalling.

The hag removed the hefty baby before Sary could stop her—even if she wanted to. Did she? Till now the child—infant—baby—she didn't know what to call it—the wretched thing was a phantom child, a "never-never." God's bitter jest. Not real. A *thing* that Julian lusted after.

Then Sary glimpsed dark ringlets and furiously kicking legs. In fact, the squalling thing was a tempest of thrusting fists and toes punching the air with boisterous kicks.

She looked off.

I can't love it!

Can't even look at it.

Oh! Wait! Its foot! Round pink toes, like peas...or pearls on a string. A tiny coral heel shaped like a ball-peen hammer...

The hag walked away with it and, in place of vanishing into the night as Sary supposed, wiped it clean.

What is it? Sary lifted up, then dropped back, studying her nails as if unconcerned. *If it's a girl...?*

Sary shuddered—her mind unable to avert from Ev'ret.

A brawny, lumpy, dull-witted, potato-faced girl? Uhgggh.

Then, the hag held out the huge curly-headed boy, so ugly he was cute. He looked at Sary with slightly cross-eyed wonder. Sary averted her eyes, revulsion stitched across her face.

The hag walked off.

The baby howled.

Sary glanced sideways. Hardened her heart. *Better not. It's better off with the hag—or Handi.*

No.

Yes. Even Julian. God blast the Devil.

Handi will look after it.

Handi and her French Pox?

The doves with the odd scabs and grimy nails?

The baby howled lustily in reproach. *Maybe once. I will just look at him, and then bury the whole episode in a graveyard of memories, well apart from sweet thought of Jonathan.*

"No. Wait! Wait! Let me see it. Him." With a crooked smile, Sary held out her arms.

"A fine healthy boy!"

Sary jumped. The hag backed as Delacorte, jubilant, blocked the flap. "Jules! Jules!" he crowed. "You should see your son!" He ignored Sary, who sat, flushed, in classic pose, arms made muscular and supple by the mine reaching determinedly for the squalling boy.

"Give him to me. Me!" Sary demanded. The hag

slanted eyes at Julian.

Julian nodded and cupped the baby's head as the infant waved potato-sized fists. He smirked. "Bare your bosoms, Swinford—for my grandson."

The hag edged close behind Sary while Julian focused hungrily on the curly head and broad button nose poking beyond rounded cheeks.

Sary stared bullets. "Leave...and I might!" Clutching the boy, Sary waved the Derringer between them.

He backed, furious. "I've seen that play-toy before! Handi has a lot to answer for. I can wait!"

At the doorway, he barked, "And he's called Jude! Jude Alexander *Delacorte*!"

Chapter 21

Somehow the name stuck.

Sary was indifferent. The child had a satisfying weight. That was all she told herself. She had no milk. The cow would have to do. Yet Ev'ret faded like a rapidly receding nightmare as Sary, Jude strapped to her chest, strode about camp righting things, chopping branches, stacking them—*strengthening*—during which the hag yet kept her blackbird eyes peering from a nest of wrinkles—and in truth Sary needed her. She concocted miracles of herb-rabbit stew and other nourishment her body craved more than before.

Once Sary alerted, seeing the hag nip into the forest, but was disappointed beyond bearing on her reappearance with yet more herbs and spring greens. Yet Sary's body ached for the iron the tender greens were rich in, and so grew stronger.

When a week old, Jude developed a cough, his little chest heaving with effort. Sary sat poker-faced as the hag pounded herbs with rabbit fat, smeared his chest, wrapped him in heated flannel, and stuck a skillet of coals under his crude bassinet. Soon, Jude sweated and his chest eased.

One night, though, was all it took.

****

Jude cried and cried as a steady rain pattered outside. Sary slept on. Her gun, kept out of habit, slipped to the earthen floor. With sturdy little fists, Jude squirmed from her side. The hag removed him. Sary murmured and snored on.

****

Down at Delacorte's Saloon, it was a full, earsplitting melee, still early by rioters' standards but made doubly beguiling by the rain icing outside walls.

The only grim face was Julian's and that of a poker player slouched as low as his chips. Julian brooded over the desultory game, watching the door and drinking heavily. He was snarling at the loser when, abruptly, the saloon mob parted like the Dead Sea and the hag's drenched figure paced through their midst with an oilskin poncho-wrapped bundle. She placed Jude before Julian, atop the pile of chips.

Whores crowded. Handi hobbled over. Ratchet, a dyspeptic onlooker, slugged back a whiskey as Delacorte clutched Jude in rough yellow hands and revolved with a look of triumph over the lustily howling baby for all to see. Never taking his eyes off Jude, he motioned to the barkeep and nodded to the hag clawing his sleeve, piercing him with adamantine eyes. If, for an instant, Julian gazed perplexed over Jude's broad features, the look melted in puddles of adoration.

"Give her something!" He barked at the barkeep.

"What?"

Julian swatted Handi and the hag aside. "Anything. That old horse of yours."

The hag shuffled to the barkeep, keeping her beady gaze steady. "Brandy. Cognac. Good cognac. And horse."

The barkeep grimaced and reached under the bar.

Ratchet slipped out unnoticed.

Chapter 22

Rain slashed outside Sary's sapling hut slackened to a fine drizzle. Inside, Sary started awake to a dead fire, groping for infant Jude. The pallet was empty beside her. His comforting milky warmth was gone. A moccasin lay abandoned on the dirt floor. She raced out, half-naked, into the rain that plastered her in a quicksilver skin.

Returning, Sary stooped, then pressed the tiny moccasin to her chest, rooted as a tall pine, her wet face a war of fear, outrage, and strange relief. She knew well where the hag had taken him, and she thought on the baby out there—cold, wet, without shelter.

Sary galvanized, gritting through clenched jaws, "No, she *won't!*" She had no idea what shortcuts the hag might have taken, but she knew where she would end up.

She bolted stew left in the pot, stuffed her mouth with flatbread. Strapped on layers of clothes, threw a scrap of oiled poncho over all, and lastly tucked the moccasin into her shirt before running out into rain. The poncho immediately sailed off like a black wing.

Sary ran to Seb's grave, where she finger-clawed saddlebags from a muddy trench, then the oilcloth-wrapped guns and bullwhip, dragging them all, along with her small trunk, onto the travois. She tossed in Seb's old shotgun, securing them. There. Ready as she would ever be.

Where's that damnable cow! She could see nothing in the drenching rain. She called to the bovine sheltering deep in pines—or, Lord knows, blundered off for her long-forgotten home—and felt sorry for the beast.

Sary jammed the travois poles deep under her armpits and strained toward the knoll. Rain still plastered her with a second skin, but her will was hot and blood heated her veins with fury and a sketchy plan. "Now...move!"

Sary scowled back at the travois. The sled stuck, then lurched over a root, slamming her Achilles. She slipped—the travois thumped her back, throwing her full length onto the mud. Sary cursed, got to her knees, her front slathered in muck, and hitched the poles more firmly, to labor on slippery leaves up the knoll, prophetically muttering, *"Thank the sweet Lord. All down hill from here..."*

Sary studied the landscape toward Big Bear as the crow flew, heaved the travois over the lip, and slid in front of it. Gripping the pole handles, she braced down-slope, trying for steady and slow, but the travois slithered faster—*faster.* She had to race, feet sliding sideways, ramming into and thudding over jagged rocks, until her face was close to the ground and she was hanging from the poles. She braced and righted herself before the travois ran over her, then started off again.

As the pitch steepened and pine needles leapt into focus, she knew the sled was close to running her down once more. She was fast losing control. At the last second, Sary rolled aside, and the whole affair rocketed past, casting her precious things aside as it went. She heard the muted crash as the travois splintered on rocks somewhere far below. She squinted, brushing rain from her face, but couldn't see. "Damnation!"

Slithering on down the near vertical hill on her fanny, tumbling over rocks and pine needles like ball bearings, she gathered the spilled load as she found it.

At the unexpected squelching, thudding sound of hoof beats, she squinted through the drizzle—she must be close to a trail. Then the unlikely figure of Ratchet galloped by, low over his horse, seen through a blowing curtain of rain like a quicksilver ghost.

His only destination must be her camp—*and her. This can't be good. Never mind—keep going. He will be disappointed. Nothing is back there, for good or ill.*

Sary tumbled, rolling and bouncing, lugging her precious saddlebags, the whip, and the shotgun, any which way. She kicked and shoved the hefty saddlebags in her slippery slide, greased by mud, until a boulder approached too fast to roll away from—propelled into it, hard, she skidded over the top and bounced, slammed into trees, and ended on a knoll with things sliding after—and far, far below the lights of Big Bear glimmered in the distance.

Chapter 23

Sary, oddly energized by the cold and her long slippery ride down, blood heated with rage and purpose, had blinders on, narrowing her vision to one goal: the gleam of Delacorte's saloon at one end of the town. Shivering, Sary limped in, torn, scraped, bruised, cleansed by intermittent gully-washers and hidden by the night. She halted, heaving, still dragging the saddlebags tumbled down the mountain with her. Fortunately, she was near the stable end, and spying the Delacorte Stables sign *whupping* in the wind, a grim Sary limped toward it.

****

Inside, Sary leaned against dry wood, breathing in the redolence of hay, horses, and relative warmth. A lone lantern flickered near wide doors fronting the main street. As she went stall-to-stall, all was quiet except the snuffling of horses. In a corner, a small chestnut mount whickered hello.

"Whoaaah, whoa. Look good, poor old feller. Just needed a speck of oats, didn't you?" she whispered, patting her old horse's newly supple flanks. "Don't we all?" She rested against its side, girding for what was to come, then moved before she regained her sanity.

Slinging saddlebags, Sary buckled a saddle tight, jamming in her poor half-broken weapons. The stock on Seb's shotgun had a crack. Oh, well, it'd have to do.

As she led the horse, Sary froze, spying the stable hand hunkered under a blanket, gently snoring. He stirred, muzzy, wriggled deeper into sleep. Sary eased past, stealing her own horse. Gripping the shotgun, bullwhip over a shoulder, Sary yanked a jacket from a hook.

Then, mounted tall, she openly rode down Big Bear's main street.

****

Smoke layered Delacorte's like a 'Frisco smog. Whores' gowns pierced the smudge—air curdled with festering brawls, discordant chatter, a raucous piano, hoarse laughter, and the inebriated belting of popular tunes.

In the midst, Julian still reveled, smoking a celebratory cigar while the doves preened and sashayed in the carnival atmosphere. In better light, one sported a mouth sore, another bad skin—a clapped-out bunch with dirty hems, necks, and spotty clothes—Handi and her ever-present French Pox crowd hanging onto Julian and cooing at infant Jude, who glowered back like a small hanging judge.

Cutting above the din, Jude squalled—a living ante kicking a pile of chips as soiled doves quarreled and fussed over him.

Julian, a kid with a new toy, roared, "Looka this kid!"

A man thrust a dripping cigar to Jude's mouth. "Here, kid." Cigar Man horse-laughed. "Suck on this."

Julian guffawed.

A pimply girl swatted Cigar Man, hauling Jude off in a tug-of-war with another dove, whining, "Give 'im to me! You always git to hold 'im. Handi! Make her give 'im to me!"

Cigar Man pinched Pimply Girl. She squawked, but let go.

A gambler growled, "Put a shot in its titty bottle. That'll shut the ugly little bastard up."

He stared down Julian's pistol. Julian's shaky finger twitched against the trigger. The gun blasted. The gambler bellowed, clutching an ear, matching Jude's howls of infant outrage.

Handi soothed Jude, who bawled protest ever louder. "There, there..." She possibly meant to take him, but drunken Julian still wanted to play.

****

Outside, still mounted, Sary grimly watched the mad, reckless chaotic scene over the saloon doors, her eyes flashing on the squalling baby on the green table amid a pile of chips.

The swing doors detonated and Sary—a cross between avenging angel and Valkyrie—crashed through with Seb's whip looped about her shoulder, lashing, kicking, the horse stamping and pawing a ragged swath through the saloon, scattering gamblers, revelers and doves alike as Sary blasted the ceiling with Seb's shotgun.

The room was immobilized.

A few doves tittered. Some ducked, shrieking, under tables. The drunks looked on, bemused. The gamblers were irritated. Julian appeared dazed at first, and then his gray face empurpled.

Handi dully watched the barkeep fire a shotgun, missing Sary but hitting a soiled dove in the arm, adding to the confusion of milling people clapping, laughing, exhorting Sary to go on.

Sary tried to fix on Jude, but it all was happening so fast, and the horse gyrated for a clear path through the mob, faces spinning, like a boat in a storm. Then the whole room exploded as Julian drunkenly drew his walrus of a pistol again. His hand rocked the poker table as the huge revolver cleared it.

Jude tumbled with a cascade of chips down green baize.

Handi snatched at him.

Sary viewed the action as from the large end of the telescope. Noise faded to buzzing like bees, cotton wool in her ears. With one desperate motion, Sary urged her horse over a felled chair, scooped Jude from Handi's shaky grasp, and twisted in the saddle as her horse gyrated to face Julian, snarling, "He may be a bastard, Delacorte! But he's *my* bastard!"

Sary bellowed it with all the denial, privation, and pain of the years behind it. "And you will never take him!"

The room stilled as Sary, clutching Jude, jerked the agitated horse around, dug in heels, and spurred through the mob.

Julian's already ashen face paled further as Sary's horse stumbled sideways and out the swing doors, scattering revelers aside. He thundered, "Wouldn't bet on it, Sary Swinford."

Sary whiplashed a support post, dragging it as she galloped off, dimly aware of the satisfying crack and groan of the porch roof caving, blocking the exit, as she cantered into a softly drizzling night, leaving behind sounds of an angry, excited throng busting out saloon windows. Gripping Jude, Sary whip-butted out, kicking townspeople, spurring on as they ran alongside dragging at her reins. Julian struck a protesting old man out of the way and stiffly mounted his horse, and left Handi to hobble after with her soiled doves and most of the saloon.

****

Ratchet, ignorant of the ruckus back at Big Bear, poked at Sary's abandoned camp, basing his actions on the kind of hunch a calculating stink-stirrer could foment, his eyes narrowed and raking the listing hut, abandoned quilts, and crusted stew pot. He poked the dead fire. Outside, Ratchet scanned disturbed rock, drawn to it.

Wiping his face beneath a dripping brim, he veered back. *Something ain't right. Something was there.* Finally his gaze riveted on a big raw hole, and he stooped, plunging his hand in. Wonderingly Ratchet withdrew a fingertip-sized nugget in the drizzle-filled night, wiped his eyes, stepped back to better see, and trod on something spongy, next to the hole. He toed the dark, alien patch, then hunkered down to claw out rotting velvet.

"Well, well, well." Ratchet's eyes gleamed as he scraped away cloth, withdrawing something hard and bone-white, dome-shaped, with hanks of black hair still clinging. Chuckling softly, he turned the skull this way and that. "Look a sight peaked, Jules. Even for you."

His laugh was long and braying, like that of a miner's mule.

Chapter 24

Sary thrust Jude inside her shirt, chinning his head close. She'd lost the sling she'd made for him. But it was futile anyway, she thought. Of a sudden, she saw the scheme for what it was, born of fury and vindication. Already Jude's silky curls were damp, yet his body, both solid weight and soft, was warm. *But for how long? Have I, in my willfulness, killed him?* But his breath came sibilant, brushing her neck, and soothing in the cool—not cold—night, a small blessing in the mountains, lulled by his heartbeat.

Sary galloped on. The rain stopped. *An omen.*

She found she was heading west. Somehow, she or the horse had automatically veered to Shay Road, rimming the dry plate of seasonal Baldwin Lake, eventually winding past Gold Mountain foothills and the abandoned mine—*her* mine—and beyond. But what was beyond?

There must be a way down. Her mount thudded the rocky trail, the urgency telegraphed by her trembling thighs as Sary slashed the beast on. *Can't care which way—only get off this blasted mountain.* Each inch of pounding hoof beat measured off victory.

She looked down at Jude. A scrap of oilcloth wedged under the bandolier was still secure against her shirt, shielding the infant somewhat.

So intent was she on Jude and the dark path ahead,

and the horses' pounding hooves against rock, that the thunder of many horses was lost until a hand gnarled as a root snaked out from nowhere, it seemed, and Julian dragged at Sary's reins, his gray face looming close. It must have taken his every effort to ride her down.

Sary kicked out desperately, goading her mount. Her horse spurted on. Julian raced after, only now Sary detected the wet slap of many reins and squeals of leather in stirrups as Julian croaked, "Don't fire!" Even as he drew.

Julian straightened his gun arm. His hand trembled. Sary's head bobbed from his vision. Unable to hold steady, the revolver sagged, firing into the earth.

Aaron bellowed behind him, "Shoot, Julian!" Catching up and reaching over Julian's shoulder, he fired.

"Don't!" Julian whipped out. An anguished look screwed his face as Sary slumped.

She felt a hot hard punch in her shoulder and arm, and one hand no longer felt the reins. Warmth soaked her shirt and leaked down her arm. She clamped the yowling Jude between her elbows in a crossed, two-handed, death-grip on the pommel. Clenching thighs and digging heels deep in stirrups, Sary cantered on.

The mob caught up easily, shying her horse, generally getting in Julian's way as he careened alongside. A few followers eyed Sary, then reined up at the gunplay and turned for home. Not much sport in this, after all.

****

Sary's mount cantered on, panicked, reinless, as Ratchet appeared like a wet ghost from a cross trail. Sary registered that he galloped from the path to her old camp as her horse raced, unstoppable, past him. Glancing left, she impulsively veered right, onto a rough trail disappearing in the tree line.

Ratchet met Julian, showed his teeth, touched his hat, and tossed Jules's skull to him.

Julian fumbled it, horrified at the empty sockets and strands of hair streaming away in the wind. Ratchet swooped by, catching it. Grinning, he lobbed it to Aaron as though in a game of ball. Aaron blanched and tossed the skull back.

Julian reined up short, staring at the skull. "It was him," he whispered.

"Him?" Ratchet scoffed. "Him who?"

Julian swatted the pommel. "That brother! That fucking brother! She lied." He clutched the skull to his chest. "Jules—Jules!"

Ratchet sighed long. "Except for one little situation. Ya see, Julian, I found the brother too, a-moldering in his grave."

"Don't mean nothin'!"

Ratchet shook his head. "Delacorte, my dear friend—"

"Ev'ret?" Julian cut in.

"All entering Heaven's reward together." Ratchet bowed, grinned, and sited his rifle at Sary's ghost, vanishing in the drizzle that had started up again. "Busy little whore."

Julian glared at Sary's vanishing figure. "Don't do nothin'." He looked away. "She's mine." Even he didn't know what he meant.

****

Forgetting the child in his red haze, Julian fired, searing the horse's withers.

Sary's horse panicked at the pain, veered off-trail, and skittered up a rise through pine. It wobbled off-stride, crashing back on-trail ahead. Julian raced, overshot, and wheeled, whooping for air, shakily aiming. Sary's horse circled and bucked. "I have Jude!" she yelled, her whip lashing out with her good arm. Jude was clamped between her ribs and her bad arm, yet the jolting shook him loose—he was sliding out! A shirt button popped, and the oilcloth flapped away, wetly crackling.

Seeing an opening between the off-stride horse and her whip arm, Julian ducked beneath and incredibly, even to him, reclaimed the infant.

"No! You'll drop him!" Sary screamed, bridging from her horse to Julian, slipping from the rain-slick saddle, hanging on Julian or she'd fall, viewing pounding hooves by her head and two mighty careening rib cages as their horses jostled side by side. She struggled up, her chin banging Julian's shoulder, and found she clutched his reins. She pushed off and regained her saddle just as Julian wrenched the reins back, clumsily gripping Jude to his side and spurring on.

"Julian!" she cried after them.

Jude was held only by a bit of quilt.

She heard Jude's outraged cry and Julian's bark in reply, "Get used to it, Jude. Be my brave little man!" Then he snarled back at Sary, "I'll never take him? Tchaaaa!"

He looked triumphantly at Jude's red howling face.

Reining around, he spurred back to Big Bear, hooves kicking mud and rock past her.

****

Sary lashed after, but feebly. Her horse was tired, stumbling off-gait. Her own strength leaked with the blood drenching her side.

"Delacorte!" she called in despair and drooped over the mane. Then the pain started.

Julian never faltered—maybe she called only in her mind, yet she saw, mistily, Ratchet gallop alongside, dipping his head to Julian's, and she watched as the two focused back on her.

****

Ratchet circled Julian's mount, taunting. "Unfinished business back there." Julian looked long in Jude's face, then at Ratchet.

"Take care of it."

"What, Delacorte?" Ratchet pressed, feeding off Julian's conflict. Hungry for his hurt.

"You know. The—*problem.*"

Ratchet whispered, seductive as a lover, "Say it, then."

Julian mumbled something, and Ratchet twisted his mount, rain whipping off his hat as he spurred back toward her.

She must go!

****

The last of the mob, until now avidly watching the drama, milled undecided. Should they follow Julian, galloping with wailing Jude for Big Bear? Or Sary, slumped over her saddle?

A few followed Sary to hector, but she was dead meat anyway, and after one look at Ratchet the stragglers jerked reins and either tagged after Julian or veered curiously off-trail to see from whence Ratchet had come. Maybe he had found the gold…

****

Sary's horse limped on. Ratchet easily caught up, playfully waggling the gun at her slumped head, cocking and uncocking it.

He peered back. *Trail's empty of that softcock Delacorte.*

His trigger finger tightened, followed by an explosion dulled by the drizzle-laden air. At that critical instant Sary sagged; the shot raked crossways down her ribs instead of through her temple.

Ratchet steadied Sary's horse and his gun hand, blasting again across his crooked elbow, again missing. "Hell's fire! Hold still, bitch!"

He tunked her skull with his gun barrel.

Sary, reeling, elbowed out, and then the hard knob of her whip handle connected, hitting the pure gold of cartilage and bone. Her whole arm twanged.

Ratchet clutched his Adam's apple as he toppled off his saddle, thumping hard to ground, gagging and grabbing his throat. He shakily kneed the ground and threw up while on all fours, head drooping, sucking air, choking.

Meanwhile, Sary's horse reared, its hooves slashing the rain. She tumbled back over its rump, thumping hard to the ground on her bad side, alongside Ratchet. She saw red, then black, then stars. After a terrifying absence, breath returned.

Dripping vomit, Ratchet grinned over at her as if they were *compadres.*

"Somethin'—ya—don't know, Swinford!" he choked out.

"Ain't just Julian's hatchet man—*chop-chop!* Gracie's brother! Makes me—little Cory's kin, don't ya know."

He dripped drool. "Not I give a tinker's fart for alla that. But it does clear me."

Despite the pain between her eyes, Sary stared down a black hole to eternity, a hole rimmed in blue steel. Ratchet advanced, the barrel steady.

She rolled aside, swinging a branch backhanded, and felt the shiver of wood, sensed the snap of Ratchet's nose as it was shoved off center. His face sprayed a fountain, already swelling, with a cross-hatch bridging his forehead.

Ratchet, gaze never leaving her face, heaved to kneeling again, swiping blood and snot, smearing his eyes. He snarled, "You just don't give up, whore! 'Cept whores have self-respect and don't act like men!"

Sary held her side and hobbled over to boot Ratchet's crotch, hating the soft, giving crunch, as he lurched half up. She bashed the branch until she could no longer stand or hold it up, and then she realized Ratchet lay still in a mud wallow.

Red gushed down her arm. It hurt so badly, and her head was floaty as a circus balloon. Using pain to stay sentient, she crawled to the horse… The stirrup played maddening games, skittering off. She looked up. *An impossible height up the barrel ribs to the saddle.*

"One last time," she whispered. *"Old friend."*

Reaching the pommel, each move shooting torment to her head, shoulder, and side, Sary managed a foot in a stirrup, and by mind-numbing degrees climbed up to fall crosswise on the saddle.

Ratchet blinked blood, water streaming his face, fanned his gun, uselessly clicking, hands slipping off the cock. But it only took one shot.

Her horse screamed, suddenly bucking off-stride. Still Sary lashed. It hobbled on, collapsing beneath her, and Sary tumbled heavily, tangled in the stirrups. Her head followed slowly, as if floating.

****

Ratchet, sighting with one eye puffed the color of gentian, wavered astride Sary. She sensed a hard whipping-singing like an angry wasp through her hair and felt the heat of it. Another shot pinged dirt beside her nose. Desperate, she whipped her head the other way as Ratchet's swollen mess of a face dripped blood on her.

He bobbed closer and sighted once more, shaking his head as if bothered by flies.

Of a sudden, still firing, Ratchet saw double, stabbing where he thought she was, 'til the pin *clacked.*

He attempted gun clipping, swinging wild, and sprawled on top of her instead, gasping, *"Now...* give up." He clamped his hand over her mouth until Sary, with a face pale as the emerging moon, lay still.

Ratchet heaved up, spitting teeth. Cupping his nose and his groin, he limped, cursing, to his mount, where he twisted to look back. *One last look.* It was painful, but satisfaction burned his face.

Sary lay in a spreading pool—dead and still as a rag doll.

Cursing all the way, Ratchet urged his horse into a careful canter to Big Bear and Julian.

****

Handi hobbled after Julian as he galloped in with Jude. Her doves ran alongside.

One burbled, "Ain't this the most excitin' thing ever?"

"Better'n old Earl playing mouth tunes on his comb or humpin' me to death!" Another laughs.

Pearl clapped her hands. "Oh, sweet Jesus, we git to play with it again!"

****

Sary's horse whinnied, nudging her, and she wheezed, squinting at her surroundings. Stars gleamed disturbingly close, as if they had swooped down to inspect and then soared up to their rightful place to coldly examine her from there.

Get up...get up...get UP! Get on your feet!

Sary dragged up, muzzily checking herself and her whereabouts.

Which way?

It mattered, somehow. Dim, rain-pocked roads melted into the distance both ways. Never mind. The important thing—*before the other important thing— chore?* She shook sense into her head, hung on the stirrup, and once more gripped the pommel, crawling up the horse's side. Another long, long process. The miracle was that the horse stood patient. His flank and shoulder had stopped bleeding for now, though she hardly recalled her horse was wounded.

Bloody saddlebags bulging with gold, pressing her inner thighs, wove into focus. Sary vaguely patted them. *They are important somehow too.*

Her body tilted to one side, then back, barely aware of the saddle and horse beneath, but it was a warm and distant comfort. She was cold...especially her arm.

She must stay on this road. Thoughts faded. Only torturous jogging remained. Up, down, jolt hard on the saddle, lurch sideways, fight back to center as her poor mount limped along, its mane soft beneath her hands.

Every cell electrified with the knowledge she needed to be far away—or at least somewhere else. It nagged her.

And so Sary sloped off, trailing blood, into the unknown.

She thought she returned to Big Bear…

Chapter 25

Julian, in his office, dry, rested, resplendent—Magnanimous! Expansive!—threw his head back, swooping down on Jude's flat little nose, crooning, "Who's the most boooful big 'trong boy? Who has Jules's eyes?"

In fact, Jude's eyes were greeny-blue and bright, not the aged tobacco-black of Jules's hot wild gleam, but Julian didn't notice as he gave Jude's broad forehead an exuberant buss. "Yes! Bright-bright eyes. Yeeesss! Who—?"

Biskits, the barkeep, Sheriff Will, and others—Orvis, and O'Malley—crowded the doorway, darting looks between Julian's seamed, gaunt visage and Jude's wide face and broad, mushroom-button nose.

"Look at this fine hefty lad!" Julian chortled. "Now let's hear some ignorant popinjay say Jules didn't have the vigor—the *iron!"*

He gestured, his arm cocked with a fist. "Not"—he searched for words—"adamantine enough! Hah!" He checked the onlookers for affirmation.

"But Jules was a skinny little shi—" Biskits began. Sheriff Will banged his ribs. "Ooooph! Er, at least once," Biskits avowed. "Maybe."

Julian looked perplexed. "Why's he bawlin'?"

Behind him, a soiled dove held an infant to bulging breasts in the doorway. Handi shoved her in—and was brushed aside by Ratchet, who looked run over by a herd of buffalo.

"Horse swung me inta a branch."

"An improvement." Julian waited. "Well? Where is she? Drag the murdering bitch-mother in!"

Ratchet smirked and whispered.

Julian squeezed the howling Jude. "Bring the"—he risked a glance at Jude—"whore in! Here! *Here!*"

Ratchet gave another urgent whisper. "Shuck of her, Julian. Took care…"

Julian looked uncertain, turning grayer. Finally he snarled, "Best pray I haven't the true thrust of what you allege—the import!"

"Good as." Ratchet grinned through split lips, and was knocked aside by Aaron pushing in bold, thunking Jules's skull on the desk.

Aaron squeaked, "Lest you forget!"

Julian thrust Jude's head to his shoulder. "Put it away! Not a thing for a…a son to see. What am I, a public forum? Get out!" He glanced sideways at the skull, planting a dearly recalled face over empty sockets.

Julian tore the star from Will's shirt and jammed it onto Ratchet, snarling, "Don't worry, Will! Still the man with the hat!"

He reached back for the hat, jamming it also on Ratchet, and thrust Jude at the nursing dove.

****

Julian knelt, creaky and hacking, over the blood splotch. Easing to his feet, he glared at Ratchet, who declared, "Not a genie in a fuckin' bottle, Delacorte. She's dead!"

"Apparently she's the fucking genie." Julian

pointed at trailing red teardrop shapes.

"That way."

****

Sary's horse stumbled across iron tracks and shuddered, buckling to its knees beneath a deserted train halt—only a bare patch of sandy ground, a sign, and tracks abutting the foothills.

Sary's arm sensed chilled metal. It lay athwart a thin rail shining blue with moonlight. *Where am I?*

Tracks faded in both directions. The horse lay inert, Sary's foot wedged under the saddle. She yanked it out but crowded the horse for warmth. Later, she unfastened the saddlebags and tugged out the blanket to huddle weak, hurting, and very cold.

A train hooted a warning before she spotted the phosphorous clouds writing on an indigo sky.

****

Julian prodded the dead horse at the train halt and peered both ways down the track, checking his watch. "'Frisco."

Ratchet kicked the horse. "'Frisco. Chicago. Place your bets, Julian."

"'Frisco. What you waiting for?"

Ratchet contemplated Julian. He touched his nose.

"Well?"

"Heard you."

"I'll send what you need. Money? You want money? Here!"

Julian dug in his duster.

"Ever eat oranges?"

"What?" Julian screwed his face. "Once or twice."

"Wanna suck oranges 'til I'm yeller."

"Oranges! More money? I'll send it."

Ratchet smirked, touching his battered nose. "I'll keep the wound green," he said, and urged his mount west up the tracks. "It better be there," floated back from the night.

"Ratchet…"

He was a black centaur-shape in the dark.

"What now?"

"I hear vengeance can be a true art form. Don't be…too creative. There's to be a trial. I'm owed a hanging."

Ratchet rode on. "Just as you say. Boss."

Ratchet galloped west after the gunmetal tracks.

Chapter 26

A Pullman car. Cinders and smoke flew past windows. A young girl named Rachel perched on a mohair seat—pretty dress, shining buttoned boots.

She stared fixedly at something across from her.

"Mama? That lady's dead."

Mother looked up from her book, annoyed, risking a glance.

Sary huddled in the seat—gray, lifeless, dirt-smeared, and disheveled. *Is that blood? Mud? She does appear dead.* A saddlebag looped tight about the unconscious woman's arm drooped under the seat. Sadly, it was the only seat totally unoccupied by males. The mother supposed this creature wasn't male under all that dirt but was probably drunk. She purposefully ignored her.

"Nonsense, Rachel. She's dru—indisposed."

Mama looked away with distaste and the hope for somewhere—anywhere—else to sit.

At the far end men drank, smoked, played cards, and bellowed jokes. She was only too happy she could not hear.

"We'll move later."

"No, Mummy, she's really dead." Rachel covered her own flat chest with both hands and piped, "Her pid-dows stopped moving."

Rachel pushed her nose close and advanced a

finger to Sary's cheek. "See? Not breathing."

"Rachel! Let me!" Mama turned Sary's head. She gasped as hair matted with congealed blood from the seared track gouging Sary's skull was exposed, and she tugged at the saddlebags, cutting into the wretched female's arm.

Sary moaned, not letting go. Frustrated, Mama stood up.

"Is there—might there be a physician on board this train? This woman's—sick!"

Men glanced up and to each other. Annoyed, they returned to their cards. Mama wove down the aisle and slapped the suitcase off their knees. Cards and money flew.

"Ah, ma'am!"

"No! You get someone!"

A man playing a mouth harp stopped his riff. "Abernathy? He's kinda a doctor, kinda."

A man with a tilted derby mugged dubiously around a mouthful of cigar. "Sometimes."

Mama nailed him with a stare.

Derby tossed cards and pushed through to the last car. Mama waited, tapping toes.

Portly, vest misbuttoned, underwear hiked above his belt, Doc lumbered up the aisle, wavered, and peered at Mama through dirty glasses. She shunted him to Sary.

"Her!"

Doc hawked into a hanky, smeared his glasses with the same, swayed judiciously, and attempted to focus. "Save'd thish for the occasion." Uncapping whiskey, Doc wavered, a ship in high winds, raising the bottle to slobbery lips.

169

Mama snatched it. *"Tchaaaa!"* She sloshed whiskey on her hanky and daubed Sary's shoulder till some of the dirt and crust fell away.

Sary twitched.

Abernathy snatched at the bottle and poked at the wound. "I'm doc here!" Sary's eyelids fluttered. "Kin see daylight through that'n." Doc held his hand out and took the whiskey, pouring a tot on the wound. Sary bucked and slumped. Doc reluctantly handed Mama the bottle and fumbled Sary's sticky hair.

"Thish here's just a bone-brusher—maybe. A bleeder, though. Not much more I can do." Abernathy latched onto his bottle and shuffled off as fast as he could while Mama watched his fat lumbering rear with disgust and gingerly lifted Sary's vest. "Don't look, Rachel!"

She gasped again and called to Abernathy. "Wait! That's all? What of her side?"

Abernathy grunted. "Used up all my med'cine, din' I?"

"Ohhh! Horrible man!" Mama hopped from a widening pool of blood. "Rachel! Fetch me my reticule and remove your petticoat."

****

In her confusion, it seemed to Sary she was stepping into a hot cloudy hell that hissed like a hundred snakes.

Someone clutched her elbow. Not an unwelcome hold—without it she'd surely fall. She staggered heavily into the unseen someone.

"Ooophhh, s'sorry," Sary mumbled, aware her arm wasn't working and her other arm was strained beyond breaking. A hard, leathery band cut her palm. *Oh, yes.*

170

Saddle bags. Heavy, heavy, as if all the pain in the world centered in her hand, her side, and her throbbing head—her muzzy, muzzy head.

She saw from one eye. *What's wrong?* Sary tugged one lid from the other on the other eye. It ripped open, as though sticky. A blot, a crust of blood, trembled in front of her vision—Sary blinked, and her spiky lashes glued shut again.

Can't draw a breath, either. Pain knitted her side as if the ribs were crocheted shut. Stitches snapped with each inhalation—she was aware too of a gumminess down her side. *So irritating, that itchy messiness.* Her clothes stuck, and something was running down her leg.

"Quite all right," she enunciated, detecting anxiety and impatience beyond her unknown companion's calm words.

The guiding hand fell away.

Sary moved limbs hammered by a blacksmith to unyielding iron, to view her companion. A lady—a true genteel lady, the likes of which Sary had not beheld since she didn't know when.

She could stand. Take unaided steps...till the fog or mist separated her from the woman and girl-child. Vaguely familiar, that young female..."*Is she dead, mommy?*"

Steam clouds thinned. Sary stepped through—and all bustling San Francisco, at least the part beyond the station, spread magically before her, full of color, with the syncopated clip-clop of horses, rattle-clack of wagons, and an unbelievable mass of people...

All alive and happy! How can there be so many in one spot, all busy-busy and...Wonder of wonders!— Sary staggered back almost run over by a carriage—

Without a horse!

She eyed its gleaming blackness and glittering metal, so blinding in its glory, as it clattered by at terrifying speed, veering at the last second with a rude back blow. Folks in all-over coats head to toe and big eye gear like bug's eyes sat high and proper, as in a buggy. Sary caught a feminine name in glittering fancy script written flamboyantly across the front of the amazing contraption.

"Mercedes..." she breathed, wondering if the female riding with her companion was Mercedes.

The automobile scuttled along, disappearing with bucking and fanfare. Sary stared until the magical conveyance was out of sight, aware of a tapping on her arm through steam clouds still billowing from the locomotive. But then a red-and-gold plaque snared Sary's eye, glossy, important, demarcating a turn in fortunes.

A lodestar.

Sary lurched toward the sign that glittered in the brilliant San Francisco sun.

The tapping came again, insistent.

She cricked her neck, irritated, and looked down at the hand.

Oh! The woman and the little girl—and what is this? Her own bosom, covered in daisy sprigs. *Never owned anything like this.* Sary's gaze roved over the ill-fitting dress, crude bandages, and her own death grip on the saddlebag.

The woman talked from inside a tunnel. "But where will you go? What will you do?"

At last Sary focused, puzzled, on the woman with the little girl. "Do?" Sary frowned then, fixated on the red sign. "Do? Win."

She scanned the dress. *Yes, still daisies.* "Appreciate the dress." Sary turned and painfully hefted the saddlebag.

"But—what's your name, anyways?" The question was only a burr behind her. Already a memory.

"Oh, never mind!" Mama yanked Rachel off, nettled, as Sary lurched across the street, dragging her dirty old bag.

Sary halted, croaking, "Wait! Little...*little girl...*"

Rachel skipped back.

Sary pressed a nugget into her palm. "Give this to your Ma. After you don't see me no more." She tried a smile, but her mouth stretched too tight.

Rachel crinkled her nose at the gritty beige rock but curtsied. "Mommy, look what the sick lady give me! A rock!" Sary smiled grimly as Mama glared after her.

Clutching the saddlebag straps, halting every few steps, Sary hitched painfully across the street.

Mama spun, resolute. She studied the rock and, her mouth open, stared back at Sary, who continued to make her way to the brick building, weaving through shoppers, foot traffic, peddlers, and families, never wavering from a path toward the brilliant red-gold sign: WELLS FARGO BANK.

Sary hauled the bags up onto the wood walkway, panting. The stain on the sprigged dress widened. She waited as a stranger, looking at her strangely, emerged and stepped aside to open and hold the door, keeping clear as if her appearance was catching. And so she entered the cool, dim, polished room, dragging the bags.

****

Tellers and customers scanned Sary—blood-stringed matted hair, hastily cleaned face, trailing bandages with alarming stains, shuffling toward them in mucky boots, the bloody saddlebag scraping wood floors.

Customers parted or shied. She eyed a guard rushing toward her as she dropped the bag at a teller window and smoothed her hair.

"I need to see someone…of importance," she grated.

Chapter 27

Sary lay naked on a bed that dipped in the middle, focusing on a ceiling crack that resembled either a pig or a basket of fruit. At times, she wondered how on God's green earth she'd gotten there. She thought perhaps she was dying, and that electrified her into hanging on, clutching the thin quilt. It kept the throbbing at bay. Otherwise it crouched on her, or bounced malevolently on her bed, or mocked her from the dim corners of the room, though at times, when she turned her neck, it waited like a one-eyed scruffy cat on the crumbling sill outside, scratching at the cloudy glass.

She groaned. The same wooly San Francisco fog throbbed in her head with each pulse beat.

From the ceiling, as she envisioned herself looking down, every bruise, swelling, and bullet wound must be evident, as was her torment as Sary sweated through sheets frayed to transparency, tossing and speaking in tongues.

The ribs scabbed but didn't heal. She felt one of them grate, not piercing a lung but making it hurtful to breath, like dragging saddlebags with each inhalation. *Concentrate. Suck in, breathe out.* She twisted for comfort that wasn't there.

One day she shrieked, not in torment, not entirely.

Sary eyed her shoulder in a clouded hand mirror,

aware for days of the hotness welling beneath taut red flesh. She had crawled from bed to fetch the dim mirror from a dusty, scarred dresser. A rare sunbeam highlit her shoulder. Sary sucked in. Sun painted her shoulder an alien green, the green of meat gone bad, puffed to bursting, radiating from a jagged, black, crusty epicenter.

Even now, as she tentatively probed, a turgid paste oozed from the gritty burnt-cinder edges—hot threads spidered from a scarlet epicenter, shiny, tumescent— and from the black hole.

She touched it—and woke up later on the floor, her skin a sheet of flame laid over bone, aware of a pounding on the door.

"What in heaven's name is goin' on in there?" A woman's voice—older, colloquial, querrelsome. Sary shrank from this presence and proof of the world out there. Her throat was raw. She must have yelled. She tried to croak something out, "Water..." But the footsteps lumbered off.

There followed a period of intense throbbing all down her arm. Her mouth was as dry as the blanket, and as rough. *Where is that girl? Some girl?* She recalled promising the drab person something. *Oh—the world!* If only she returned. Skinny little thing. Stick wrists and fingers.

Someone else, too—fat under iron stays, and a wobbly chin. She had directed Sary upstairs, with the thin girl guiding her. How many days ago, hours ago was that? Sary felt herself sliding away...

Oh, please! She watched the door—the knob. *To die here alone...*Listened for footfalls, creak of boards. *Am I the only one? Oh. There it is!*

A pitcher. Brimmed to overflowing with cloudy water. Cold rivulets dripped from it. When did that come? Who brought it?

She woke on the floor again.

The fingerprinted pitcher was now dry. *Still thirsty.* She looked to a drear oblong of window. Water obliterated the panes.

She would break them. Smash her head through, face the skies, and drink, cool her blazing skin, cleanse her matted itching scalp... She was aware, too, that she smelled. A stench emanated from her burning flesh and clothes.

Ahhh, good! She had raised the loose window. With her head out, she luxuriated in a bone-chilling stream, inundated with cold wet diamonds.

Later, on the floor again but this time under the window sash, her face and hair wet, her shoulder seared. She looked down. Dark yellow muck oozed from a burst center, like pollen from an evil flower.

Much later, she was aware her shoulder had crusted over again. It should be cleansed and rebound. And then her ribs. She pressed her side; there was yet a dull grating throb. She explored her face. A scab slanting above her right brow and hairline formed an odd part under Sary's probing fingers.

Not too painful. Not puffed. She could ignore that.

She risked a glance at the ghastly area once more, gently exploring the epicenter. Something unyielding— not bone. A bullet? She recalled the round tins of balm her mother used to buy from tinkers back in Indiana. Touted to cure all.

She laughed, in the dark on the floor, looking upside down at the moon through the dirty window.

She must have slept. It was still dark. She was half on the bed. The girl had brought more water. Sary elbow-hitched over. She spilled most, gulping the rest from the spout.

Should have saved some.

No matter. Sink back. Rest.

When next she roused, the cat on the sill blinked huge blank green eyes. Did she imagine it? It was gone, and she closed her eyes...*heavy, heavy*...and woke wailing. Her shoulder exploded with another bursting, ripping pain, and hot gruel volcanoed out, running down her arm. The reek was horrendous. She bit her lip. Slowly the hurt receded to a ragged, throbbing echo.

Another dark period. Somewhere a coil of hunger unwound in her stomach. *So hot...* She threw back the covers.

A moon knifed across her body. Sweat chilled her shift. Fitfully, Sary plucked at brown scratchy covers. Her face was outside the glass now, peering in with big cat eyes, she thought. Pain crouched in the corner, waiting. *I must do something!*

****

Sary continued to fade in and out of consciousness. When she tentatively probed her shoulder, watching in the hand mirror, daring the torment, the last expulsion of yellow exposed something in the ragged hole. Gently, gently, Sary's fingers probed deeper, ignoring the tenderness.

Yes. Hard. It moved. Not bone. She jackknifed, hanging onto consciousness, as hot glass shards seemed to pierce her bones, zipping along jagged neural paths clear to her feet. She gritted her teeth and dug her forefinger and thumb down into the wet tunnel of flesh. Fingernails grown long scratched metal.

Yes, a bullet. *No, no! Don't push! Pull!*

Gently, oh, very, very gently, Sary pincer-nailed the hard thing, drawing the pellet out, accompanied with a sucking gush of thin brown blood and more green.

The pain was less throbbing now, though, more a numbness. The area around the hole was paler. When Sary next roused, her palm cradled a squashed brass dome.

Chapter 28

Sary swung thin legs over the edge of the mattress by degrees, cringing as her toes hit splintered boards and tripped on a thready rug. Dragging the blanket to the window, she twisted to peer in the occluded mirror at her wounds—their edges were red and puffed but healing.

The day was bright for once, and Sary bathed in sunlight. Her eyes flew to a dim corner behind the washstand. Her poor bundle was yet there, most likely too impoverished-looking to tempt anyone, and her saddlebags rested in the basement of the Wells Fargo Bank, save for a few nuggets and ready cash in the bottom of her bundle.

She poured water into the cracked bowl and wet the cloth next to it. Scraping away the last residue of crusted blood and serum, she scrubbed a thin bar of brown soap into the wound and all around it. No clean cloth to rip for bandaging. It took a long time, using her teeth and good hand, to tear strips off the towel.

Tired again, she longed to crawl onto the saggy mattress or run shrieking from the fetid room. The chamber pot hadn't been changed in a while.

She scratched. A rare smile formed. *My ribs itch. A good sign.* Sary waved the mirror before her face, not recognizing hollow eyes circled in claret or caved-in cheeks. Even her poor hair was thinner. She finger-traced the welt of scar. *Ah well, never was a beauty. I now have a permanent part.*

Chapter 29

Ratchet himself still showed badges of his own encounter with Sary. Though his bruises and scrapes had faded to a sick lemon color, they seared his memory with ignominy and odium. He fidgeted in line, attempting to push ahead of the brash San Francisco crowd—and was shoved aside by a female, no less!

He snatched the flimsy yellow paper offered by the clerk, reading it regardless of others in the great train station's Western Union line, and grinned, crushing the telegram.

In the bank, a teller counted Ratchet a wad of money.

At the postal office, Ratchet ripped a tube, sliding out Delacorte's sketch of Sarabande Swinford.

Freshly shaved and in stiff city clothes so natty even Delacorte would be taken aback, Ratchet showed Sary's sketch to anyone he snagged. He showed some initiative, too. No sheriffs—not that the lily-fingers were *called* that in the city. Ratchet scoured the train stations, the tram lines, the poorer sections, guessing rightly but for the wrong reason that this was where she'd hole up.

He could smell her in the tawdry rooming houses, in the bars. Anyone who would have her.

****

At Sary's room, there was rain. Again.

Raising the warped window, she stuck her head out. She was cleaner, rested, and healing somewhat. It must be soon, or she would never leave. She knew this.

Tall masts studding the sky were a reminder of *"jasmine, velvet, and long skinny boats—sunny cobbled streets and gleaming white walls..."*

The images beckoned, nigh irresistible.

Jude seemed far away and insubstantial as a daguerreotype, flat or shiny as one tipped it to the light.

Today Jude's image was dull and therefore unreal.

The drab knocked and brought whiskey and clean rags. Sary gulped as much as she poured on her shoulder.

"What happened to yuh?" The drab asked her. Sary wondered why. Solicitousness? No. That was answered by her lack of aid. She slugged from the bottle. Knowledge sometimes meant rewards. She must leave.

Vigor and a muzzy sense of well-being forged brave old roads. She regarded the bottle fondly and carefully peeled the bandage off, ripping the last bit. *"Owww-waw!"* With a fruit knife, brought to her next to a wizened orange, she slit her shoulder and daubed at the pus. There wasn't so much of it now. Her pins were still wobbly, but by hanging onto first the wall and then a chair, she made it to the washstand and bathed all over with the stale water, a scrap of soap, and the thin towel.

****

Ratchet purchased oranges, complaining of the cost, and bit through rind and all as he roved his hungry eyes everywhere.

****

Sary sat up ten times, lifted a chair, and paced end

to end of the room. She stretched from a door. Ripped a scab. Re-bandaged. Earlier the drab had dropped paper bundles on her bed, curious but unmoved. Sary waved her out, diving into greasy fried cod and cold boiled potatoes and an apple.

She faced the remaining bundles, tediously lacing a cheap corset tight over both ribs and bandages. She suspected the corset was second hand—or even the drab's own, and the girl had pocketed the change.

The arm Sary had thought merely stiff seemed permanently hooked and slightly withered. Sary grabbed her wrist and pressed, but try as she might she could not force it straight.

A wheeling gull snared her eye, and so Sary didn't catch Ratchet turning a far corner, showing her portrait to landladies down a row of tenements across the way. They nodded, hitched a shoulder, or flirted.

Then, the drab pointed her way.

Sary glanced out again, studying the street she must navigate. *I should be already gone from this room.* Only then did she notice the approaching man, flashy-dressed like an Eastern dandy—and she backed onto the bed after the man, showing a paper to a woman wielding a broom, metamorphosed into Ratchet.

The woman waved her broom across and up.

Sary ducked, landing on her bottom, and snatched the sprigged dress, now rinsed out. It seemed alien, this act of fitting on a garment. Her arm wouldn't bend into its sleeve! She ripped it, shoving through. Never mind buttons…*Never mind anything.*

She threw objects into her precious bag, hoping she didn't miss anything of import, dug her boots from under the bed, and flung open the door, bolting into the hall, shoeless, pelting down the back way, the endless narrow winding stairs made to hinder at every hairpin turn.

Half the way down the landlady emerged, protesting, from what seemed to be a kitchen, judging from the fish and cabbage smells. Sary, hopping, struggling with boots, shoved at her and reached the back door. The landlady held her back, shouting, "Pay me!"

"I'll send it to you," Sary snarled, trying for a smile and elbowing the landlady in her ample stomach.

Behind her, a distant cracking and splintering somewhere in the house. Then the thump of the hefty landlady being thrust into a wall behind her and more protests.

Sary yanked at the balky door and risked a look back—*Ratchet*, stumbling over the landlady, tangling with the dumpy woman's feet, shoving her face. She fell and screeched as Sary groped a skeleton key and flipped it around with fumbling hands. It turned rustily and then gave with a loud *clack*, and Sary fell out, slamming the door. Ratchet yanked a cleaver from the scullery and crashed after Sary, while the landlady fell back, her eyes huge. Limping as fast as she could across the narrow yard and through laundry, tangling in a wet sheet, Sary was suddenly free, beyond the outer line, bursting out into an alley.

Ratchet was wound in the same damp, flapping barrier as Sary squeaked through a half-hinged gate and then heard another squawk of hinges fast behind her as she limped on, bootless, down the alley. Ratchet tore the gate off, fell over a burner barrel, cursing, and was followed by the clatter of disturbed garbage cans.

Sary went as fast as she could, any which way, ducking finally around a corner to where, in the foggy distance, a steel wall of steamship blocked her horizon. Whistles sounded, and gulls screamed. Passengers called and were given excited farewells. Just a glimpse, then all was lost in another maze of dead-end alleys.

Sary wavered at a crossroads, then tore off in the general direction of the sounds of the departing ship. Sary could still hear the passenger's farewells as she hobbled up another street. Turned a corner—three dogs watched her, curious. Edged past them. There—so close—a wall of ship cut the alley off, and she skidded short. The alley actually T'd at a tall wood fence. Scraps of rusty metal rose beyond the two-block barrier of a junkyard. The sound was fainter.

Oh, Lord, her side hitched where a bone was knitting crooked. The unaccustomed activity had winded her, and her shoulder throbbed with each jolt, eased somewhat if she tucked her arm close. For want of a direction, she veered into a trashy, serpentine alleyway.

She lost the gray horizon of ship and halted, gasping, at sight of a small boy still sailing his boat in a gutter—she was going circles. Then Ratchet's boots pounded somewhere behind her, with the crash of cans and crack of crates.

She craned her neck for a glimpse of the ships and tall masts between two tenements—*farther away now!* She turned, helpless, checking the maze of alleys. *How do I get there?* She heard Ratchet snarl at the boy with the boat, a cold wind on her neck. She imagined the swish of the knife cutting the air. Her neck prickled as she ducked into a yard, breathless, clutching her ribs as she knelt to lace her boots and, through a split in the old fence, watched him plunge past.

****

Her energy had dissolved like mist by the time she thrust out into the open, vulnerable. Plunging into crocodiles of children, she veered round another corner. *Right there*. Ratchet was looking the other way. Yet, at the opposite end of the block, there was a sailor and his girl and more wheeling gulls.

Ducking, Sary headed that way and was soon lost in the crowd, weaving through meaner sections, slowing in bewilderment as she burst into Chinatown— a colorful confection, apparently part traveling circus, part market, and—to Sary's delight—deliciously foreign. Smoke, dried fungus, ginger, pungent teas, hot oils, fish—the incenses perfumed her nose. Her mouth watered.

"Where you diggin', China...?" She heard Delacorte's words in her mind and realized what an odd sight she must be, with her wild light hair, taller than the sleek-eyed, licorice-haired denizens bustling around her in their lush black and bright silks and chattering a liquid singsong as seabirds whooped and *screed* about her head. The target for the birds was a white dough ball like those sold in stacks, but this one now lay on the dirty cobbles.

She bolted it, tasteless and gluey, and filched a sliver of dried fish, then wished she hadn't. Now thirsty, Sary was nevertheless heartened by a flotilla of gulls marking the waterways.

Another glimpse of brown, slapping water—*at last!* She sucked in the fetid tang like rare perfume, but a frieze of bright flags, hung like laundry and crisscrossing the massed streets, maddeningly obscured the wharves.

With a glance over her shoulder, she glimpsed Ratchet crashing into a clot of carts and sliding on bricks slimy with old vegetables and fish scales.

He grabbed at two oranges rolling past, ignoring an irate Chinese vendor, and ripped into one as he looked wildly about.

Sary crouched below the shorter people, slipping between racks of lovely silks. *Ohhh, wouldn't it be wonderful to feel them, to wind myself in such colorful...*

The sound of splintering wood intruded on her thought. Things crashed in waves. Incensed shouts arose. She risked a look.

Ratchet had literally disappeared beneath an irate mob of flying pigtails like tarred rope, padded coats, and venders' straw hats.

She smiled—the first time in months—pelting to a stop, sniffing water again, scanning only more bars, one-night hostels, doss houses…

If I could only board a ship—any ship!

Another glimpse of Ratchet's rangy figure above the melee.

How did he find me? I must change appearance—one of these colorful silks, maybe, and wind it about my head... With that thought, she swerved into another passage, hating to leave the sea front.

Gulls wheeled more distantly, and the scent was more refuse than salt.

She was near dropping—yet here was another opening—clutching her side, as she burst out onto a wide street. Passersby swiveled to look after the limping, hitching, gasping, wild-haired, half-dressed Sary.

Ratchet skidded along, scrutinizing, shoving, pushing against the tide, and spotted calico sprigged with daisies...

"Got you!" he snarled.

Sary slip-slided on fish heads and rainwater, ripping down a passage so constricted it was more of a gap between shops—her elbows and bags scraped the sides. It narrowed further, as if the buildings were tired, and she was trapped like a mouse in a box.

Ratchet crossed one end of the passage, blotting out the light—a mere blip, a Morse code for danger. Sary stumbled over bricks lying in a heap and pressed into the cavity they had left, while Ratchet retraced steps and scowled down the slot, shading his eyes.

Sary kept on, stumbling through the door she'd found, into a snug of coal fire, old ale, and the thick odor of damp clothing.

The imbibers in residence didn't spare a glance at the filthy female dragging a bag. One finally looked her up and down.

"Can see why you no come in tha front way, darlin', ta be waylaid by one a these randy mates! A little beauty such as yerself!"

She heard someone snigger. *"Scag..."* And wicked laughter followed. She drew in a breath, adjusting her eyes.

The room was noisy with diverse chatter—Irish and other dialects more guttural, as sailors, women, and laborers drank and wolfed down greasy fish, bread, and stew. Her stomach rumbled.

If I stay small, by the fire, where it is mostly quiet,

with little nosegays of laughter, except for a noisy group postulating and gesturing in a far corner, no one will notice. I'll stay away from them, too.

She edged over. At least her flight had summoned unsuspected energies, and she hugged the knowledge tight.

Perhaps there is a tomorrow, free from pain, free from—what?

She was rich, but her wealth lay in moldering saddlebags in a vault. Beyond a few nuggets and bits of cash rapidly dwindling in this expensive city, and not easily accessible except by written note, or cheque as they were called, that was all she had.

She'd lost Jonathan, never to be replaced. And the brother, not that she had much of one, but he *was* kin. She'd mislaid a child—he too was beyond reach. Gone were her youth, her looks—well, she'd never really considered looks. Jonathan had loved her... She was presentable.

Then, there was the arm. Fancy feathers and a few laces wouldn't fix that.

What was left? She wouldn't think on it now. For the first time, drying her hair by the fire, spreading her skirts to dry, sagging against the warm brick, she felt the lightening wings of hope lifting her spirits.

Her eyes drooped. *Warm...nice...but perhaps one side uncomfortably hot...* Her dress steamed. A door banged open with a wind that blasted her skirts in welcome gust of chill air. Sary peeked through tangled hair and sucked a breath. The rangy, wolflike man, hunched to spring, scoured the room with his gaze. Ratchet's feral eyes raked the crowd, jerking from face to face with crazed intensity, and then another group burst in, thrusting him forward.

Ratchet hadn't spied her yet.

Easing away, Sary neared the knot of noisy folk at the back of the room.

****

A hand holding a grease pencil snagged her.

"Let go!" she hissed, making for the door she'd fallen through earlier as Ratchet's craggy head showed above the crowd, zeroing in on the boisterous group with eyes the color of lead. But the hand with the grease pencil, yanked her with a surprising grip into the midst of a sweaty band. Sary caught a blur of laces, bosoms, and veils, all ages, with bright-crayoned faces. The scents of tallow, onion, unwashed clothes, and old grease, with underlying whiffs of cloying jasmine, enveloped her like a warm, smelly cloak.

And then she saw Malcolm the Midget shine a mirrored lantern at Ratchet. "Oops, sorry, mate." He bobbed humbly.

Ratchet squinted under a crook of his elbow, snarling. "Shine it up your bung hole, hunchback!"

A voice still hissed annoyingly in Sary's ear, *"Do something! It's* Midsummer Night's Dream*!"* The troupe pressed close, and someone tossed a veil over her head.

Ratchet beheld Puck and the fairies' prancing action for a moment, with a look of dazed unreality, before he spun and knocked taverners aside in his rush out.

****

The actor winked, darkening his other brow.

Sary squinted.

Hamlet?

Sary took in the man who was a boy. Lines divided his forehead, now, that weren't there in her memory. More lines bracketed the still beautiful mouth and straight nose she had recalled in troublesome, fevered moments before sleep finally swept her away.

The actor, Tommy, was shaggier than she remembered him, with more rips and stains on a velvet tunic skinned bare at the elbows, no longer a romantic dream, tho appealing—but then, neither was she.

Hamlet/Tommy grinned, showing his amazingly strong white teeth and tossing a greasy lock of hair. "Now. Where were we?"

"I didn't...exactly make it to the nunnery," she managed.

"What a wicked, *wicked*—and might I add *filthy*—nun you'd make."

A mature actress swatted him.

"Have a care! The poor, half drowned—" Sary was aware of the others then: "Lovely to see you again, love..." And, "You all right, dearie?" And, "How's about a cuppa?" She heard their muddle of voices.

"I wouldn't mind." Sary snatched the mug of hot tea, bobbing her thanks.

****

It was the boisterous troupe she had met so long before: Caine, Tommy, Luigi, the King Lear type, Malcolm the Midget. The older woman with hair varying in hue from boiled beet to iodine was new. Together they relished their meal and discreetly eyed Sary.

"Part of our bounteous remuneration," Tommy slurred through bread dredged in "stew"—pulled gristle—and signaled for more.

Sary gnawed bread, veering from the redhead whose over-zealous attention was apparently an assessment: *How is this wet feline going to shift me— what roles will she usurp?* was writ plain on the face like melting pink tallow.

Sary shrank, assessing them in turn. *Malcolm: slick fingered, impudent, how much of that cheekiness is fake?* She eyed Tommy. *Seedier Tommy. On the cliff edge of destitute. So different from Big Bear's charming roué. Lear is assuredly leering.*

They could even sell me. I've heard of such tales. Perhaps they think the law chased me here. They could use the money. Better keep myself to myself...And then? A day—two at the most, surely—until Ratchet moves on. Make my way to the docks and...then...

All Europe...!

Suddenly aware Tommy studied her from the corner of his eye, his gaze roving over the scar in her hair and the one where the noose had dug in. She casually brushed her hand across her neck, hiding it, giving a stiff smile.

"Unrequited passion? Or do you always affect men in such a mettlesome manner?"

"It would seem so," Sary grated.

"On the dodge? The fiddle? Come on, me darlin'. You can tell your old mates." That from Malcolm the Midget.

Redhead swatted him. "We take care of our own and our business, ya nosey ha'-penny."

Tommy shook a cigarillo from an ornate case, clamping Malcolm's wrist as he reached. Malcolm mugged cheekily and stage-whispered, "Our Tommy dast not besmirch the one token of his *solamente* conquest. The broke-down Marquesa with the mole. Where was it? The mole, I mean."

Redhead bellowed. "Marquesa! Hah! Baroness, if ever was one! Then wrong side of the sheets!"

King Lear intoned: "Knowing our Thomas, the wench assuredly had a wrong'un herself, nine months gone!"

Their laughter turned ribald and loud. Then Caine burbled, "If one put a bag over her 'ead!" Followed by pounding.

Sary made a face. *Even the rest of the tavern watches them.* "Really shouldn't stay. So kind. I'm very—"

"Oh, terribly good! Most horribly kind. In-*dub-*itably caring!" Tommy sneered, trapping her hand. "Wager you're not exactly spoiled for choice. Sit. *Queenie!"*

Malcolm waggled brows. Sary plunked down hard.

"Still out there, you know. Ahhhh, Sary, was it?" Tommy mocked.

Sary jerked a yes.

"Safe with us. We won't sell you to the gypsies."

Sary flushed.

"All California and you!" Tommy heckled.

Oh, Lord, I want to sleep. To lie on something soft and dry.

"Cor, Sary!" he nagged. "Open roads! The heat! Rain! Dust! Sour wine, greasy bacon sarnies…"

And wagons stuck in muddy wallows, breaking down in gully washers, raucous sweaty shows. More starving. Why did it seem so alluring a thousand years ago? Sary yearned to say it.

Tommy still prattled, oblivious. "Ruddy stinking

costumes after another rousing, yet *frightfully* nuanced performance given in some goat-encrusted hovel of a town—"

"Honoring us with eggs and chickens, not to mention the odd overripe tomato," Lear interjected.

"Gawd! Can't wait!" This from Redhead.

Malcolm piped up. "Me? I likes the odd overripe egg…"

Tommy plucked his tunic. "Cor! Costumes so weighted with salt-sweat one could float the bloody Thames."

He waited. Sary looked down her nose. "Well?" Tommy nudged her nearly off the bench. "We have need of a dogsbody, some baud to help wash up, clean costumes, do the odd walk-on—no spoken lines, mind you—"

"See the world from the rear end of a horse!" Sary snapped back. Tired, hungry, she couldn't get the stew's gristle down. She shivered with damp. Couldn't they see she had the ague? Her head thudded with hammer blows, and the man rambled on.

"Does it matter?" Tommy asked. "Back end of the horse…and me? *All* of me? Back end…front end?"

"I'll manage!" Sary snapped.

I'm going to lose even the gristle if he doesn't stop. And where's Ratchet? Outside?

Tommy dug into another plate of stew. "Got a better offer, Duchess?"

"Anything." She wanted to hurt him. She'd be on the ship by now if they hadn't waylaid her. That glorious…

Sary stopped, arrested by the troupe's fallen faces, and mumbled, "No offense."

Chapter 30

An endless evening. Too much song, crude jest, greasy food, sour beer, and harsh tobacco scoured her throat and clouded her brain. At last, the promise of a bed. Tommy led an almost tearfully grateful Sary past cheap doors over the bar. In one: a half-dressed woman unhooked a chemise, breasts nearly spilling out. The man there cupped them and scowled at Sary. Sary flushed, half-wistful. Then Tommy reached past her to open a door to a low-ceiling room.

"Perks of the manager." Tommy jabbed at the troupe entering a similar room down the hall. "We don't bunk with that lot."

"We?"

He flashed his charming crooked grin that deepened a cleft near his mouth and one in his chin as he thrust fingers through the famously floppy hair.

Sary entered, scrutinizing the limp bed and tattered quilts. Had anything looked so heavenly? She checked the window—rotting wharfs, canneries, rooming houses, and bars fronted the bay, stretching both ways, but nothing else. And what was more important, no Ratchet.

"I'll take the bed."

"By your most excellent leave." He cocked a brow and tossed her a playbook. "Earn your rest. We haul our own cart here." He flopped on the floor, bunching his cape under his head. "You *can* read?"

Sary slapped the playbook down and blew out the candle.

Tommy called in the dark. "You're welcome here with us, Sary. We won't bother you. You are safe." A silence. "Long as you—want—or need." Then, "You looked trampled by a herd of buffalo—or my numerous fans." Silence. "What happened?" Disgusted. "Yeah, well. And the horse they rode in on…"

Tears wet Sary's face in the dark. She bit her lip. *I don't care, I don't care.*

Chapter 31

Sailors and a rough bar crowd gaped, bemused. Tommy and the troupe danced with broad humor across a stage of yet another venue.

Sary, in a blonde wig and tattered velvet, fanned herself in the wings, awaiting her cue. Days somehow sped into weeks—different bars, once a small theater, a girl's school, a whirl of rehearsal—for Tommy took his troupe seriously—with color, laughing faces, and pugnacious drunks, and chores mundane as mending costumes.

In an odd way, Sary infused the traveling show with fresh blood, she being the new audience to conquer. The skits were more spontaneous, and the troupe reveled in audiences more robust than usual. Managers paid less grudgingly and meals improved.

She flinched as Lear, now awaiting his cue, brushed her shoulder. She checked the seeping wound—an underlying infection, healed but like a good patch over a worn quilt, made foolhardy any plan other than this easy confluence of days.

Fever was her constant companion now, with flushing cheeks and lips, lending her eyes a certain irresistible madness.

Her gaiety was hysteria, but the mob wasn't in on it, so Sary earned her keep, hiding her bad arm by holding things in the crook of it, and if the troupe noticed, they kindly left it alone. Sary scratched her side where a knob had formed, with aching as fresh as if the fracture were green, but at least her ribs healed. The redhead said kindly one night, "Fleas, is it? I have somethin for that, darlin'."

Sary thought she might find she enjoyed all this and be sucked down the rabbit hole of casual warmth, zeal, and camaraderie. She wished she could...

A little more time. Jasmine and laces and long skinny boats. Castles and...and maybe little Jude... She whispered her mantra. Her mind shied from the noisome saloon and Handi and diseases, and Julian and his putrid cough. *Does Jude yet live?*

"Sary!" Tommy hissed.

She started. Tommy, on stage, edged awkwardly toward the wings, glaring at her. The audience was restless, and so Sary barged on as shrewish Katherina one more night, snarling, "If I be waspish, best beware my sting!"

Sary was not bad as an actress, yet she seemed to take personal delight in stinging Tommy beyond the waspish *Taming of the Shrew* dialogue.

Now Katharina/Sary, in bedraggled velvet cut daringly low, swatted Tommy extra hard, venting frustration beyond stage direction with each blow. *Swat!*

Petruchio/Tommy hissed, "A tad harsh! Sweet Katherina!" and pinched her in turn. "Have a care!" He chased her, pincering his fingers. "My remedy is then to pluck it out." Tommy leered at the titillated audience.

Sary looked daggers and, as Katherina, sashaying before the mob, smirked back. "Ay, if the fool could find it where it lies."

The crowd sniggered, goading her on. They were in an actual theater for once, and the gallery roared approval.

Petruchio: "Who knows not where a wasp does wear his sting? In his tail." Tommy performed a crude bump and grind. He whispered, "Give 'em what they want. A bit more bosom, sweet Katherina. An ankle perhaps. Eh?"

Katharina swirled. "In his tongue!"

Petruchio pranced across stage, broadly posturing. "Whose tongue?"

Katharina's foot darted from under her gown. Tommy stumbled into a stool, skittering it into the audience. They tossed it back. Tommy raised the stool, threatening.

Sary, her hips swaying, tittered behind her hand.

"Yours, if you talk of tails, and so farewell." Sary trod on his foot and swivel-hipped away.

Tommy kicked at her backside, missing. "What, with my tongue in your tail?" And he roughly swung her back. "Nay, come again, Good Kate; I am a gentleman."

Ribald snickers from the mob as Tommy thoroughly kissed Sary, then dropped her. Sary staggered, swinging her arm wide.

Suddenly Tommy sank to his knees under the swing, mugging to the audience. "Marry, so I mean, sweet Katherina, in thy bed..." Tommy leered blatantly, tried for another kiss, and jumped back holding his lip and his groin, to the mob's raunchy delight. He strutted the stage with effort, as if it were all act and his privates didn't hurt.

Sary looked contrite. Sort of.

Chapter 32

A scruffy Ratchet tossed Sary's drawing, so creased it was almost quartered, at the desk sergeant. He shunted it back as if Ratchet smelled.

Cursing, digging into his pockets for an orange, Ratchet left the station. He huddled in a 'Frisco downpour at the tram stop, still cursing the eternal San Francisco penchant for moisture. Fog, rain, mist, drizzle, drool, gully-washers. Oh, for the sere heat and dry chill of Big Bear City.

Behind him, frayed soggy posters plastered brick walls higgledy-piggledy. He had little patience for them. One, however…

The peculiar yellow of some long ago stock from a forgotten printer snagged his attention, darkened by rain and one day from sluicing off to join gutter flotsam gushing to a cistern. Tommy had reams of them, dated but cheap. They still depicted Tommy in tights, with the troupe, and read:

"Sleight of Hand! Jugglers. Fire Eaters!
Feats of Strength!
Rousing Recreations of William Shakespeare's Hamlet!
Starring Headliners of All Europe!
Seen by Royalty!"

Ratchet did a double-take, snapping lantern jaws closed. More wolflike than ever, his gray-yellow eyes narrowed as he inwardly recalled that blasted clot of gypsy actors at that first saloon. *Damn! And the puddle of water.* They did seem familiar. His mind flashed to Big Bear and Delacorte and—Sary.

"Rained that day, too," Ratchet snarled savagely, with long, bared teeth. He ripped down the wet poster.

****

Pots and jars jumped as Tommy pounded the table of a makeshift space jammed with wigs and costumes. The troupe was buttock to buttock, cramming on costumes, elbowing for makeup.

"Have a care!" Lear fretted. A black line of grease pencil shot to his forehead.

"You owe us!" Tommy raged at Sary's image.

Sary smeared orange cream across cheeks, stippling on greasy rouge. She enjoyed the new range of freedom in her shoulder. At last the wound had healed properly, with a shiny scar to show it was better, and she was anxious to try her wings no matter where they took her. *Enough bolted meals and greasy stew and smelly backrooms...enough of Tommy goading and chiding and—oh, damnation. Look what I've done.* She'd wiped a line of carmine past the boundaries of her lip.

The troupe ignored Tommy's raging at Sary as if it were commonplace.

"Every night. I'm practically—advertising," she mumbled finally.

"Bloody hell! What? What do you advertise? Not sainthood! Under three pounds of paint and wigs, you belong in a bloody music hall burlesque. Not a prestigious traveling Shakespeare exhibition, lending erudition to the masses..."

Sary tightened her lips.

"Moreover, you're not concentrating! Last night you—"

"Bother last night! I…think…I think…I *saw* someone," Sary blurted.

Nevertheless, Tommy rolled on. "I had to strangle you twice! Far as I recall, Desdemona does *not* study the audience *after* she expires. Who's the phantom lover? Someone we know?"

Sary dived under a bench for a slipper, showing her backside. "You wouldn't want to."

Tommy eyed her bottom with interest as he continued, "We never meddle in affairs, Sary." The troupe nodded vigorously, although they were not much listening, except Malcolm, who always perked his ears for gossip.

"Who chases you? The Hounds of Hell? You a pickpocket? Murder some poor wretch?"

She sucked in a breath, rubbed her still stiff arm, and muttered, "It's all wrong, that's all. I *feel* it."

"Stuff and nonsense!"

Tommy slammed more lip grease in front of her.

"Tomorrow's opening night! You rehearsed—not Becky, you! No matter what, if we're sick or bloody bleeding dead, we theater folk have a tradition called dependability. Gratitude! Loyalty! We need the money, Sary."

****

Ratchet trekked office to office, thrusting the poster at theater managers. One bored manager finally tapped it, shrugged, nodded, and checked a ledger.

****

Julian dealt cards for a strapping eighteen-month-old Jude, while Handi hovered in the background. She edged forward with a winning smile, holding a tiny velvet, fur-trimmed coat for the sturdy toddler with the tousle of glossy curls and clear green eyes above plump, freckled cheeks.

Julian twitched, petulant. "What's in your craw?"

"Air. He needs out, Julian. The new pony?" Handi wheedled.

"And have my boy thrown and his neck broke? Jealous cow! You'd like that."

Jude giggled. Then he said, "Pony, Grampa? Where pony?"

"In yer grandma's bustle. Ain't no pony! Just a crazy old woman. Don't need pay her no mind."

Handi flinched and watched Baby Jude pick up his messy spread of cards, inexpertly fanning them in imitation. Julian poured whiskey into his milk, and Jude greedily reached for it.

"That'll grow hair on your chest." Julian thumped his chest, added a tiny drop of milk in his own glass, and tinked Jude's glass. Jude giggled and coughed from the blast of smoke from Julian's cigar.

Handi drooped and left.

****

Sary shut her eyes, blotting out the garish image in the cloudy traveling mirror. "A little longer then, Tommy." She rubbed her head and picked up the tube, slashing more carmine across her mouth, making herself unrecognizable, unless she were a Jack the Ripper victim, she fancied.

As she daubed shadow above each eye, Sary wondered, gazing in the mirror, who that woman was in the red wig and green, heavily mascaraed eyes staring from a bleak face. Perhaps someone as scattered as the false parts she shed each night, one part yearning to revel in the fabled glories of Europe, another darkly pondering the fate of one ill-favored little boy, innocent as a spring dandelion and forever, as dandelion fluff, blown away. On the other hand, should she sink into the day-to-day bawdy geniality and shelter of the troupe—and Tommy—until the other life faded with wear and time? But would that be real or merely happenstance?

She was so weary of life just *happening* to her. Sary desperately wanted to pick up the reins herself and gallop hell-for-leather in a direction she herself chose. She blotted more face rouge. She must make a decision regarding Tommy. If she had to decide. It wasn't really a choice. Deep down, she feared his touch would be the touch that might bind her to him forever—her body betrayed her and yearned for that touch—

"Katherina!" Tommy's voice broke in—he always called her by the name of the character she played. "You going to moon over yourself all night? The audience cares little if one has a pound or a half pound of grease paint on your face. Really, Kate!"

And so a red-cheeked female named Sary, in a stained purple gown and red wig, bounced on a makeshift stage.

****

"Peeka-boo! Where's my sweet sugarboy? Where's he hidin' at?"

Jude giggled, covering his broad freckled face under widespread chubby fingers. One green eye peeked through them, while Pearl lounged on a pillowed bed, dividing her attentions between satisfying a red-faced customer and amusing the curly-headed little boy.

As she toddled little Jude to a potty, she cooed, "Does my little man need to go winky-wink…?"

The customer flopped on his back and groaned.

****

Ratchet sucked oranges, inwardly groaning at the sign across the street, a sign all tarted up in blue and gold: Anchor's Rest

Flowers in boxes. Sparkling glass. He checked the names on the slip of paper. Another saloon, but the perverted band of gypsies might have come up in the world. He hoped they hadn't moved on. He'd swear they knew, by God, how much he was in a fever to be back in Big Bear, where folks didn't knock you down without a fare-ye-well, and a man knows *without* yankin' down a fella's BVDs if a fella's a man and not a woman—and the bona fide females here, were so *unwomanly.*

Aware of how he looked, Ratchet had practiced till one look was as good as a knife to the gizzard. Men quaked and women quailed. But females here just laughed and made faces back.

He pushed from the wall, his long yellow teeth exposed, lupine, as cheers, clapping, and banging of tankards came from within. He would make her pay.

Spilling out the door came the pansy actor, a slatternly redhead towering over the men, a perversion of God's plan in the depraved shape of a dwarf, the old fart with the long beard, and—Christ! that murdering slut, cowering just like she done before.

Not this time. Not this time. Murdering whore! First, I'll carve the gold outa her.

He quickened as the troupe scattered, leaving Sary arguing with the same nancy boy in velvet bloomers.

"Never mind sugary words! You deliberately trod on my hem...!" Ratchet heard Sary yelling like a fishwife. "You *wished* me mortified. I'm leaving, Tommy. I swear I will!"

The catamite waved his arms like a semaphore. "Sary! You were on fire tonight. Blazing! Incendiary! How can you even entertain—?"

"If I were on fire, it's because I wished that damnable play over!" They were walking away. He would follow a mite. This was better than a tent show.

"I received a *pourboire* tonight," he heard the catamite say, like he was all proud. *'Poor bwore'* he heard—more fancy words, nailing him for certain sure as a nancy boy, a fairy lad. Eyes narrowed, the one she called Tommy showed the witch a coin. Ratchet would relieve him of it later. A little molasses for his efforts. He critically assessed Sary. One arm was kinked, and she held it close to her side. She was plumper, kind of toothsome, as females go. Her hair, Ratchet grudgingly conceded, was fetching, hanging down like that. A female Lazarus rising from the dead could do no worse, he supposed, savoring these few seconds before the kill.

****

Sary looked about, uneasy. Ghost fingers surrounded her neck.

"Are you even listening?"

"Yes, Tommy."

"We deserve a slap-up meal."

Sary looked over her shoulder.

"No one pursues you, your highness! You're not *that* illustrious."

Ratchet grinned, ducking.

"Suit yourself!" Tommy sulked, pocketing the tip.

Ratchet nodded approval—*Fairy-boy might have brass in him yet*—and stepped out clapping. "Excellent day for a hanging, Swinford." She spun, wide-eyed. *Looks ready to run.* Ratchet spat pips, pocketed them, and sauntered over, grinning. Fairy-boy frowned, until Ratchet's long hand flashed his knife. The bitch tried to tug the boy off.

"My wrangle's not with fellers in purple bloomers, sugarplum. Wait your turn."

"Tommy!" Sary tried to yank him, but he waded in with fists cocked like an English gentleman. "Tommy! You can't fight him that way!" *This isn't a play,* Sary wanted to yell, as Ratchet slammed him, one-armed, against brick.

"Don't piss with me, *boy!*"

Tommy doubled. "Ooooph! Run, Sary!" he managed and rushed back in, awkwardly flailing, as Ratchet's knife sang. Tommy didn't care for the tune after all, falling back while Sary looked about for a weapon, any weapon, and snatched up a broken brick, raising it high. *This is all too familiar.* Ratchet seemed to sense her and reached back and grabbed her wrist, twisting the brick out of her hand and yanking Sary to him. She dragged her weight, clawing with her other hand, as Ratchet advanced on Tommy. "You wanna save sugarplum fairy here, move, dammit, or I'll cut you here!" Sary had hope when she noticed a crowd of stragglers appearing in the gap. She didn't notice the animated looks on their faces. Ratchet threw Tommy, the beautiful Tommy, off.

Sary sadly watched Tommy, with the scallop of hair falling over his forehead and the perfect mouth, edge back, heard his feet slap around a corner and pound off, fading. Ratchet, with a look of evil triumph, scraped her against the brick, his hand clamped about her mouth, drawing her deeper into the dank alley, more a narrow passage, that stank of fish, cabbage, and rotting potatoes.

A British sailor leered after them and was the last sane thought Sary had. "'at's right, mate, give it to her proper!" He rammed his arm in the air.

Trapped in the narrow slice between a bar and a butcher shop—*stale beer…raw blood*—Sary opened her mouth to scream, but Ratchet drove his fist into her stomach. She doubled, breathless. Stretching a long-toothed grin, Ratchet shoved her between the refuse and barrels plugging the rear of the alley, effectively trapping her, and then, as she was afraid of the worst, he did something surprising. Ratchet, watching her face expectantly, dragged out a paper, and forced her head down for her to see it.

Sary stilled. *What is this?* She dared look up.

Ratchet yanked her neck until her nose touched the paper. Sary scanned it, paling, glad her hair now covered her face as the wretched man turned an official-looking sheet over, and began reading, savoring each word as if an especially juicy piece of meat.

"Blah blah…representing…" he drawled, "State of California… Yes, yes, here 'tis"—he flashed another weird and gleeful look at her—"'Full power and authority of the United States Government…' "

He halted, waiting for her reaction, and was disappointed when she had no such thing. "Here's the best part." Ratchet flashed a badge with a star. Sary frowned. Ratchet a sheriff? In this world? But then he finished, and her mind froze. "I arrest you for the murder of one Cora May Doheny, female child"—he waited—"Jules Alexander Delacorte"—Ratchet smirked—"who you had carnal knowledge with, and one Everett Elliot Eckhardt, both adult males, and will take you as remanded for incarceration...until your eventual"—Ratchet flashed strong yellow teeth—*"hanging..."* The long-toothed grin spread all over his face. "Yes, ma'am, we found 'em all right. That brother help you? Too bad he ain't 'round to share the verdict." And he chuckled that rats-in-the-wall laugh of his.

"I've come up in the world!" Sary lashed out. She didn't know where the foolhardy courage came from. "They used a tree, last time," Sary snarled, kicking, but because of the closeness, it was a feeble blow on his shin.

"No more a tha—"

Ratchet swiveled to the crash of crates and bricks, and the effluvium of old fish kicked up. Sary's heart gladdened. They had never looked lovelier. There were Caine, Luigi, a glimpse of Tommy in the rear, all boiling in, with Luigi brass-knuckled and Caine swinging a bar of some kind.

Ratchet shoved Sary back into a stack of crates, madly grinning, waving the knife in wild scythes and jabs. He relished their interference, Sary saw in a sick flash. Caine ducked and swung the bar, smashing brick. He couldn't get a proper arc in the narrow space and barreled headlong into Ratchet instead.

Ratchet grappled Caine's back, and Luigi swung over Caine, slicing knuckles down Ratchet's jaw. Ratchet threw both of them off. Luigi was down. Caine's head smashed on the opposite wall, but he got up, swiping his eyes, and waded back in.

Sary picked up a crate from behind a barrel that caged her in, trying to bring it up. Ratchet surged forward, and she had her chance, but Tommy jumped in, hauling up short. "'Get behind me, Sary," he yelled. "Run when you can. I'll—"

Tommy still acts as if he's playing a part and his wooden sword is real, Sary had time to think.

Ratchet spun, laughing from the belly. "Back for more lessons, eh, in the art of manliness?" Ratchet sneered. "This one might cost you dearly." His fist, with the knife, slashed underhand in a crude jab meant to gut Tommy.

Sary swung the crate, just brushing Ratchet's shoulder, but it nudged his knife arm enough. Over his shoulder, she saw Caine rushing back and Luigi bent low and advancing, swinging his arms like an ape, and Tommy, painfully rising from the litter-strewn alley. Sary was angrily aware of catcalls from a mob at the end of the alley, blotting out the street, jamming the intersection. It all happened fast, then.

Ratchet elbowed her and, whipping the knife around him, backed to the nether end. She ducked as Caine continued to swing—iron ringing off brick and red dust spraying. Sary searched for a proper weapon, sparing a glance at Tommy as Caine's bar scraped across his beautiful nose. Tommy staggered back, holding his bloodied face, into Luigi, attempting a flying leap at Ratchet.

Ratchet swung from Sary to Caine and then to Luigi, smirked at Tommy, and grated, *"This ain't over."* With that he vanished, eeling his long body past the trash barricading the far end, and Sary heard his boots pound off just like Tommy's had. Caine gave chase, leaping over the trash, but soon reappeared, flushed and grinning and ready for another scrap. "Some dust-up, eh, Sary?"

Sary nodded, numb. This wouldn't be the end. She slid back up the wall and eyed the two battlers, Caine and Luigi, with speculation.

Chapter 33

Gasping, Sary leaned out yet another floor-to-ceiling window of yet another cheap room, over more fetid, lapping water, close to both laughing and weeping.

They found the bodies. Apparently not Seb's—likely no one in that misbegotten town cared—*but the little girl, little Cora! She did not harm that child. She would never!* Even though Sary scoured her heart for culpability, she felt none, at least about Cora. Still she felt drenching pain and guilt. Could she ever run from it? Again she raked the tall masts sketching *freedom* against a fresh-air canvas of sky that stretched clean to fabled Europe. They represented ships with the ghost shapes of furled sails—or some powered by vast steam engines, she'd heard. The monotonous *slap-slap* of water lapping pilings intruded. She eyed a dead gull spread on the wharf below, and she was back to rotting garbage and reality.

"I'll *destroy* him, Tommy…"

"Him?" Poor Tommy, still shaken, examining his swollen face, looked bewildered. "That—ruffian? That poltroon? That—scalawag!"

Sary gave a bitter laugh.

Scalawag! Ratchet as a *scalawag!* Only Tommy would not see danger as anything beyond dramatic words in a play and stage villains. She had put the whole child-like troupe in danger. Next time, Caine and Luigi wouldn't be so lucky. They too had a sprinkle of fairy dust in their eyes, thrown by their craft.

Ratchet was a stone killer. He thrived on pain like blight on rye. It was mother's milk to him. He would never return her to be hanged. She would not make it that far, if he found her again. She heartened. It must be a ruse, the arrest part, she thought. No one was hunting her but Julian. Would he not have proper bailiffs? Either way, her trip to Big Bear would have no return. Her mind skittered like blown paper across the wharf below.

Tommy shrugged. "I have no knowledge of whom you speak, sweeting. Yet, quoting Marlowe: 'He that is born to be hanged shall never be drowned...' "

"Oh, do shut up, Tommy. Let me think."

Tommy pointed manfully to the door. "I know you are upset. Don't! Open!" She smiled faintly. It was as if Tommy still played Petruchio in *Taming of the Shrew.* He slammed out before she could react to the sound of locks clicking. *He never locks the doors!* A careless habit.

"Tommy!" Sary rammed the door and beat on it. "Tommy! *Confound* you!" She kicked and shouted through it. "And poetry doesn't help!" Running to the window, she studied the drop to the bay. "Hell's fire." Sary flopped onto the bed, sighed, sat up, and reached behind to take off the heavy costume she yet wore, fumbling for the buttons.

Behind her, a wardrobe door cracked open.

Long, calloused, spatulate fingers appeared in the notch.

Eyes glowed in the slice of light.

Sary kept reaching, anxious to wash off and think and plan. Already her eyes searched out her trunks and cases.

A second later a hand brushed her hand. Yanked her buttons.

For a flash, she thought it was Tommy, a thought dashed by a bicep in rough tweed smashing her bent elbow hard against her cheek, locking her face and mouth tight—*salt and oranges and body odor...*

Galvanized, Sary thrashed side to side, kicking, twisting. Her eyes caught her face in the mirror, and she despised the frightened look above Ratchet's muscled hand that gripped her mouth like a malignant growth. His rangy body pressed her spine, his face obscured. *But she knew.* Stiffening, she pulled with all her strength, then feinted and slumped, but he merely tightened his grip with an amused grunt. Sary stopped, snared by the sight of his other hand hovering before her.

Incongruously, the fingers delicately pincered a perfect pearl-drop earring. The soft gleaming sphere floated in the gloaming of the room, pinked in candlelight.

She saw her face in the mirror, with her frightened eyes watching the small swinging globe, mesmerized. Then Ratchet hovered low beside her, and gravely held the pearl drop to Sary's ear.

She clawed the steel grip clamping her mouth and tried to bite the tough leather of his hand, tasting tobacco and tweed and oddly—oranges.

"Delacorte tells me—and I *always* obey Mister Delacorte"—Ratchet snickered—"'Bring Sary, earrings in her ears,' he says to me." A chuckle grated like moss-covered rock.

"But I figure, why not just—her *ears*?"

Ratchet flicked a sharp blade, splintering silver in candlelight, and touched his nose. "Didn't improve none on my good looks, Swinford. Consider this a return favor." He waved the blade over her ear, chuckling as she watched disbelieving. "Oh! Don't concern yourself none with any pesky talk of *hangin'*. Doubtful you'll make it that far, if I was a bettin' kind, least all one piece." He threw his head back. The laugh was a rusty hinge.

Sary bolted upright.

"Un-un-uhhh!" Ratchet rammed her back, tightening his grip, and held the blade aloft while bizarrely continuing his folksy chat. "Yep, been trackin' you and your filthy gypsies too long. I knew right where to find you."

Sary tracked the piercingly sharp point, imagining it slicing her ear clean off, or in bloody sawing cuts.

"Before that?" Ratchet jerked an impatient shrug. "But enough palaver." Crushing her tighter, he straightened his stance, checked the mirror with the dark image of his bony hand and above it Sary's enraged eyes and wild hair. Lifting the blade like a straightedge razor, he lowered it, gently making a trial stroke, just nicking the tender bridge of skin meeting her hairline. Blood trickled onto her cheek. She tried to shoot up through his embrace and avoid the blade. He jammed her back down with spine-jolting strength and halted. Savoring the moment. At the stretched silence, she raised hopeful eyes.

Ratchet gazed to a far corner at nothing—giving nothing. "Saw a two-headed snake oncet," Ratchet finally grated.

Ratchet suddenly pinched the knife blade and one calloused thumb around a hank of her hair, roughly sawing. Hacked-off hair rained thick before Sary's eyes, and she was too outraged to be frightened. She twisted and bucked and jammed his thigh with her elbow. Ratchet halted again, knife hovering, his folksy talk dragging on, as she looked on, helpless. "Looks like you and that consumptive soft-cock both got snake-bit," he chuckled reminiscently. "Yeah, yeah, I prob'ly ain't bringin' you back. I already got the money." He winked at her.

As he looked off, congratulating himself, Sary renewed her kicking, twisting, wriggling, ramming upright—never mind the knife, or her ear—shouting, *Tommy!* in her mind.

"Come now. Rest easy! Long ways 'tween here and ole Delacorte. Anything can happen."

Hack, hack, hack. More hair dropped heavily into her lap. Sary stared, appalled. Her scalp was all ragged tufts and bare patches, yet it was the unholy gleam in his eye, like the fever of an illicit lover, that made her buck and lunge, wrenching her head from his rigid grasp in one desperate act, opening her mouth to scream.

He snapped her head back.

Futile. Ratchet clamped her nose now. *I can't breathe!* Saliva made his hand slide an inch, and he grumbled, "Easier putting earbobs in first, I reckon..." He yanked her head and managed to snag a wire through her left earlobe. His mood changed. She saw Ratchet batted the earring, lost in admiring his work.

Both seemed mesmerized. Sary's eyes were huge

in the clouded mirror, watching the soft gleam of the pearl in candle glow, swinging from her lobe.

Then her gaze flashed to his face. His body shook. He was amused. He laughed. A mistake. Sensing a lessening pressure, she wrenched her trapped arm down, jerked her other shoulder up and then down, planting feet, and rammed up with all her might.

Taken aback, Ratchet pivoted her into the iron bedpost—hard. The knob struck the base of her skull. Sary saw stars, then blinked into focus.

Ratchet dragged her up like a rag doll, flipped the blade over her ear, and sawed grimly, without ceremony. She sensed blood trickling down her neck before she felt the searing cut. Gathering all her life force, Sary, tears streaming, nose filling, kicked a sharp heel back and hooked her fingers overhead. Sucking air through his horny palm, she saw in the mirror a pale, nearly bald oval with two black holes for eyes, and then they too dimmed as her mirror-image faded and Ratchet tilted to avoid Sary's nails. His knife jolted aside, he lowered the blade, careless with impatience, flicking looks at the door, and grunted, constricting his grip so her teeth ached. He lowered the blade, all pretense drowned in a pool of fury.

Using all her waning powers, Sary jerked straight up, locking her knees, sensing she had only this one chance, and lunged sideways, dragging Ratchet with her, gyrating in an awkward dance and wrestling them closer to the floor-to-ceiling window. Collapsing in on herself, Sary threw him off-balance, hip-butting him even as he still held on.

He lurched, back-pedaling, tangling with her skirts—her ankle, the low sill catching his shin. His arms flew out, pinwheeling. Wavering, he looked at her with shock and hatred, clutched at her, grabbed her sleeve, her arm, then soared windmilling into space, dragging Sary with him. Both hovered in midair as they plummeted to the bay lapping with floating detritus.

****

In those few seconds as she plunged, Sary saw warped planks, fish-stained with dried entrails and shining scales, speeding toward her and envisioned her face splintering into wood, smashing bone…smelling the putrid breath of fish long dead…

The wharf's weathered edge skimmed past Sary. Strands of errant hair Ratchet had missed snagged on rotted wood—she felt the irritating tug seconds before her piebald head connected with the bay water as Sary plunged alongside Ratchet a second later, a surge of foul cold water marking the spot.

Ratchet popped up alone.

Brought up in the dry arms of Big Bear, he couldn't swim. He flailed like a long bony child, spewing bay water foul and olive, slipping further below with each effort.

A late fisherman wearily rowed for the wharf, oblivious of Ratchet, or of Sary beneath his boat as his oars thrashed.

Water exploded up Sary's nose, rushing down her throat as she arrowed to the bottom beneath Ratchet, weighted by her heavy costume. Velvety water plastered her face, blinding, suffocating, and she forced herself to calm as ambient light eclipsed to ink. She battled her voluminous skirts down, yearning to open her mouth.

As Sary plummeted down through murky salt,

Ratchet thrashed to the surface. His head tunked the fisherman's boat hard, and then he was bobbing in its wake, confused and furious, when a returning oar smashed him in the ear. Plunging, dazed, Ratchet caught the rapidly descending tail of Sary's skirts. Sary still struggled with the weight tangling about her head, darkening the already green twilight, when her skirts were yanked sharply down, almost dragged off her body, as Ratchet's affrighted face rushed past, her skirts clenched in his white-knuckled fist. Immediately Sary felt his hands claw up her body and found his face abreast with hers, mimicking a lover's embrace. He still clawed, pushing himself up and her deeper still. A foot booted her head, and he shot up, striving for the surface. She was too surprised to be angry. A wavering moon blinked out. A cork plugged her neck. She craved to suck water deep into her lungs. The spark of rage exploded, instantly extinguished by the tons of water enfolding Sary in death's clammy arms and dragging her to the deeps.

Sary retreated—two thousand miles east, and three years back, to a sunny room, warm, safe, dry—oh, so very dry, and bright, alongside Jonathan…

No. Jonathan's face…?

That isn't right.

It's Tommy's face. Tommy's face beyond a watery veil…

That absurdity shocked her, and her eyes sprang open to green, brackish water. *The weight of it. Lungs bursting. Does it end like this?* Her greed? Her doomed child? Brother's hopes? *In this polluted, pressing nothingness?* Her heart raged. *Why did I not leave? Why leave it all too late? But, you were sick and mending. Recall? But now I am drowned!* With thoughts black as marl, Sary's body plunged toward untold fathoms, deeper still.

She pressed her mouth tight against the persistent icy fingers wrenching, trying to open it. She strained for the surface. Velvet skirts, heavy as concrete, had soaked water like a sponge. Petticoats slapped, tangling legs like wet bandages. She couldn't even kick!

As water bloomed darker, it embraced, welcomed, entombed her in a liquid shroud, pressing, invading her nose, ears, mouth...lungs. The water warmed now...comforting...

Go limp. Float...don't breathe...!

Sary dwindled, limp, to the bottom. Inky blackness pressed her wide-open eyes. She groped as a blind woman, mildly shocked when her boots thudded on a hard sharp thing. When they slipped off, her feet sank into velvety muck—soft gluey marl sucked her calves with a lover's constriction. Aching for air, Sary tugged, but her legs stuck fast.

****

Ratchet's terrified face surged above the surface. Below, Sary undulated on a junk-filled bottom. Her body lightened, and a black shape drifted past her eyes, billowing like a dark angel. Her anchoring skirts, ripped loose by Ratchet's tugging, finally—miraculously—floated off.

Even lightened, she sank deeper with each tug of her leg into the floor of the bay. *Where is that hard thing?* With her last bit of oxygen, she probed mud. Yes! Her fingers groped gritty metal—*Push hard.* Something, maybe a barnacle, sliced her palm, still the ocean floor claimed her leg. *Did the left foot slip? A lessening of pressure?* She pushed hard against metal. Sary felt her foot's blessed release from the strangulating muck. *Thrust hard!* Reluctantly, the mud let go, and Sary drifted, blind, with all the force of thistledown, for the top. Her chest was bursting to release. Bubbles trickled from her nose. *Air. Must have—*

Her face popped to the surface.

Fall back; suck in wet stars come out while you were between Hell and Earth.

After bobbing, pleasantly languid, hauling in air deliciously tangy with fish and seaweed, Sary checked her bearings.

The wharf and an uneven row of gaslights were to her right, the dark ocean, stretching to the strange island of Japan, to her left. Sary shivered, not from cold, entirely, in her wet floating petticoats, but at how close she had come to *not* being a part of either, or of anything on earth except as a permanent member waving like seaweed in the bilge waste, old bedsprings, and gutter effluvium at the bottom of San Francisco Bay.

Sary paddled on her last strength to wharves with staggered rows of tenements and warehouses lining them like weary sentries.

Sary's arms, like lead sash weights, groped slimy pilings studded with razor-sharp barnacles. The pilings loomed up to the wharf's underside, impossibly high. She paddled in circles. *No Ratchet.* Half expecting him, she looked back at the empty tide, which glinted reproof.

Can't just leave him down there.
Yes, you can. He did it.

Sary flinched. *No. No more deaths.*

Then Ratchet washed up, knocking into pilings, sloshed in with the waves. He was under the wharf, choking, eyes rolling like a frightened horse. When he caught sight of Sary's face, he floundered to her in wild overarm swings.

Sary pushed against a sluggish tide, and Ratchet washed up again, tangling amid cross braces under the quay. There he bounced with the waves but jerkily, *against* the tide, slamming posts, fumbling at the knife attached to his gun belt. She saw his belt was hooked on something, dragging him under. Already the rising tide slopped across his nose, and he tugged frantically, striving to keep his head up, fixed on her, imploring.

Sary paddled warily closer. She could not watch him drown. Could she wrench his belt loose before the next tide surged in? She circled. He still had that wicked knife, but trapped awkwardly behind him. She motioned, still paddling herself, as each wave threatened to sunder her and heave more water in her face and down her throat, tasting bitter salt. *Surely he will let me go now.* He leaned, compliant, from the post. "You won't bother me? You will forget me?" Sary yelled between waves. "You promise?"

"Yes, yes, please, for God's sake!" Ratchet appeared satisfyingly terrified, Sary thought. The rest was lost as waves crashed over Ratchet's head and didn't recede. Sary inserted her hand in the space and wriggled his belt free. She backstroked quickly.

Hand over hand, Ratchet now clutched pilings with evil in his face, kicking out viciously at Sary's head. He slipped, grabbed a slime-covered brace. Barnacles sliced his fingers. Blood barely stained the water as he sank beneath. His wild eyes widened under water. The next roller swept his feet out from under him as Sary clung to a cross brace to keep from getting swept out with the tidal pull. Ratchet's reserve of air exploded out. Bubbles galloped past Sary. Then he sucked for air where there was nothing but water and let go. His hands thrashed, tangling in seaweed. Sary watched where his coat billowed and bumped to rest in a maze of wood. The last bubble escaped, and Ratchet hung limp, swaying amid the pilings.

Chapter 34

Tommy fell into their room laughing and calling, clutching a long loaf, paper-wrapped fish, and a wine jug evidently meant for a private celebration—just the two of them, Sary registered, before he just stood there and gaped.

Sary, dripping wet, nearly bald, her hair hacked off and left in tufts, seaweed strung across one shoulder, furiously scrubbed her arms in the room's poor washbasin, a petticoat puddled about her ankles.

He sagged against the jamb. *Now what?*

Sary cried, rubbing her arms raw, "Damn him! Look what he made me do!"

"Inamora—"

"Do be quiet, Tommy! Don't say a word! Not one platitude, or fancy phrase. It's too *easy!*" she wailed.

"Inamorata!" He stopped at her look. 'What? What's too easy?" Moving to her, he ducked Sary's thrashing arms as she stabbed a pointing finger out at the bay.

"Ratchet! Down there! He...*drowned!*"

"Who? Who the hell's Ratchet?"

"Ratchet!"

"You mean that—?"

"Yes! Open your ears, Tommy!"

Tommy watched her warily. Her face was pale, and tears leaked off her chin to white breasts, oddly stuck with seaweed. She was drenched and shuddering. "But—" His eyes swept back, caressing the milky white round of breast with the nipples pale as tea roses.

Tommy tore his eyes away. Up to now they had been modest with each other, and his gaze swept the room, bewildered, taking in the open wardrobe, the blood drops, the rucked-up sheets.

He dropped the bread and wine and went clumsily to embrace a body shuddering so hard he could barely contain it—partly to shelter her nakedness and partly, Sary sensed, to shield himself from wanting her.

She revolved, melding her freezing self to him.

Oh! This feels so good. If he weren't so hateful! She pressed close as Tommy tenderly stroked her hacked-off hair and kissed her forehead, brushing the hacked-off ends with his cheek, Sary raised her face. It had been so long since she'd felt a man's hardness, his comforting, enveloping embrace. How safe it felt. The action turned into a long fumbling kiss, with mouth and teeth and tongue, as Tommy tore the last soggy petticoat down.

"Later," he mumbled between searching kisses, "I want to hear all about this. But for now, let me warm you," he muttered thickly.

Breathing hard, Sary whispered something harsh and throaty back, lost on Tommy.

Sary, in nothing but pantaloons, transparent and clinging, yanked at the buttons and shimmied out of them as he ripped off his clothes, slamming her naked body into his. Sary wound a cold leg around his warm muscular hairy one, wrapping chill arms about his hot neck, glorying in his rough warm comfort. Tommy picked her up, cradled her close to his chest, and Sary knew nothing coherent after that. Only her body knew. Tommy dropped her backward onto the bed, entwined them both in coverlets, chafed her hands, and let their breathing warm the bed and her body. Slowly Tommy slid his lips over every inch of her. Holding her face in his hands, he kissed her long and deep, warming her cold mouth with his tongue, cupping her body with urgent hands, heating her with his weight.

Even her memories of Jonathan and their little room warmed by sun sailed away in this endless rapture. It had been so long since a man loved her in all the right ways. She was not a possession or taken in naked lust or as a workhorse. Later, wrapped in sheets, they sank intertwined to the floor, all in a heap by the low window, looking upside down at the stars.

After a moment, Sary grinned and flipped on top, feverishly kissing Tommy as if she starved, and then she was on the bottom, and Tommy pressed his delicious strength once again into her.

****

A candle burned low.

Sary, wound in a sheet, her bottom flaming from floor burns and her back against the frame of the tall open window, studied Tommy's face. His beautiful chiseled features were thinned by hardships, his complexion roughened by long rough roads and weather. His eyes, sadder if not wiser, were yet infinitely warm. She began talking as she sipped wine from the bottle and found she could not stop. Tommy lay with his head in her lap, kissing every part he could reach easily. He finally focused on her words. She leaned to him, at last, gave a bursting sigh, and bussed him, ruffling his hair. Then, hesitantly, defiantly, she asked, "So what do think of your gallows bird now?"

She finished the last of the bottle. Her throat bobbed as she dared to look at him.

Tommy hitched up, checked the night, and slumped back, gazing bemused up at her. "Affliction is enamored of thy admittedly lovely parts, Sary, and thou art wedded to calamity…" He turned to look away and did not see Sary's impatience. "I'd rather you'd told me. Have you—you *did* reveal everything?"

Sary jumped up, letting his head thump to the floor, trailing sheets. He gazed with interest at her pinked bottom and flash of thigh as she stalked to the window and addressed the night.

"Plagued with scars—nearly hung—gimpy armed—and you didn't think there might be a past?" She glanced, contrite, over her shoulder. "Sorry, Tommy."

Tommy reached for the other bottle. "This Ratchet—he's the end of it, then? Whatever *it* is."

"Maybe." Sary claimed the wine and returned to the night. "You don't know me." Then, bitterly, she whispered, "How can it be over?"

She realized he'd risen and thrown on trousers, and she frowned, wanting him to return and comfort her. She was greedy for it now.

"Afraid they're waiting, sweeting. Make haste," Tommy fretted instead. *As if we never had this, this magic, this closeness…*

She knew she was unfair. *This is what happens when you let love stalk back into your life, hounding you, making you scared and silly—and needy…*

"We've tarried too long." His eyes softened as he gestured to the floor. "Let's *tarry* again soon."

He stuffed her trunks any which way.

Sary stubbornly kept drinking, pointing the bottle accusingly between gulps. "I've done it your way! I've danced *everyone's* tune. Every man-jack's, tinker-tailor's misbegotten fancy, whimsy, hankering, thirst, yen, or slightest wisp of a dream, of a desire for…"

Tommy yanked a drying stocking. "You've had enough of that for now. Hurry. *Sweeting*."

She shook her head, wordless, and tilted the bottle upside down over her mouth, sucking the last dregs.

Gasping, Sary swiped her mouth. "…my entire, meek-as-milk existence." She finished groping her rope burn scar, and slurred, "I've *paid*, Tommy."

"No doubt…" He ducked as Sary lurched and drunkenly waved the bottle. "And that stinking, curdled, smelly, conniving, underhanded, assassinating whore's son will pay even more. Oh, he'll *pay,* Tommy!" She staggered and narrowed her eyes. "With everything he's got!" She wiped at her nose. *Why am I acting this way? I, who always keep my own counsel?*

Tommy checked the room, distracted. "We feed our bellies with rage now, do we?"

Sary stumbled, giggling.

"Oh, Tommy," she cried. "Money is one thing I *do* have!"

Tommy reacted. "Money? What the hell you talking about?" He tossed her a gaudy costume.

Sary waved the bottle wildly. "But, Tommy. Where's my things?"

"In a hurry, Inamorata—"

"Tommy! Where's my *things*?"

"One step ahead of an extremely rapacious landlord. Rather afraid some of it got…" Tommy looked around confused. "Tossed? Besides..." He checked the window. "It's more than time!"

Sary sank to the floor, pawing her old clothes, clutching to her chest hard-won bank papers, the Derringer, and Jude's tiny moccasin, things Tommy had never before seen. He threw cases out the door and checked under the bed. "Barely scarpered with props and costumes as it is. Ah, well." He laughed, with his head under the trailing sheet. "Experienced, we lot, in disappearing acts..."

Sary hardly heard him as she ducked away from the window. A policeman and a knot of people pointed at the water and then swiveled, scanning windows as if trying to select one. Still clutching the bottle, Sary swung wildly as Tommy rose from under the bed. The bottle connected with a dull thunk. She flinched, softening the blow, but still Tommy slumped hard, wordless. She dropped beside him, shaking him.

"Tommy! No death scenes!" She peered above the sill. The knot of people approached the tenement. "Dam*na*tion!" Sary heard doors opening, and footsteps, below, four floors down. Voices. A clatter of doorknobs. A door slammed. Feet pounded up stairs. More voices. She eyed their suddenly flimsy door. *Is it locked?* She recalled Tommy throwing their cases out. *Probably not.* All the while she kept shaking him. "Not now! Tommy! Wake up!" Tommy mumbled something, rolled his eyes, and breathed slow and steady.

The pounding was right below them now—garbled voices and grumbles of people answering. Footsteps clattered on steps, ever closer. Sary yanked at a pillow and jammed it under Tommy's head as feet walked their hall, multiple feet. She heard rapping, police calling. A door opened. More voices, complaints this time. Another slam, and locks clicked. Feet pounded closer. A door opened after knocking. Sary heard a long angry protest. The next room faced the bay, too.

Sary scrambled into the other gaudy red costume, the one used for Katherina, haphazardly fitted on the red wig, laced shoes, and grabbed up her precious case.

At the door, she looked both ways and turned. "Tommy. I'm sorry. I'm *so sorry!*" Quickly she ran over and brushed his lips. Tommy groaned, his eyes fluttering awake. "Sary...?" And he slumped back. Once again, at the door, Sary looked back.

"Oh, Tommy! You may not *like* where I go. What I need—*have* to do."

Police and a small knot of curious followers rounded the bend.

Sary, in her red wig, smiled and brushed a policeman on her flight down.

Chapter 35

Another maze of alleyways. It seemed she always ran away from somewhere half dressed, unprepared. Sary couldn't see where she placed one racing foot after another, stumbling, tripping over garbage, cobbles, and things rushing past. More shouts—this time an excited cacophony of exhortations was just ahead.

Not far now.

Bursting out on the scene, Sary approached chaos—raucous yells of encouragement and heckling, as the alley widened on a alley intersection of an ale house, laundry, and restaurant, odors of bleach admixing with those of beer, sour refuse, and sewers.

A light rain was falling, but that didn't stop the ragged mob jamming the passageways—men, women, and even toddlers—from exhorting Caine and Luigi to beat each other to bloody death.

Sary saw Caine cold-cocking Luigi amid a frenzy of onlookers absorbed in the flurry of bloody action, connecting fists, and money slapping down.

Sprays of blood spattered bettors and spectators alike in gouts of red rain, mixed with boxer-sweat, until Luigi landed on his backside with a nose like a beet. "Owwww!"

Caine grinned, slipped a horseshoe from his fist, and held a hand out to Luigi, still groggy on the cobbles. He halted his hand midair, following Sary's slim one as it pressed a gold nugget to his bloody matted chest.

"Thought I'd find you two here," she said, making her eyes merry.

Caine ignored the nugget and stepped aside to accept a small purse from a promoter. "Ta." He touched his forehead, and only then did he finger Sary's costume, scanning the wig.

"Why you wearin' 'at? 'At's the Shrew's last-act costume. What you all tarted up for, Duchess? We're not on?"

Crouching on the cobbles, Sary bounced the nugget, ignoring his question. Then Luigi viewed the moon of her face rising over him. "You too," she told him, upside down. "Twenty-one rounds of horseshoes qualify any man, I should think."

****

The boxers slouched, bloody and defiant, against a brick wall. Luigi sucked a loose tooth. "For what?" he slurred.

Caine queried, "And why can't we tell our mates?"

"This is why." Sary held up another nugget, turning it in the gaslight. "Acquainted with killing, then?"

Luigi mumbled, "Self defense."

"Of course."

"Twice."

Caine spread three fingers. Sary stared.

"Just 'appens." He shrugged. "So 'oo do we murder-late, and 'ow much? That chap 'oo…?"

Sary smiled grimly and flipped him the nugget. "Not as it happens." She scrutinized their lumpy faces.

"You'll do. We leave. Now."

"Hold on, Duchess," Caine hedged. "Where to?"

"You'll be remunerated. Well!" Sary tugged, irritated. "We must make haste." Even to her that sounded imperious. The nugget was worth more than they would see in years, but Caine stood like a wooden Indian. Luigi looked from one to the other. "Re-mun… re-mooner…what?" he asked.

"And where's our Tommy?" from Caine.

"He's fine!" *Is he?* Sary, now she had made up her mind, was obsessed with leaving. It was more than time, yet Caine was stubborn as a farm mule. "All right!" Exasperated. "Big Bear."

"Tommy's in Big Bear?" Luigi wondered.

"No!" *Oh, why are they so pigheaded?*

Luigi wavered, uncertain, a frown bunching his low forehead below a floss of black oily curls.

Caine forced the nugget back. "Hate the ruddy mountains, I do. All them trees pressin' in. Couldn't get me proper wind, 'ole bleedin' time." He thumped Luigi. "C'mon, mate." And he steered Luigi off.

Sary ran ahead, walking backward. "I need you, though!" She watched them plow on past. "You get used to the air. Please, I *need* you!"

Luigi stopped and said simply, "So do Tommy, Sary."

She flashed a guilty look. "I hope not." *Damn!* She watched them back as police entered the alley, focusing on her, it seemed. The red dress flamed like firecrackers on Independence Day, but the fight was illicit. The mob melted. So did she, the red gown, so piercingly bright in the alley, extinguished around a corner.

****

Ratchet hung, limp and dripping, over the

fisherman's boat as the fisherman dug through Ratchet's pockets. Ratchet blinked, spewing water, coughing, and turning a bloody eye to the man with his hand in his pocket.

Chapter 36

Shaking, Julian plunged the needle into the withered crook of his elbow, turned away from Jude, a strapping toddler who played with his Noah's Ark on the floor.

Handi entered, casting a weary eye at the kit. Julian scowled over his shoulder. "You're in bed."

Handi motioned to the fitted velvet kit, faded tubing, and hypodermics. "Not fitting, Julian."

"Your keen perception startles me, Hannah. You are correct. Something ain't right." Julian stared outside. "I feel it. Here." He rubbed his knotted wrists and fingers.

Jude climbed into his lap, digging for candy.

Julian ruffled his curls. "Kept all this intact, Jude. Shuffled cards, till my hands—Look! Knots on cedar! All for you, Jude, my treasure." He cough-laughed, holding out lumpy hands, clenching his fist. "And it'll stay that way."

Handi hobbled out, shaking her stringy silver curls. Baby Jude was supposed to lighten their latter days, but the saloon suffered despite Julian's words. The doves were impudent. They had run out of a popular whiskey last month, sending old customers to the saloon down the way, a place little more than a plank on two barrels.

Jude held up a wooden camel to Julian. *"Cam-o!"* he chortled. Then he offered him a wooden zebra and a lion. *"Zeb-o! Wi-on!"* Jude lisped and tossed them in the air, commanding them to, "Fwyyyy, Zebo. Fwyyyy, Wion!"

Julian knelt, stiff, stuffing animals back in the ark. "And the camels make four?"

Jude held up four fingers, crying, "Four!"

"And the monkeys? How many, Jude, my boy? My *clever* boy?"

Jude held up six fingers. Julian hugged him, absently wandering to the window as if besieged. Behind him, Jude chugged a monkey in a wooden train up the ark's ramp.

Chapter 37

It was a fine hot day in the Redlands foothills of the Big Bear Mountains.

In the shade of the Redlands Saloon's porch, O'Malley slugged whiskey from a bottle. Orvis swung out with a sullen bar girl and claimed the bottle for himself, looking mid-gulp at the locomotive squealing up amid hissing bellows of steam. "Here she comes."

Cooley, tagging after Orvis, eyeballed the train too, sneering as only a horseman could as men offloaded the 1901 Mercedes. He scratched his acne and eyed the large cylinder tank riding high on the rear of the automobile before his gaze swung to the fancy woman just descending the steps.

Even to his untrained eye, the hat was, well, *gaudy.* But that red velvety dress, rouged makeup, and big curls bouncing like scarlet sausages? *Hunh! Don't need to knock on Cooley's door more'n oncet.*

He saw all this as Sary stepped from the Pullman car, checked her surroundings from under the sweeping hat, and froze at the sight of the three, biting her lip, recalling them from Delacorte's. *Well, that's why the big hat and butter crock of makeup.* She felt foolish in this getup, but her instincts were correct. *What damning luck, though. A bad omen. Shush, Sary. No bad thoughts. You are a machine, like this automobile.* Plastering a bright smile, Sary spun, overtly gay, to the waiting mechanic, resplendent in city spats and a boater hat, tapping him on the shoulder with her glove.

Cooley watched Sary openly flirting, chattering, trilling, flashing her fan at every man in pants. "Hie, there, Orvis, looka over there."

Orvis still messed with the saloon girl and stubbornly wouldn't look. Cooley snorted as men hoisted heavy cases and baggage to the car's open tonneau. One dropped a wooden crate, revealing a gleam of metal. Sary froze her smile like a statue and quickly stepped in front of it as they loaded the two long boxes into the rear of the vehicle.

"Why, I cannot thank you enough," the three heard the redhead say to the man, her crimson lips wide, showing her teeth. Emerging from a blast of steam, the hovering man tipped his boater and led her to the machine all gleaming red and warm chrome, blinding in the sun.

"Hunhh!" Cooley sniggered, watching the slicked-up dandy demonstrate the mercilessly bright auto to the fancy woman. *Like teachin' bears how to play poker.*

Cooley wanted attention. "Now that's some fancy candy box!"

Orvis squinted, taking in the sleek flashy auto and the female. "What, the fancy woman, or the automobile? Think she'll pass it around, though? Someone like you, looks like a dead porky-pine with all the quills pulled out?"

Cooley, touched his acne, pained, stiffly ignored him, but that didn't last. The dandy cranked some kinda handle, while the fancy lady looked on oohing and aahing. "Get a horse!" Cooley snorted. "Hie, Orvis, looka there. Horses don't need no crankin'!"

"That's right," Orvis grunted. "And ain't you forgetting Delacorte's horses? Let's git."

"I ain't the one hangin' around." Cooley looked to Orvis's girl, but Orvis and O'Malley were already headed to the boxcars, where two fine horses and a pony were being off-loaded. He tarried. The flashy lady bent, showing a fine rear, and gave the crank-thing a go, and they all watched. Cooley giggled, but after a couple of false starts, the handle-thing jerked from her hands and the whole abomination hopped like a dog with fleas. The female—*Funny, she turned her head just so, and danged if he didn't think he knowed her*—thanked the man, all smiley-like, hitched her dress—*nice ankles*—and climbed behind the automobile's big wooden wheel.

Sary smiled grimly. *That's right, men. I scarcely look like the muddy, half-demented female you starved out of Big Bear, do I?*

The Mercedes lurched forward. As the contraption jolted away, she raised eyebrows at wood blocks, ropes, and a lantern in the rear. "But what are these?"

The mechanic hustled after, enveloped in dust, yelling, "Emergencies! I meant to tell…"

But Sary had already lurched and juddered away and was waving back. "I think I have the feel of it, Mr.—? Dare not stop now. Thank you for everything," she called from within a cloud of dust.

Orvis scowled. "Damn fool female—where in thunder does she think she's goin'?"

Sary hung on as the mechanic ran along beside. She had gotten the general gist of it, ascertained she had enough fuel, and shut her ears to any admonitions, impatient to be on her way—to death and doom or retribution and triumph. The outcome rested partly on this bit of frippery. But she was a machine, recall? She ran on grit and intuition—no more thinking.

That dandied-up mechanic caused attention.

Oh, and you don't?

But it is all, as Tommy has lectured, distraction, Sary...Distraction.

O'Malley nodded. "Old Julian may a got hisself some competition there in the whore-mongerin' business, Orvis. Wouldn't mind a taste myself."

Orvis spat. "Ain't our concern. Or wallet." He eyeballed the car lurching past and away in a trail of dust devils. Across from them stood an establishment that was part undertaker, part lumber and junk yard, with a decrepit Gatling gun stenciled US ARMY listing on a cart in front of it.

He wiped his mouth. "Mind the store." He handed the horses' reins to O'Malley. "Gonna re-wet my whistle."

Cooley licked his lips, contemplating the back of red-haired Sary, waiting till Orvis entered the saloon. To O'Malley he announced, "Them beans. Goin' to the privy."

O'Malley said, "Hurry back. I had them beans, too."

****

Cooley had the bar girl slammed against the privy—and he giggled as, looking over her shoulder, he glimpsed a sailing red cartwheel, Sary's red hat soaring above the trees.

****

Sary had flicked a puzzled glance at the Gatling gun with its iron-rimmed wheels—one rim gone—long multiple barrels, and cartridge loops as she jittered by, threading the Mercedes inexpertly through Redlands' rough-laid streets, practicing the unfamiliar controls.

As establishments and houses dwindled, Sary checked behind her—*no one, hah!*—and cranked the enormous wheel hard, a sharp left, skirting the foothills, wandering vaguely up, until well past the settlement of Redlands, and then forcing the auto into another sharp right between clumps of bushes loaded with yellow blossoms to bump over tracks at the little-used train halt. The power was exhilarating as the Mercedes jolted onto a disused ox trail the old miners used for hauling ore and supplies, corkscrewing abruptly up. It was a useless smidgeon of information Seb had liked to show off with, and Lord knew where he'd picked it up. Still, if she hadn't known where to look, she might have missed the rocky turnoff, even if there was a glimpse of a washed-out trail beyond. The important part was that it led to Big Bear by the back way. Her mind winged back to the last time she'd traveled this trail, unknowingly leaving Big Bear in a haze of jolting pain as her valiant horse lurched downward.

The wheel took on a life of its own as the powerful auto bumped and swerved abruptly over rocks. The exotic machine passed its first test, powerfully grinding up the climb.

Sary scrutinized the four gears and, wincing, selected one, thrust the right one forward, and successfully powered up a sheer incline, more rocks than road, feeling exhilarated and proud.

She warily eyed the first hard bend. Her conveyance was already slanted down forty-five degrees. The track, rough but passable, barely, was a steep straight grade her car had skittered up with ease so far. Yet rock slides, downed trees, washouts—all were possible around that unseen bend.

Sary's heart dropped as she overshot the first hairpin, wildly overcompensating with the huge steering wheel. The auto tilted on two wheels, rocketing to the edge of the dropoff. Sary swung hard right to the mountain face, her foot and hand working with brakes and clutches, the effect of panic, and managed to jolt back on course without going over. Dismayed, Sary scanned the gouged-out, washed-out downward-canted defile ahead.

Mountains on her right, a sheer drop to her left, she judged the gap of good road left between the washed-out drop and the mountain. Was it wide enough for her car?

"In for a penny…"

Trodding on the fuel pedal, Sary jounced over ruts and spurted around the first small avalanche. *So much for being followed. Rotten luck, the three henchmen should be there. A person would need be demented…*

****

Over the bar girl's shoulder, after spying the scarlet hat sailing like an errant flame, Cooley glimpsed Sary and the red horseless carriage for a flash, between a maze of buildings.

"What's humorin' you?" the bar girl snapped. "Sure ain't me!"

"City folk!" Cooley snickered. "Old ox trail's washed to shit—plum petered out. Ain't been used since Moses was a baby. She shoulda took the—"

The bar girl shoved down her dress. "So be you! Petered out!" Cooley buttoned up, moseying to gawk up the cut after the automobile's dust cloud. Scratching his head, he strove to puzzle it out.

****

Cooley took time in the Redlands Saloon, dragging out the rich tale of the female taking the hard way, as he told it to Orvis, who did his best to ignore him.

"If mam raised idjit boys, I'd swear it were that Sary-woman," Cooley ended with a flourish. "What was dead?"

Orvis stared, frozen, into his glass, apparently looking for the secret of life.

O'Malley contributed, "Said she died, though. Got shot up."

"Tall tales…" Orvis said. He thumped Cooley, dousing his sore face with the dregs of his whiskey.

"Owww! Dang, Orvis!"

"Why didn't ya tell us before? This could mean money. Old Delacorte's got his long johns twisted around his balls a-lookin' for this Sary woman…wants her dead and gone."

****

At the foot of the old miner's trail, Orvis poked thin tire tracks. He looked from the town to the station and back up the ox trail, scowling at Cooley. "Dang! She's dead. And if that ain't her…"

****

The Mercedes corkscrewed past another washout. Sary's hand flashed for the brakes, and the car jittered, near stalling. She scanned the way ahead. The track, indistinguishable because of another washout, sloped at the same slant as the mountain. She let out the clutch. Oh, Lord, is it to be this way the entire trip up? The car jounced over the hump almost sideways… "Easy,

Mercedes." Sary bit her lip, not breathing, leaning as far to her right and the mountain face as she could. As the axle bumped and scraped over humped rocks, the car pivoted at forty-five degrees to the dropoff, wheels scratching for purchase.

Her conveyance slithered further slanchways, with a small spill of gravel, as Sary frantically yanked the handbrake, tromped on the extra footbrake, and peeked down the sheer drop. She was so close to the edge she could not spy any ground beneath the auto at all, only the sheer drop and a spindly pine to stay her fall into the nameless gorge dizzyingly far below.

Gently, she tapped the gas—the car had a habit of leaping ahead like a jackrabbit—and held her breath as she let out the clutch. The car ground past one more crumpling edge.

****

O'Malley continued haranguing Cooley. "...and we saddle up the wrong horse, Julian ain't gonna like it, and we're the south end of a north-goin' jackass."

Orvis glared at O'Malley. "No shit." He mounted up. "Box her in," he grunted. "Use the new horses. Delacorte ain't gonna like it, but use 'em anyways." He spun on Cooley. "And if we're milking a billy goat, you'll be drinkin' a bucketful of pain, Porky-pine!"

"Why don't we just *take* her!" Cooley whined.

"Already answered that. She's a fancy whore! Got herself a real pricey gewgaw there. Looks like Julian-business. I don't mess with it! He wouldn't take kindly. And, before you wrangle any more, that candy box probably got herself lost." He sneered. "Females ain't got the brain power God give a goose."

Cooley and O'Malley unhappily eyeballed Orvis

spurring off on the new, relatively short and easy way back up to Big Bear. O'Malley looked up the cut, swearing at Cooley.

****

Sary jounced steeper and higher, making good time, considering the first pitch was more rock than trail, scarcely feeling the jolts up her spine or thumps to her backside. She'd be in Big Bear City long before sunset. Suddenly her eyes widened.

She flipped the wheel, making frantic manipulations—*brakes—wheel—right—left. Stomp the clutch. Pull the hand brake. Stomp the foot brake*— amazed she recalled it all. Still the Mercedes stalled, skidding to a stop an eyelash short of a boulder squatting solid as a five-ton elephant, blocking her path.

She gripped the wheel and stood on the brake, pulling the handbrake, willing the car to *not* judder backward. The whole machine perversely veered as tires whirred, gritted, and ground for purchase, sliding back over the dropoff, and sputtered there with the back left wheel off the side.

Rope and chocks. Sary didn't think. She groped. Funny how terror could so readily tell one what to do. *Rope-tie the wheel straight. Reach down, gingerly chock the pedal, leave the car running. Next, climb over the windscreen. Carefully.* Sary stood on the seat and straddled the slippery glass, slipping down over what the mechanic had named the bonnet.

The auto canted further, with a horrible grinding. Sary slithered sideways, hanging onto the windscreen by her fingertips, with her feet dangling over the drop. The auto whined and—*dear Lord!*—slipped another foot before it shivered and settled, silent.

Sary gripped the fanciful hood ornament, feet still dangling in space, fighting gravity, then swung her body straight across over the hood, the bonnet.

Stretching, she toed the earth beyond the front bumper, dropped off, jammed a rock behind the right front wheel, and cranked the starter back to life.

As the motor juddered, Sary crawled up the hood and back over the windscreen. She slithered out the driver's side and, teetering with her feet wedged sideways over the fall, she reached in, un-chocking the pedal.

Press hard on the fuel. Move the clutch. The auto lurched and rolled back. Then three tires gripped and ground, spitting rock, dragging her up-slope while afraid it would take off and smash somewhere ahead…or below. *Go, go,* Sary pleaded. *Almost there…* The undercarriage caught on something, and the Mercedes rocked to a halt but, thank the Lord, still jittered away.

Sary gritted her teeth. She hung outside, shoved the doorframe with all she had, and rammed the fuel pedal with her hands. "Move, damn you!" Her arms quivered and her feet scrabbled for purchase off the edge as she sweated and strained. Why had she supposed this blamed automobile was a good idea? She hated herself at that moment.

The auto strained, too, making a horrendous roar, lurching with a pop of gravel back onto the trail—only just—and yanking Sary with it. Pulling herself through the frame, she regained the seat and jammed the gears, sort of, into place, backed way back, jerked the wheel straight, closed her eyes as the car rushed at the immovable mountain of a boulder, twice her height, and course-adjusted at the last second. The car bounced between the boulder and the mountain. With her rear fender scraping rock, she jounced through to the far side and an open track with a bend just ahead. Lord knew what was beyond that one.

****

Sary halted. She'd been on the trail an hour. It was still early, but she felt uneasy. The trail rippled behind her, and with it, a throaty growl—she ducked as rocks thundered past her in a battering, pinging avalanche that ended almost as soon as it started. The auto's vibration must have set something off.

Sary froze. In the silence, *somewhere* unseen hoof beats clattered against rock. A bobcat sprinted across the gap. As Sary followed its flight, Cooley and O'Malley cantered around the hairpin turn below her, on horses made skittish by the fall.

The boulder was still there, its top littered with debris. The two eyed the rubble and headed their mounts to the same gap she had passed through.

Sary stomped the accelerator, mindlessly crashing through gear exchanges. The doughty Mercedes jittered past another bend and out of sight as the riders flashed looks and eased their mounts. *"Whoa, whoaaaaaa, easy, boy."*

The auto couldn't outrace horses on a rough twisting trail. Sary set the handbrakes. She bashed a gun case with the brass starter handle, hearing the hoof beats more sharply now, and spilled rifles to the ground, scattering a few. She grabbed two, and a box of ammo, and in long skirts scaled a watershed up the side, yanking the velvet skirt from spiky shrubs, before Cooley and O'Malley came into view. She scrambled over a slab overhanging like a table and from there scanned the two right below her as they reined up short.

They gazed at the shaking contraption, all red and gleaming, with its big glass headlamps like bug eyes.

She smiled grimly as the two edged toward the Mercedes. It was sputtering like a kettle on the boil, as if it might explode.

O'Malley peered in, then chortled. "Well, sweet daughter a joy. Looka what Candy Box left behind!"

Sary had Cooley in her sights as he gripped the two new rifles, forgetting all about her.

"Hooo-ey! Look what else Candy Box brung us, O'Malley!" Cooley waved the rifles, his cracked young voice clear in the mountain air. She swung her sight.

O'Malley was in the driver's seat now. Messing with controls. *Her* controls. The car lurched. O'Malley jerked his hands from the steering wheel. She grinned. *Purely hate you to go flying off the mountain now, mister whoever you are. O'Malley?* Then she frowned. *It could do just that. Then where'd I be? Better not tempt God.* She bit her lip until O'Malley eased out, backing up as if her automobile was the Devil's chariot, running on fumes of hellfire. Her car sputtered to a stop.

"Well, it ain't Christmas." O'Malley turned quarrelsome. "Where is Candy Box, anyways?"

Sary scowled as Cooley pranced and mimicked hiking skirts.

O'Malley snorted, firing up the mountain. "Hey, sugarplum! Cooley an me just wanna taste!" Rocks splintered. Twigs snapped all around her. She cringed. *Too much like before.* Spying Cooley scrambling rock to rock, nearing her hiding place, Sary fired a warning and swung back to O'Malley. *He jumps like a schoolgirl.*

Cooley fell on his rump in his haste to retreat.

In her deepest voice Sary ordered, "Put 'em down."

O'Malley ducked behind his horse, then swaggered out. "Candy Box is right. Come on out, li'l darlin'!" Coldly, she watched him motion Cooley up one side. He took the other side.

"Yeah, come on out here." Cooley smirked, cocking a pistol. "Won't hurt ya none." A brush of Cooley's strawlike hair stuck up past the rock he crouched behind. The yellow tuft moved.

"That's right. You won't." Sary answered in her own high clear voice and took aim, blasting away. Cooley's hair ruffled, and below him, a hole appeared high in the Mercedes' cylindrical tank.

"Hie, there! Y'almost hit me!" Cooley whined. Boots scrabbled shale as Cooley bulled back up the mountain, closer.

"On the ground!" Sary yelled, triggering off another warning.

Cooley yelped. "Git *you* on the ground, little girlie." He contemplated O'Malley, undecided. O'Malley hit dirt as he edged beneath her overhanging slab.

"As I reco-member," O'Malley hissed, "she always was free with ammunition, if I surmise rightly who this bitch is."

Cooley flattened halfway to the overhang. "Lettin' a female get away with this horse shit?" The two eyed each other and rushed Sary, red-faced and furious, bumping into each other. One slid—she didn't know which one but heard boot heels digging in. There was silence, then furious whispering. She could sense as well as hear them creeping up, gaining ground, dropping behind a shrub and then a boulder. There was a roll of pebble, a slip of shale, and a crackle of dried prickle bush. Sary sighted a bead on spurs glinting in hot noonday sun.

Cooley's boot poking past scrub made a tempting target, and her fingers, still a bit stiff, tightened on the trigger. The blast rocked the mountain air. Spurs spun like a whirligig. Cooley jerked his boot to safety.

"Ow! Told you! Quit firin'!" He whispered to O'Malley, "What's wrong with this female?"

O'Malley grunted. "What's wrong with most women? Whatever, we can fix this un, permanent." He sat back, uncapping a canteen. "Let her stew."

Cooley rolled a smoke, and Sary smelled the scent of harsh tobacco.

****

Sun slanted through trees. It was around three, Sary judged. Sweat dripped off her nose. She heard one of the men snoring for a while. The velvet she wore was hot, and sticking, so she shrugged off the top, feeling vulnerable in a chemise. An errant wrap of chill wound her shoulders now and then. A Mexican standoff. What was a lark for the two ruffians was now serious. They would never let her off the mountain. Their pride was hurt. They would have their fun and then kill her, bash her head in with a rock, or worse. Sary licked dry lips, eyeing her canteen in the Mercedes. Eyed the sun. At night, anything could happen, whatever their slow wits could dream up. So far, they hadn't thought of damaging the automobile. They didn't understand it, possibly feared it. That wouldn't last. She studied it with longing as it glittered like a red jewel below. Still, smashing the steering mechanism would ruin her. The machine had seemed so brilliant back in San Francisco. She'd been fascinated by the power and magic the car represented. Besides, the money, as Mama would've scolded, "scorched a hole in her apron pocket." And—admit it—she wished, after Tommy had shown her how, to make a grand entrance, if that was the most useful strategy. She couldn't now, what with the third man pounding away for Big Bear and Julian Delacorte. *Delacorte will send killers down the trail, and I'll be trapped on both ends.*

She slid off the overhang. The slab teetered the tiniest bit and gently settled. A small trickle of rock skittered down. Sary slipped down the side, hoping she was hidden from the two. In the shade, Sary scrutinized the slab's underpinnings. Only a third of the huge rock seemed to be embedded.

She flattened, crawled under the slab, and looked up at the expanse of lip. Where it entered the mountain, talus, small rocks, one jagged stone, and a decayed cedar root wedged it in place. It vastly overhung. Still, too much counterweighted the slab for her to simply shove it over.

Frustrated, she eyed the sun's passage.

Where were they? She heard occasional gripes and grumbling. She thought they were still beneath her, somewhere, probably behind that clump of blasted cedar and felled trunk to her left.

Back above the overhang, Sary raked and jabbed the rifle barrel where the slab was sunk in rubble.

"Whatcha up to, Candy Box?" One of them, the older, she thought, yelled up.

Let them wonder. Viciously Sary booted gravel on either side, rewarded with a whispered conference. Was it still to the left or right under her?

They separated, and she spotted O'Malley. Sary waited until he crept past, his green shirt and red bandanna exposed against ocher and dun strata. Sary loaded and fired, aiming high. O'Malley ducked. She heard an oath and spotted him limping for cover far beneath the overhang, but she couldn't get a shot. Sary crawled back up, grunted, braced against the mountain with knees locked, planted her boots, and shoved with all she had.

****

Dirt trickled onto Cooley's head, furiously jacking a round. His acne flared hot. "Sick a this horse shit," she heard him mutter.

He jumped out, firing straight up. The shot twanged, echoing off her rock. He fired two more angry bursts.

O'Malley grumbled, spitting a brown splotch. Coughing dust, Cooley blasted away, hitting more rubble. Pellets zinged back at the two in the lazy mountain air. More dirt trickled in a small slide past them. Then O'Malley fired as he ducked, and the bullet split the cedar root beneath the slab.

The enormous boulder grated an inch. Rock pulverized into grit. She felt it tremble.

From below her came the clear clicking of O'Malley cocking the new rifle, and she saw Cooley pick at his acne and squint at the lowering sun. Neither saw the slab shift as Sary wrathfully booted it. They were arguing in hoarse whispers while Sary jammed cartridges, dropping some that gave a message of shaky nerves past the two whose guns were cocked and ready. Smirking, they watched the shells bounce and wink red past them in the sun. 'Til now they hadn't been sure where she was.

Reload! By the sound of the boot scuffs, the two were rushing up, careless. Sary took a slow breath and rammed shells in true as the two men's heads came into view above the rock—her rock. She fired. They scrambled for cover under the overhang. *Now or never.* She booted the huge slab in frantic tattoos, and the stone moved, gritting rock against rock. The root fell away with a slither of shale, and Sary felt her support shudder and tip. Almost Biblical, this hope, as gravel worked like ball bearings and the slab loosened in its socket.

Yes! It shifted down. Sary hitched back. *Where are they?*

The slab settled with a ground-shaking *whump,* amidst billows of choking dust. She heard their coughing, their shouted curses, and watched the sky. She must steal down somehow. Oh, this was going all wrong. For the first time she allowed the thought to creep in—she should have stayed. She should have... *Oh, do shut up, Sary!* She pulled at the sticky velvet and wished she could just toss it all off and stay cool in cotton underpinnings, but that would be small protection against sharp rocks and scrub.

Sary slithered on the tilted rock and spied the tops of their heads. Any second they would rush her. She had five shells left. Sary crawled to the side while they scrutinized the base. The gigantic stone was definitely canted. On her top side, exposed dirt showed. A rim of weed, where the base had been, was now a six-inch gap.

Not caring where they were—if they caught her they would kill her, or take her to Julian—Sary, hot and parched, gouged loose shale on both sides of the gap, using the rifle barrel, and shoved for what must be the last time, using up a saved reservoir of strength, her back to the mountain, her boot heels rammed against the overhanging rock. It moved a bit more. Yes, a definite downward tilt now. Then she climbed atop it to gently bounce up and down. The huge, delicately balanced stone teetered and grated with her weight. A lizard zigzagged off, tail cocked.

The massive stone tipped farther.

Over tipped. Teetered. Wobbled.

She fell off backwards.

Shale dust showered the two men. "Hie!" Cooley spat, coughing.

"Damn!" O'Malley shouted. "We ain't leavin', Candy Box. That what you thinkin'? No one'll find your scrawny-ass bones when we get through with ya. You can throw all the dirt at us ya want."

Their shots blasted to smithereens the one stone still securing the base. She felt the huge slab slide farther, and she desperately rammed the rifle barrel into the crack at the same time. The barrel bent, screeching against rock. *Glory be.* The massive boulder shuddered and scraped off its pivot as she thrust, gouged, and fell back, sweating and dust-covered in her red velvet. From below came shouts of outrage and fright, the sound of boots scrabbling. *Jump, you idiots,* she had time to think, as the boulder groaned and at last began its ponderous course down the mountain, at first sluggish, then thunderously loud as it bounced and dragged her in its wake.

O'Malley, lost in dust and rock fall, bellowed until his curses were cut short with a sickening *thunk*. Sary hung on as the boulder bounded across the trail behind her automobile and on down Big Bear Mountain, smashing small trees as it went. She was a part of the slide herself.

****

Haze settled. Sary woke with her face in shadow. A man in a hat bent over her, upside down. He held a huge stone.

Sary jerked, head butting a furious Cooley. Cooley dropped the stone and staggered back as Sary rolled away.

"Women ain't s'posed to do that! What kinda unnatural…" Wincing, Cooley looked at the splotch that was O'Malley, below. Enraged, he gritted his teeth and raised the rock again.

"You mean this kind?" Sary kicked a sharp-toed boot at his chin. Cooley pinwheeled back, still holding the rock but losing his balance, his body no longer over his seat. Falling heavily, Cooley backslid, head down, careening off rocks and saplings end over teakettle, snatching futilely at weeds and thudding in a heap next to O'Malley's body, with Sary not far behind.

Cooley picked himself up and, after a glance at his erstwhile companion—O'Malley looked like dog's dinner—gagged and limped to his horse, not sparing a glance at Sary. She threw the bent rifle after him as he galloped up the trail to Big Bear.

"Damnation!" Gathering the rest of her belongings, she dashed past O'Malley, who had been flattened like a bloody inkblot, and paused to look back. *Too easy,*

Tommy! No time!

Sary raced to the automobile. *It's darkening.* Hoping the headlamps worked as promised, she fumbled for the switch, flicked levers, and two cones of blinding, startling light illuminated trees ahead in stark color, more green than real. She switched them off and let out the handbrake, and the Mercedes spurted ahead as if eager for Big Bear too. At each lurch up the trail, the huge cylinder tank riding the rear sloshed out a trickle of fuel.

Chapter 38

The Mercedes' round headlights arced across her old camp, a place more desolate, more embarrassing than ever. The iron kettle was gone. The fire pit was scattered. The hut—No, Seb hadn't built a hut, they'd sat under a tarp, and their coffee was cold bitter acorn, more than not.

No time. Eyes danced away from the disturbed gravesites. *Enough! Deal with the dead later.*

Sary knelt on dusty torn velvet, feverishly clawed oilcloth bundles, palm-weighed ammunition, and checked the odd assortment of weapons for rust. Mountain air was dry. They looked the same as when she'd buried them, another lifetime ago. Her fingers brushed rotted, spongy wicker. They stopped.

She clapped her ears, hearing Tommy. "I know! I ken, Tommy. I have enough for the siege of Carthage already. We've—*I've*—lost the surprise. Delacorte knows!"

Sary unearthed the wicker, gingerly brushing dirt from caked green glass. Her hands shook as she lifted it out. She could scarce breathe.

"Do shut up, Tommy!" She studied the pear-shaped bottle. Liquid moved sluggishly within. "But it can't hurt—much. If I'm careful." Gently she laid the pear-shaped bottle aside. "It's not as if we're spoiled for choice," she told Tommy's carping phantom. "Quit nagging!"

****

Sary yanked off the wig. Nearly bald, and nicked where Ratchet had hacked her hair, she stepped from the red velvet, rubbed dirt on her face, and put on men's clothes from the car's open tonneau. Ripping velvet strips, she rebound the green bottle and tucked it into her shirt.

"No, not good," she decided and cradled the bottle in the rear of the car. Then, crouched by the tires, she muttered and drew with a stick Big Bear's main streets, soon crisscrossed with lines. Savagely she scratched them out and hunkered back.

"Remember when I forgot my lines, Tommy? And I made them up? But I knew the play, and the end of it. Well, it's all made up from here on in, Tommy. So hold onto your hat."

More fuel jolted out as the car sputtered under the moon, down from the highest point to Big Bear's high-desert valley. Behind her, fresh rock covered Seb's grave.

Chapter 39

Oblivious of all, Julian tucked little Jude into his son's old oppressively masculine bedroom, while down in the saloon Orvis downed a glass, poured again from a half-empty bottle, and flicked glances at Julian's table, wondering where the hell the man was. He slugged a final shot of courage.

****

Orvis fidgeted outside Jules's bedroom, now Jude's, souring his mouth at the unexpected sound of Delacorte croaking out a lullaby.

"Hush, little baby, don't say a word, Grampa's gonna buy you a mocking bird, and if that mockin' bird don't sing, Grampa's gonna buy you a..." Julian crooned raspily.

Orvis tiptoed off.

Julian halted and, without looking, barked, "Herd a buffalo out there? Quitcher stompin'!"

Orvis ducked in. "Oh. Hey. Mister Delacorte."

Julian gave him a look.

"Wanna hear something humorous-like?"

Julian, finger to lips, tiptoed out. "Well! Got my horses? 'Bout time."

Orvis shuffled. "Uh, yup, better'n 'at. This female"—he chuckled—"Sneakin' up the old miner's trail, Cooley and me—"

Footsteps pounded, and Cooley himself crashed up,

winded.

Julian winced at his acned face. "Shush!"

Orvis scowled at Cooley and turned back to Delacorte.

"But here's the humorous part, like—"

"This better be good!" Julian snarled, just before Cooley butted in.

"Had one of them auto-mo-biles, Mister Delacorte, loaded with fire power. Ten, twenty gunsels, shootin' from the hills—come up the back way, either lost or sneakin' in, like."

Orvis cast a sour look at Cooley, then checked behind him. "Where's O'Malley?"

"Lord! Ain't human what she done to that man! And lookit!" Cooley held his nose.

Julian grabbed it. "Get on with it!"

Cooley blubbered. "Ow!"

Jude awoke, snuffling, and Julian picked him up. "Shhhhh! Be my little man. No one dare harm a pinkie…" Scowling at the two, he kissed Jude's fingers and jerked his head.

****

In Julian's office, Julian gazed hungrily at the velvet case and hypodermic. He tapped his fingers. "I'm waiting."

Orvis jabbed Cooley. "Quit caterwaulin'. I'll tell!" To Julian. "Yes, sir. Cooley's right there. It were nine, ten shooters. At least."

Cooley nodded.

"The best, and been around. Looked like someone dropped 'im down a mine shaft," Orvis elaborated.

Cooley said, "Six jumped me. I shot—I shot *three* of 'em. She run off. The rest—"

"Hold on! She? *She!* You keep sayin' she."

"What I'm—we—been sayin', Mister Delacorte," Orvis said, "is she looked like that dead woman. That Sary woman from the mine what got shot up and hung? I mean, she's dead, ain't she? Come again, s'posed she mighta been one a your new gals." He glanced over at the skull with the black hair still attached, nudging Cooley.

Julian wheezed, "Swinford. And she's hired unknowns? Well, let her come," he barked. Then strangeness passed over his raddled face. Orvis looked at Cooley as Julian's eyes brightened with a faraway look. Sary. Sary had come back, and he'd not heard a scrap from Ratchet.

The men shuffled. "Just thought to tell, case you wanted…" Orvis faded off. Julian stared at unseen demons and knotted his hands, changing once again. "At her old camp. She'd like me to ride up there. Oh, yes!" He nodded vigorous to Cooley and Orvis. "Just walk right in." He fingered the skull. "Eater of the dead. Revenge is her executioner," Julian gritted. "We'll be ready. She won't take *my* boy."

Orvis ventured uneasily, "How—how you want to end this then, Mister Delacorte?"

Julian strode out. "Sieved and leaking."

Orvis and Cooley hastened after. "Mister Delacorte. Might not be that many. Just seemed like a passel of 'em, what with…with all the guns, and all." Orvis nudged Cooley. "Didn't it, Cooley?"

"Don't matter," Julian shouted. "You done good. Good men!" He clapped their backs, bellowing, "Handi!" And Pearl came running. Julian bawled, "Where's Handi!"

Pearl flinched. "Poorly, Julian."

He thrust Jude at her, muttering, "Useless cow!" and rummaged a revolver from a drawer. "He don't go two toes from you!" Tossing the weapon at her, he pointed a long arthritic finger. "Anything happens to that sweet boy, use it on yourself. Cooley! You!" He thrust Cooley to the window and strode to the hall with borrowed vigor. "Orvis!"

Orvis ran after him.

Cooley hooked a chair, smirking at Pearl.

****

Ratchet's suit was shrunk, scratchy, and odiferous from his dip in the San Francisco Bay, and it was still slightly damp, adding to his irritability as he prodded what was left of O'Malley and swatted flies. Touching knife to nose, he scowled.

"I'll keep the wound green, Delacorte." Ratchet lashed his horse up the trail.

****

In the saloon, Julian thumped the piano. "Play!" he bellowed.

The piano player pounded out a jolly syncopated tune. Julian slapped a poker table. "Sing! Want ta hear cacophony!" He pointed and jabbed at cynical gamblers, hardscrabble ranchers, weathered panners, trappers, and the down and out, alike. "You and you! Out! Come round and back in—keep doing that. Show some life. Fucking icehouse morgue in here! Where's the poxied girls?"

More soiled doves, hooking and buttoning, rushed down, followed by sickly Handi.

Chapter 40

The sputtering Mercedes coasted, juiceless and silent, onto a bluff overlooking Big Bear as the last of Sary's fuel jolted out.

She left the vehicle back at the tree line and went to crouch at the edge. Dropping, Sary scanned the main street lined with saloons, mercantiles, ironmongers, and a new bank. The buildings dwindled into houses, a blacksmith, and lastly, the stable at the far end, with the water tower facing her at the near end.

Gay piano music tinkled up, hanging in the air like fairy music. The bouncy ragtime and the lit-up cluster of so-called civilization seemed cozy and welcoming, but Sary knew all too well the mockery of *that* scene. She promised herself, "I won't let my boy turn into a keeper for a polluted old man in a rotting town—a cheat, drunk, card shark, consorting with whores, or worse. Never to know anything but Big Bear!" *Where are you, Jude? How are you? Are you alive?*

She panned with her binoculars.

Men, casually holding rifles or resting twitchy hands on gun belts, melting from doorways or in and out of porches, around buildings, most especially Delacorte's, snapped into focus. She spotted Orvis among them. Even from her high vantage point he appeared antsy, as if something brewed. Sary eyed him as he shrank into the host of milling men and disappeared. Whatever the storm, he wanted no part of it. Maybe one less to worry over.

"A church social down there, Tommy." She resented the way they joked and slapped, their guffaws raking the night. Not many were privy to the jokes, but it made for a change, she surmised.

"There are so many…"

Her resolve weakened like cloth too many times darned and fretted over. Then, arrested by a motion, Sary swung the glasses.

A sign flapped loose—*Handi's*. She'd never let a thing like that go. Sary briefly considered what, or even if, that meant anything.

Panned to the left. One of Delacorte's or Handi's soiled doves was silhouetted in a window above the saloon—probably a bedroom. Sary swung the binoculars over the uneven roof and back again, her mouth open. Removing the eyepieces, Sary squinted at a huge unfinished Victorian house crouching like a monstrous cat over a mouse. It was a buffoon of a house, even unfinished as it was, a crazy quilt of half-floors, with staircases climbing, it seemed, for no destination in particular but wide-open sky. A half-finished turret lent the structure a lopsided look, like a hat perched on the side of a clown head, and odd ells, portcullises, and bays bulging like tumors seemed afterthoughts, as if someone sketched plans daily to a cobbled blueprint. She dipped the eyepieces to a dark maw of cellar dimly guessed at below. A chill crept up her back. *Never mind that!* Sary laid the binoculars aside, chewing her lip. Tommy once again intruded.

"Sary. There's always a curtain between me and the audience. This is real. Isn't it?"

"Act like you're not afraid, Tommy. Act like you've never acted before," she answered. Suddenly she sucked in a breath and drew back—a shadowy man crawled around the water tower, staring stonily right at her, or so it seemed.

She edged to the Mercedes, feeling eyes on her back, unloaded rifles, and crept to the bluff in relays, careful not to let them clink. The man was gone. No, still there, on the other side of a rickety catwalk, looking the other way. Sinking in scrub, Sary turned to figures moving across lit windows below as she loaded rifles, placing them at intervals along the bluff edge and sweating her next move.

****

In Jules's old bedroom, Cooley winked at Pearl, suggestively waggling his gun.

Pearl cuddled Jude, ignoring the man at first.

Julian watched the street. *Damnable party out there!* He burst out, gasping, onto the porch with the patched posts, swatting doves, shoving men to four corners, bawling, "Keep watch! Line up! Don't piss around like gawping halfwits!"

"But Delacorte, what the Sam Hill we lookin' for?" a panner groused. He was obviously bemoaning his one night in town, when he couldn't get even a sniff of a poxied gal, leave alone a hard drink.

"Her! Hell's bells! You blind, deaf *and* dumb? *Her!"* Julian registered the shrugs and side glances, concern evaporating the moment he turned, wild-eyed, to other anxieties. Most joined in the mugging chorus, but an unknown predator grown huge in small imaginations still worried a few. Julian seeming to suppose the danger so self-evident checked them.

Besides, all this was a change from mountain gossip racing like a forest fire, from one end of town to the other, so fast that fifteen minutes after you et morning oatmeal the whole town knowed if you put sorghum or honey on it.

However, Cooley and a few young bucks looked for more. A half-Indian trapper with a road map of authority in his face, brown and weathered from the hills, staked his rifle and wouldn't let Julian pass.

"Delacorte. How we know who to kill?"

Julian stared at him, wild. "Oh, you'll know by her traitorous face." He nodded vigorously.

The trapper spat. "All this about some female?"

Julian shoved him aside. "Don't let nobody through!" He subsided choking. "You won't know what shape she takes!"

A shade of superstitious memory passed over the trapper, and he gripped his gun and his knife scabbard tightly.

****

Julian fell into his office before they could see the weakness. He smoothed Jules's skull against his chest, kissing the ivory-slick bony prominence, tucking it back into its satin-lined box.

Yanking drawers and cupboards, spilling weapons, he took up a relic—a long-barreled, bulky, army revolver from the French and Indian wars—and loaded bullets big as his thumb. His hands wouldn't work. He dropped the gun. Bullets scattered. Shakily, Julian shot up and reloaded.

****

The unseen piano player still thumped tunes as Sary finished with the rifles along the bluff edge. She had methodically loaded each one. Once again, she heard Tommy.

"How do we play it, Sary? Comedy? Or 'The Scottish Play'?"

"Oh, definitely comedy, Tommy," she answered his wraith and hunkered down to wait—and plan. All dark except the saloon. Quieter, too. Still, Sary sensed townsfolk peering like ferrets from dens, eyes glowing with the moon in them, all with preternatural sight, seeking her out.

The assembly—gaunt-faced bar bums to weathered panners, ranchers, drunks, and corpse-white gamblers—seemed more focused, ringing the saloon in a ragged wall facing out or on watch atop the saloon, with silhouettes of bristling rifles. Pearl the dove leaned out the window, this time with Cooley.

"I grasp it, Tommy. I can't get them all."

One man atop the saloon turned. She dropped the rifle. It was the fourteen-year-old.

"Let me think!" She fiercely addressed tufts of weed.

"You should'na bonked me on the head. I should be there," Tommy nagged. Sary flattened her belly to the ground.

"Don't need anyone! And, I didn't mean to hit you, Tommy!"

A cigarette glow rounded the tower. As the watcher sucked in, she saw a dissipated face, young but brutal.

Sary slugged from the canteen, cudgeling her brain, gulped a fistful of raisins and stuffed more into her shirt pocket, and watched the water tower—all clear. She crawled back to the Mercedes and returned clutching the green bottle.

"That's not in the play!" Tommy spoke in her head, alarmed. *"And just what mayhem do you plan with that mischief? You're stalling, Sary!"*

It was a delaying tactic. What was she to do with gelignite? Blow up the town? In that short span, more men milled with purpose. Their prey was her, and they were eager for the first showing. Men on roofs, doorways, lining the porch, stalking three abreast, some raking the bluff with their ferret eyes.

"Well, what you waiting for? Gabriel's trumpet?" Tommy again. She panned a last time. Pearl. Only now she held something. Sary stopped breathing.

A small boy—*Jude,* by the child's curls and round cheeks. He was no longer the infant kept in her memory-vault these strange months, and she gazed, mesmerized, as the toddler clapped chubby hands. His excited crow cut though the rinky-tink piano, the clip-clop of horses, and the stamping boots.

Pearl, breasts spilling from her chemise, giggled, pointing at a mob enlarged by ordinary folk, wives and shop owners, as fast as news reached their quiet kitchens. Gently Sary laid the bottle on the ground, desperately thinking.

"Tommy? Remember? Before the play? How Luigi did that magic act? It was all the art of misdirection or something. Illusion, you said."

"Bravo!" Tommy's irritating wraith applauded. *"And when does this sparkling bit of legerdemain begin?"*

Tightening the weighty gunbelt low about hips made thinner of late, Sary shouldered a rifle and shoved the Derringer into her boot. "Watch me."

Tenderly she tucked the green bottle into her shirt

and crouched at the edge of the bluff. Slipping over, she hung on tough weeds, crab-crawling down to the stable set a little apart from the last straggle of buildings, until she was above the smithy. Sliding the last few feet where the bluff sloped, the stable three yards to her left, she ducked into the shadowed lee of rough wood, redolent of hay, horses, and manure.

****

Nesting the pear-shaped bottle in weeds, Sary peeked through the back way, squinting in the lantern glow that turned littered straw and hay bales to dull gold not unlike her swath of ore.

An omen, if she trusted such things.

A water-pumper wagon squatted just inside double doors standing open to the main street.

Sary cringed at a dry whine of hinges as she entered. She paced past the same stalls as before, when she had stolen her own horse. The stable was alive now with whickering and the thud of many hooves. She halted mid step. Standing in the wide doorway was the boy who breathed through his mouth, who had worn a startled blue-eyed expression the last time she saw him. Lured to the action, the stable hand danced out, feet pattering away. He wouldn't be back.

Sary raced stall to stall, shooing horses out, no doubt alerting the town. Soon it wouldn't matter. She flung the lamp, firing the hay. After decades of arid air, the brittle-dry stable caught and bloomed with a shocking roar. Sary leaped back, suddenly aware through the crackle that it was Grace, among others outside, yelling, "Ya sleepin' with your long johns undone? We're on fire here!" Sary glimpsed her dashing from the dry-goods store, apron flapping, waving her arms as she bee-lined for the saloon.

Sary raced for the rear of the stable—and rammed right into Ratchet, who looked like the Devil come alive, his gaunt features animated by the flames. He resembled a ghost with an aura of flickering light surrounding him. Supernatural, straight from Hell. *But he drowned. He drowned!* Sary realized on one level that he must have been in one of the stalls. Without thought, Sary stifled a scream and flung the last of the kerosene. With the stench of burning tweed in her nose, Sary grabbed the green bottle of gelignite and ran for her life. Behind her, Ratchet slapped his pant legs and sprinted after her on his long legs, murder in the red glint of his eyes.

****

The saloon still rocked, revel-makers on the Titanic, soon to go down. Sary darted past shop owners dashing from homes and stores and making for the blazing stable, avoiding the panicked horses. They backed, shielding faces with bent elbows as tongues of fire licked from the door.

The foolhardy dragged the pumper, blazing now too, swatting the burning hose, yanking it, stumbling, grunting and cursing, flags of fire snapping behind it, to the water tower. With the ease at which they rolled it, rattling and bumping, Sary surmised the pumper's reservoir was empty. She was stunned by the implication. Why would they store the pumper in the stable and not below the water tower, she wondered, as a sail of fire whipped and crackled over the blacksmith's bark roof. The wind had risen.

"What have we done?" Sary breathed.

"We?" Tommy carped.

"Bigger than I thought, Tommy. They won't be able to stop it."

"Then you'd best make haste, Sary Swinford…"

The wind picked up, helped by a vortex of heat, blowing perversely west into the town.

Jude!

Firemen struggled back with the filled reservoir, manning the pumper. A thin arterial spout ineffectively sprayed, turning to steam and smoke and obscuring the street as Sary wove though people who milled, agog, changing focus in ragged waves but aiming generally for the stable, getting in the way of the wagon and tattered bucket brigade.

"But it was just a diversion!"

"You're on, Sary. Do you know your lines? Your part?" Tommy demanded.

"No! I told you, it's all ad lib! Now don't bother me!"

"It's all for nothing, if you don't go on now! Your audience awaits."

Sary wended, ducking and darting, through sparking coals. She attracted a little abstract startled recognition when she didn't keep her head tucked or ran into a townsperson vaguely recalled, but they were soon diverted by the fire, as pleasure takers wandered from the saloon to ogle or help fill the clumsy brigade. It was a circus atmosphere. Sary skimmed through a thinning in the mob as more drifted to the stable end, while some ran back home or to their store. Someone thrust a dishpan sloshing with water at her. She passed it along, getting another puzzled look, and melted away. Sary looked ahead. The windy conflagration was well away from the saloon and Jude—so far. At the gap in the buildings, between the new bank and Doheney's, it would die out.

****

Sary darted under the tower, craning to study the fat wooden underbelly, briefly considering the man on top and the volunteer filling buckets from a loose hose hanging outside. In the shadow of the bulge's underside, she tucked the bottle by a strut—it just *seemed* right—and stepped aside. Shotgun to her shoulder, she blasted the underbelly with buckshot, over and under. *There, that's done.* One more diversion.

Pellets penetrated a few holes in the thick damp wood, the sound lost in the melee, which included a few cowboys letting loose, shooting at the moon. Her shot must be weak from being underground. Far better the newer rifles with their one shot. Still, it would take longer for the water to deplete, and by that time, the stable—okay, she amended, the stable and the blacksmith's—fire would be doused. Not that she wished the town's burning, at least not until Jude was safe. Then it could stoke Hell's fire for all she cared.

A diversion. Only!

Sary dashed out into a town turning red, as water needled down from the tower's underside, and was immediately besieged by a gaggle of doves dancing from the saloon, flowing past, giggling and oblivious. They didn't stop.

Neither did she, hearing them shriek as they cavorted under the spray, screeching at the coldness of it.

Sary rammed into a hefty woman waddling like a duck trailing chicks. The woman squawked. A cinder fell on her hair. Shrieking, she patted it out and yanked her brood along, spinning Sary into a pack of boys.

Ratchet's tall figure thrust people aside. Until now, so focused on her plan, Sary had been blind to the chaos, babble, shouts, and imprecations. The town's atmosphere was part holiday, part a fop to boredom, and she had been buffeted by the mass whose attentions were now snared by fresh explosions—the dry goods store caught fire, and Sary was whipped out on the other side of the mob by this new surge, in full view of those guarding the saloon porch.

She judged this last barrier, only two feet away, from below her cap. Brutal men. Gap-toothed, leathered from mountain winters and scorching summers, they ringed the porch, gripping weapons, intent as coyotes, undistracted by anarchy as their narrowed eyes, dead beneath their hat brims, hungrily roved the streets and the bluff.

They were the worst.

Ratchet's friends. Julian's henchmen, certainly. And where was Ratchet? Hands jerked and flexed on gun butts. These were the ones thirsting for death, who wouldn't quit until she was riddled with shot or dragged through the streets and hung. She little resembled how she once was, though. Perhaps that alone made her invisible. A grizzled miner raked her face with his gaze, veering back and nailing her.

Sary lowered her head and nodded jerkily. The miner was bumped from behind and turned in anger to confront whoever had jostled him, away from Sary.

Almost there. Only steps now to the weedy gap between Handi's derelict hotel and Delacorte's saloon. Sary darted a glance—Pearl and Cooley still leaned out the window, half-dressed, gawking at the circus. Jude was nowhere in sight. *Where is he?* She was almost run into by a woman pelting past carrying a quilt, one boot, and a baby, but the little episode effectively concealed Sary as the miner searched for her. He spat tobacco, and the man behind him complained, wiping his shirt—and Sary was safe in the gap. Hastening down the shadowy way, she raced to the open back stairs and up them, heart pounding with her feet. Sary stopped and listened, opened the door, hastened down a passage to where faint light bled from the main hallway to the gallery from which she had sensed Delacorte's morbid presence a lifetime ago, when she was still young and relatively innocent.

Jude was in front, somewhere. She must get down that main hall. Rows of doors. A few of them open.

Chapter 41

Julian gun-butted Cooley off Pearl with his walrus revolver. His precious Jude was on the floor playing with Pearl's pistol. He nodded, apoplectic—he'd take care of her later—and scooped the toddler up.

Pearl, straightening her clothes, pleaded, "I'll keep 'im, Julian! I will!"

Cooley hesitated. "Mister Delacorte, sir?"

"What?!"

"What if I tole you it were just that measly old female? Warn't no guns. No—no others. Just like a jest, like?"

Julian glared, snarling, "Looks like you been buck-shot," and careened out with Jude in his grip, heading down a side gallery just as Sary entered the upstairs hall leading to it.

****

She backtracked, fingering fully open a door that had been slightly ajar. With a sense of wonder Sary entered an overweening nursery, touching things as Handi had done but with distaste in place of reverence. She started to stroke the hobbyhorse with gaudy feathers and gilded reins but spun awkwardly at the sound of boots stumbling down the hall—a body banged against the wall.

Then Julian blocked the door. He seemed bigger, like a gaunt giant.

Both he and Sary gaped, stunned, yet Sary was riveted on the round-faced, sturdy, curly-headed boy Julian gripped in long gray-veined hands. The child's chubby bottom stuck out past the crook of Julian's arm.

Jude peered at Sary over his shoulder with long-lashed, wondering eyes. Green eyes—her eyes.

Julian, in turn, wavered the hefty revolver, trying to steady it, to hold it up, his gargoyle mouth twisting at Sary's grimy face and hacked hair, visible as it poked from under the cap she wore. Sary had eyes only for Jude, who was a dead weight in Julian's suddenly frail-looking arm.

"Ya come down in the world, Swinford," Julian snarled. There was something about Julian's eyes. In the dim light reflected from a nursery lamp, his rheumy eyes were black, jittery, and quite mad.

"Give me my baby. I want him now, Julian. Please. I came back. He's not yours. He's not—"

It all happened at once. Sary, alarmed, saw the smoke coiling through the nursery just as little Jude sneezed like a kitten and Julian hacked a cough. With the cough he lurched sideways, wildly waving his revolver as it exploded, spitting fire.

Little Jude jumped, wide-eyed, as the cradle behind Sary blew feathers and a fist-sized hole opened in the wall.

"Julian!" Sary screamed.

Julian's hand sagged, weighted by the gun. He gazed at her and waved his hand feebly.

"Julian..." he grated slowly and dropped the gun hand. "Speak it again," he murmured, vague.

"Yes." Sary faltered. "Julian." Another step. "Julian," she whispered. "Julian."

"See? Not difficult." His eyes glittered with wetness. His voice was a wraith, filled with longing.

Sary glided closer. Then the eyes were lost to her as he jerked his head up and backed to the hall, haunted and mad. "Julian!" Sary chased after him. His coattails whipped around the corner, his boots clattered down, and a door echoed while Sary bounded down three steps at a time. She saw him struggling up the rocky slope behind the saloon to the half-finished monster of a house.

****

As Sary clawed the slight rise to head him off, Julian abruptly changed course, skidding back down past her with Jude bouncing in his arms. Too late, Sary spied the rickety plank spanning from the saloon to the slope on which the enormous house loomed. She veered as Julian hitched sideways on the flimsy plank. It wobbled as he balanced his weight with Jude's.

A wheelbarrow squatted like a sentry at the far end, and the ravine below was littered with bent nails, kegs, and bits of lumber. *He can't make it!* But, somehow, he was over, hitched up to an unfinished veranda, pounded across hollow boards, and vanished like smoke in among a forest of studs.

Sary looked up. This close to the towering hodgepodge, Sary couldn't see the sky.

Chapter 42

Raw pine perfume wrapped Sary's face as she pelted into a space of shadowy bars and moonlight where broad, half-finished stairs dwindled to an ebony void and steps ended abruptly halfway.

To one side, a hall melted, deep in gloom. To either side, vast spaces meant to be salons and reception rooms were demarcated by a confusing jungle of uprights and ghostly studs. Other rooms were barely hinted at, while above them a crazy quilt of joists, beams, rafters, whatever they called them, and random spans of unfinished floors ascended, layer after jumbled layer, to the stars.

She paced farther in, straining to hear where Julian and Jude had gone.

A hammer sailed end over end, skipping off rafters, skimming past her head, and thudding, after long seconds, somewhere below. She squinted down. The moon bounced off boulders, raw earth, and workers' detritus in a rough, dimly seen cellar.

Sary peered up past the joists. Nothing. Listened. No sound. She poked her head through a raw frame, scrutinizing a stud-jungle of cross braces and unfinished lathing. A nail keg whizzed past with a *whushhh*, and she heard a grunt of laughter. The keg too bounced, splintering with a metallic crash somewhere below.

Sary rotated. "Where? Where's the, as Tommy'd say, 'the bloody stairs'?" Backtracking through more raw openings, she wandered deeper in confusing warrens of half-rooms with a welter of open and floored-over joists, hallways opening to the woods, and stairs to the sky, with always the rock-strewn cellar crouching in wait for her mis-step. And what about Jude?

The whole crazy-patch seemed as if each time workers returned—from lunch, or on another day— carpenters who probably couldn't read anyway—they began anew on differing levels, at their own whimsy.

Sary stopped, surrounded by creaks and rustles that pecked like blind birds from overhead, beside her, *everywhere*. She waited. Maddening silence. Not a footstep or cough.

She entered yet another raw opening to the right rear of the monster house, into a darker labyrinth of angles, shadows, and dead dreams, stopping at the tinkling snap of bullets dropping somewhere above, rolling with musical clatter, but nothing thudded past her head.

Then, the sound of sweet high childish prattle.
"But, Grampa, where we go-ing?"
"Shhhh, shhhhhh... Shush up!"
****

Ratchet cast a moon shadow through the raw front entrance. Sary and Ratchet both heard the clang of a gun reloaded, and Julian's voice, "Stay there, my little man. Don't move!"

Ratchet grinned in the dark and edged in swiftly. The real two-headed snake was there.
****

Don't move?! "Delacorte!" Sary shouted. "Don't leave him!" Flicking her gaze through the open spaces and empty rafters destined to become twelve-foot ceilings above her—"Don't put Jude down!"—she pinpointed their location. But how was she to get there? Swiveling, disoriented, Sary backtracked, she thought, to find only the unfinished stairway.

"Grampa be right back," she heard above her. Twirling, she raked through the tortuous angles of bright moon and dark latitudes for the way up. Veering left, she skidded to a stop and hung onto a doorframe in shock. The room beyond was ceiling-ed with stars and floored with space, and she could see, in her mind's eye, Jude toddling off, crawling to that black hole, and somersaulting below.

"Jude! Stay where you are!" she yelled as she tripped over a keg of nails and skidded on her hands and knees.

Gruff laughter came from above. "Careful, Swinford."

Sary pulled splinters, frantically eyeing the dizzying well of ebony nothingness linking endless stars and sky to the night abyss below, where unseen monsters of rock lay in wait to mangle anyone who dared fall amongst them, ready to leave shattered bone and heads bloodied like gourds.

Jude, crushed...broken...

She whirled, dizzy. Jude whimpered. Above her? No. Jude was farther off now. Left again, going in circles, fixed on the ceiling, following voices.

"Grampa? Canny, Grampa. Jude want canny."

She laughed weakly. *Over there now.* This time the voices were drowned by something exploding, and Sary was aware of a background cacophony of yells, rushing feet, and iron wheels clattering amid a hubbub of thudding horses.

There's life out there…

"Delacorte? Stop. I won't come farther. Please, show yourself. Jude isn't safe!" Her throat felt cut from yelling. "You'll do Jude—and yourself—an injury."

Above her there was more laughter, ending in coughs, curses, and Jude's trebly protests. "Grampa. Want down! Put me down! Now!"

She leapt over dimly seen planks and tools toward what seemed to be a slanted board floating in air.

A banister.

No steps! Damn! Skidding to within an inch of the dropoff, she peered up at open risers waiting for treads. Planting a boot on each side, Sary straddled the gap on sawtooth risers and, hanging onto the makeshift banister, hitched up, peering between her boot toes. *Don't look down! Nothing but air. Cold, dead, black air.* At last, fingering a ceiling beam, she hung on for dear life, ducking as a thin blur swished past her head— a raw beam somersaulted to crash in the cellar. Delacorte's gray ghost peered down, gleeful, and ducked back.

"Delacorte! I'm still here, and I am coming after you!" Her challenge was answered by phlegmy laughter and the creak of a board. Sary hitched faster. Never mind the nothingness beneath. She vaulted up and over rafters stretching out like train tracks, and like a tightrope dancer she wobbled across the mostly open space, leaping joists as quickly as a circus performer in order to not lose balance, until she came to a rough square opening.

Her boot slid, fanning air, and she rammed a heel onto the two-by-four behind her and wavered outstretched arms, overbalancing. Both feet slid off. Sary plunged through, scraping her shoulders, and an up-flung hand, her rifle hitting rock below with a muffled clang while her outflung hand caught rough wood. More angry than scared, Sary hauled herself up, biceps and shoulders quivering. One leg went over the beam. She flipped prone on the thin edge, rested, inched along the strip, groping ahead with hands, using thighs, knees, feet. She kept tipping one way and then the other, swinging upside down, holding on like a monkey. She threw herself onto a half-floor, scanning a welter of studs.

"Jude? Sweet baby! Dammit! Where are you?"

Jude's babble was louder, then fainter. "Put me down, Grampa…too fast!"

Sounds of big boots pounding away and boards rattling.

"Shhhhh, my little man."

"Dark, Grampa! Want Han-di! Want Pearl!" Only it came out as, 'Wan Hani' and 'Pull.'

"Where we go, Grampa?"

"Hush, Jude!" Then a ringing slap. Jude wailed.

Sary spun, furious, and addressed the dark. "Stop! Don't you *dare* hurt my baby!"

"What do you know? You didn't raise him," Julian snarled.

A desperate Sary taunted, "Are you scared, Delacorte? Why not show yourself? I'm just a woman."

"Woman!" he scorned. Delacorte hesitated. Silence stretched thin as a wisp of smoke coiling in. She thought he was done. Then, quietly, he asked, "Did you murder my boy...my Jules?" It came almost on an intake, as if sucking back words he wished unanswered.

She heard boots shuffle away. "You wanted me once. I'm here. Delacorte, come back!"

Sary spied a closed door—an actual framed doorway, with a door and handle. At last. Thudding over loose planks, she yanked it and strode out—into black wind. She grabbed the frame, maneuvering her palm to the inside, and braced, looking down stunned at rocks inviting her with their hard knuckles and cold jagged stone fingers. More shocking, she saw it all by the light of the fire she'd started. Hurling herself back, Sary landed hard on her bottom. *"Oooouw!"* She rolled onto her back and gritted out, "How the hell did you get up there?"

****

Another maddening stairwell waiting for steps, more unfinished levels. Another banister led to a dark coffin-shaped oblong overhead, and again she wondered how workers got to the upper levels.

She studied the open stairwell's dead air, and backed, judging distance across the void to the hodgepodge banister, and leapt, grabbed hold of the banister, her slick palms losing traction, feet dangling. *Quick! Hand over hand—cross-over, cross-over, another six inches—latch on!* Her shoulders screamed in their sockets, but it was only a foot away, now, to the ceiling. *Seize the landing hole. Pull! Pull!* Her muscles writhed. *Swing a leg up.* She missed the edge. *Higher.* She hooked the landing with a boot heel.

For a minute Sary viewed the dark, upside down, shutting her eyes at the inky well below. Then, swinging up, she stomached the rim where balustrades should be but weren't, kneed the lip, and tumbled across the finished flooring. Blessedly, she lay there, galvanized for action—at last she was closing in.

Sary checked the closed doors of future bedrooms on all four sides. Then Julian Delacorte's muffled hack. "You want him, come fetch him, Swinford!" Startlingly close.

She rammed the nearest door.

"Sary Swinford? I'm waiting," Julian sing-songed. "Recall those words? You come to me now!"

Sary raced around the hole to another door on the far side, sliding up to it. She nudged the door with her gun barrel and entered a room open to the stars and swirls of sparking haze. *It's empty. The rooms must be interconnected, in a square around the landing.* Her thought was belied by a hogshead of nails smashing into her face. Jagged light-rings flickered under her lids, faded to bolts, then to orange and yellow stars. She sat hard, aware of nails beneath her backside.

Blind and deaf, Sary clutched a handful. Flinging the nails low, she rolled sluggishly aside, absently pocketing more nails. Pinpoints of vision expanded too gradually, but, as through a tunnel, Julian's coat-rack figure manifested, raising a massive revolver— unbelievably aiming it at Jude's curls instead of at her.

She rolled as big boots, viewed through a jagged ring, stepped over her. Julian sneered down. "Recollect, Swinford? You bet this once. I'm calling."

Sary revolved in a crouch, wavering her own gun. "But I didn't!"

She viewed them through a tiny hole in her vision as Julian backed to the landing, holding his walrus revolver steady. Sight returned enough for her to measure the distance to the rail-less drop, and she cried, "Watch out!"

His face twisted like a gargoyle's in a slice of moon that highlighted silver stubble, crevices, and sunken eyes raging at her trickery. Still Julian hesitated, uncertain, faltering at the very edge—and regained his footing to lurch right and slip through yet another door and bang it shut. A curtain floated lazily before her. She choked. The smoke was thick and furling up through the open rafters now.

A high scream erupted. Sary froze. Piercing. Almost a woman's shriek, followed by sickening diminishing thuds and a final smashing thunk...

There was something wrong with that hoarse cry. She'd forgotten all about Ratchet. *Jude? Delacorte?* "Jude! Sweeting! Talk to me. Tell Mama. Where are you?"

Raw pine will burn like a box of lucifer matches.

"Oh, please answer!"

"Ma-ma?" Jude's trebly question hung in the night.

Julian rasped, "Keep still!"

The moon melted like yellow cheese behind clouds of hot smoke. Sary frantically groped past the landing hole on hands and knees. Smoke skirled like ghosts of buildings past risen to this third—*fourth?—level.* She'd lost count. Then she saw it.

A door smaller than most, hidden until now by a brick chimney, showed itself in a draft, revealing a latch still swinging like a tiny pendulum.

Sary poked inside the narrow door to an equally narrow chute and crept up pokey steps with her gun in a two-handed grip. *So, this is how. Worker's stairs, destined to be the servants' way.* Delacorte knew exactly where it was, the first one finished. Wind whipped the door shut. *Trapped,* her mind babbled, *in this narrow stairway. No one will know. The house will burn...a burning coffin... Stop it!* Her mind shrieked like the wind, urging her to go up.

Groping the narrow stairs, Sary touched hinges in the low slanted ceiling. Carefully pushing, she let her head rise above the trap door. Sensing cooler air and a lighter slice of dark, Sary faced acres of drafty space where wind moaned through rafters and whipped about her bare head. Joists set sixteen inches apart stretched over the entire house. Either a lazy carpenter had done his worst, or scrap lumber was simply hauled and nailed for a rough finish. Split, loose, warped flooring abruptly ended and began in six-foot-wide gaps in a haphazard checkerboard. Some spaces, she realized, dropped directly to the basement.

Could Jude possibly be here? Was Julian laughing, even now racing from the house to the saloon?

Suddenly Sary was so tired. It seemed forever since she'd left Big Bear and all her shredded dreams behind. She dug deep for anger, found it waiting, and with refueled strength she knew that if she was to rescue Jude it must be in the next few seconds.

A warm gush of air exploded with a geyser of fire, hungrily feeding, at a corner of the house. A red tongue jetted from the maw of cellar, searching for random food to feed its heat.

Should have left well enough alone. All my fault. Jude was alive here, even cosseted.

A ladder straggled up in the dead center of the space. Easing along a joist, now five or six levels over the cellar, Sary made it to another trap door where the flimsy ladder ended. With a *whump* the door thudded up and back, and Sary clambered through, turning in a gale skirling around the boxy widow's walk with its four open window sockets.

And there was Julian, with half his arthritic body swaying out one of the four windows yet to be glassed, holding on with one knuckly hand, rheumatic knobs showing bone as he gripped so tight. The cold was penetrating, yet Jude faced the windy void over Julian's shoulder, his little face crinkled, trying for brave, but Sary fixated on Julian's hand trembling with strain.

She tore her gaze away and focused on his face.

"Together." Julian was speaking to her. "It's fitting."

Sary waded into the wind howling past her.

"Just the two of us, Julian. You and me. Put him down. Over there. Please." Sary waved to a space between the windows. "I beg you. We don't have time." She stretched out a hand, smiling in what she hoped was an appealing way.

"No, no time at all," he agreed, and smiled serenely back, but his eyes were jigging and glittery. Still hanging on one-handed, he peered over his shoulder, twisted, not quite ready to go.

Jude whimpered, clutching him fiercely.

"Please!"

"Drop 'em!" Julian ordered, motioning at her.

"Yes. Yes. I am. I will. And if I do?" Sary unbuckled her gun belts, feeling behind for something half-recalled as she entered, something lying carelessly on a ledge. A hammer? A plank propped between windows? Something. She groped behind her.

Julian still fixed on Sary with a peculiar mixture of

love, hate, evil, and frustration. Bracing, he thrust Jude out to the wind. His yellow-toothed grin was calculating, challenging...vengeful. Jude kicked and clasped Julian's neck.

"Yes, Julian..." Sary stepped closer. "Anything for you. Whatever you want." The hammer dropped back to the sill from her fingers with a dull telltale clunk.

Julian, wavering on the sill, didn't notice. "Shhh! Shhh. Be my brave little Jude."

Sary giant-stepped, reaching.

"Back off!" he snarled.

Sary backed to another window in the cramped space. "It's me you want. I'm here, Julian. Look at me!"

His vision wavered between her—he blinked—between this thing, this witch in filthy men's gear and butchered hair, and the fresh, cream-fleshed, wide-eyed girl she was once.

Sary smiled angelically, arms wide.

Blink. It's the filthy, half-bald female once more, not the woman of his mind. Fighting a gust, Julian glanced out at the drop, calculating, and veered back.

Blink. Sary, the angel of the Christmas tree...

"Your turn to...come...to me, Julian," Sary croaked. "I always...loved you...*Julian,*" she managed.

The words were a bone thrust sideways in her throat. Carefully she dragged an earring from a pocket. Her fingers brushed the nails she had placed there.

With a nail—more of a stud—concealed in her fist, she slowly wriggled the wire through a lobe as Julian watched, transfixed.

Sary—by his fire. The actual fire was beating at his face now from outside...*Sary, wearing pearl earrings, his earrings. Smiling—at him, Julian. Each pearl reflecting the flame warming her cheek, her breasts— those soft breasts—all cream velvet...*

Julian smiled, unaware of the conflagration outside but his face warmed and his raddled and sagging cheeks reddened instead by the imaginary fire. His smile mutated to what he deemed, with lips open wide, encouraging, even roguish.

Sary saw only a stretched mouth—cracked and crusted, phlegmy corners flecked with blood, yellow tusks showing. She could smell his putrefying lungs, mixed with the fresh sweet scent of little Jude.

"This what you want?" she pleaded. "Come. Come to me, Julian." Sary half-moaned the last, retreating, with one hand groping for the hammer. Her other reached out for him and she plastered a tender smile on her face. Even to her it seemed as fake as the rosebud simper on a painted china doll.

At last, her fingers brushed the hammer lying slantwise on the unfinished sill.

****

Julian gaped at his hand, shrieking a second after Sary's outstretched fist rammed the stud into his crepe-like flesh raised with worms of vein. With one fluid swing born of desperation, Sary slammed the hammer true on the broad nailhead, fastening his hand, with a thud and a great welling of blood, to the raw frame he clutched.

The hammer dropped. "I'm taking my child," she said. She crossed the narrow space.

One of Julian's hands still gripped the frame. The other held Jude. So focused was she on getting the little boy to safety that Sary hardly noticed the hammer bouncing to land cock-up against the wall by Julian's knee.

Julian doubled over his hand, pulling instinctively, yowling, squeezing Jude in a spasm of pain. Tears coursed the raddled cheeks as he glared red-eyed at Sary. Still clutching Jude, whose little face was screwed with outrage, Julian bent his knees and slid down the frame to his scrawny rump.

They both eyed the hammer at the same time.

She watched, disbelieving, lunging as he finger tipped it with his trapped hand, but he had it, manipulated it, his face twisted in a gargoyle of maddened torment while Jude lustfully howled and kicked him with sturdy little boots.

"Put me down, Grampa! Don't *wike* it here!" He beat with fat little fists.

Julian trapped Jude between his crooked arm and his chest in answer. Reaching across, he maneuvered the hammer around, dragging the claw end under the nail head and levering it up by painful wrenches, howling at each impact on his flesh.

Sary couldn't tear her eyes away. Julian ripped his hand free in a fountain of released blood, enfolding it to his chest like a wounded bird. Nailing her with crazed eyes, Julian lurched across the floor, trailing blood, with murder and betrayal written plainly on his face, as Sary crashed back down through the trap door.

Julian tumbled down the ladder after her, lifting a heavy boot to stomp, aiming for her neck. She rolled into Julian's legs in the last second, terrified at the thought of Jude flying from his arms and landing God knows where, aware she smelled raw pine burning, and watched, disbelieving, as he placed a boot sideways on a rafter, attempting to scootch across to safe flooring and the other trap door leading down to the house across flames shooting up in spiteful jets and wraiths of smoke.

She had to stop him. Now, before his strength oozed out with the blood pouring from his hand. She took a deep breath.

"Not worth it, Delacorte! He never was Jules's. He doesn't belong to you..."

Julian hesitated, wavering, one foot over the drop.

What have I done? At this height, a fall through floors of joists would cut Jude in half.

She breathed again as Julian managed to sidle off the rafter to a solid section.

"Look at him," she screamed across. "He's just a little ordinary boy. Who? Who does he look like, Julian?" She couldn't help it. Her nerves were paper thin and tearing. It was Jude's last chance.

Julian flicked an eye at Jude, hacked a rope of sputum, and snarled back, "Don't need to! My son's blood. Bone of my bone, blood of my blood. Living on after. My...*heart."*

She crawled up, limping now, edging across the same rafter. They were two lame beasts stalking each other as she hawked Julian, inching dangerously along. His big boots overlapped rattling planks bridging a gap to another whole section. The fall had done something to her knee. They were equal. Ahead, Julian hit a dead end and had to backtrack.

"It's not worth it!" she yelled. "He never was Jules's. He doesn't belong to you!" Oh, sweet Jesus— She eyed the trap and saw Julian had somehow, teetering madly, made it to another rafter. If he made it down, Julian could end up anywhere, lost in the crowd, and the long search must begin anew, with all her destruction behind it. *Where's the fire now? Somewhere nearer.* She could hear its crackled voice and feel the hot breath.

Gripping a truss overhead, Julian minced along one-handed, sixty feet above a cellar that was beginning to resemble Hell. Blood poured from a hand dispersing red rain that was buffeted by wind and bounced off layers of rafters to patter somewhere on unseen oblivion. She daren't distract him. He still had five feet to go.

Sary slid a foot forward and buckled. She eyed Jude. Jude was very still. He had stopped kicking. The plank Julian inched across knocked and shuddered, not tacked down. He was still two feet from the door. Sary called desperately above the wind, "He looks like Ev'ret!"

Julian snarled, "You didn't say that!"

"Look at him!" she cried.

Julian wavered over the drop, in obvious pain, ignoring it all. "No! Jude's sharp as spurs! He don't miss a card. He's...he's..."

"NOT YOUR BLOOD!" Sary screamed, and limped rapidly after him as Julian spared a glance to see Jude's broad little nose and sprinkle of nutmeg freckles. Sun had never had a chance with Jules's porcelain pale flesh. Jules always burned.

Julian tottered, balancing on an updraft whipping his coat tails. He giggled shrilly, raised one big booted foot, and taunted, "Hazards of the die, Sary! The cards! The whole filthy horse race, Sarabande Swinford! Ya bet more'n you could lose!" Wheezing his diatribe, he continued, "You ken that sickenin' feeling when the grin's plastered all over your face an' ya just lost daddy's gold watch?"

His long gray face stretched into a leer as he chuckled bitterly. "Wager you do *now!*"

Julian backed another foot. And another. "I wagered for a halfwit pumpkin head!" He batted a ribbon of tarpaper, swaying wildly, one long arm jerking at the last second for the overhead beam. "But you held a pair of deuces all along! You *knew!* You parlayed me a taint-blood bastard! Very good!" he panted.

His astringent words howled off in a whippet of breeze as Julian suddenly realized Sary loomed quite close now, fairly skipping over thin blades of wood.

Lifting a large boot, Julian stomped it astride two rafters in a standoff and raised the revolver to Jude's curls. Once more his eyes bored into her with an admixture of rage, hurt, and foundered dreams as Jude watched his granddad with frightened wonder.

Julian's face was red-lit, she realized. The same carmine flicker warmed the attic. They were trapped, both coughing in gagging paroxysms behind a pinkish smoky curtain.

"Julian!"

They both flinched and look down into the Hell below. Handi in her nightdress dragged a rifle at the very rim of an abyss of shifting, swirling, bloody haze. Falling beams, blazing like faggots, crashed to the cellar through a maze of uprights, cross braces, and rafters. Through it all, Handi's face was whiter than the lead paint she wore.

"The *other* succubus!" Julian raged, swinging wide

with the revolver and losing his stability altogether.

Sary lunged for Jude—and *missed*. He was held by his little neck clamped in Julian's arm, squirming, kicking, red-faced, trying to howl his outrage, when Julian back-stepped, tripped a weird *schottische,* and, in the end, lost his dance of life.

As Julian instinctively grabbed for safety, he let go of Jude and plunged, smashing through levels, cracking boards and bouncing off joists, thudding like dead meat with a terrible crack of bone and pulverizing of muscle.

Sary saw him sprawling, broken like a wizened plaything, draped across boulders and partly on Ratchet, who had preceded him in death and now, Sary saw, had preserved him in life. Her mind flashed to the odd scream heard earlier. Her attention was torn to a flutter of an eyelid, a faint moan, and involuntary stirring of legs below. Julian yet lived, broken as he was.

But Sary pondered none of that. She had lunged, frantic, for Jude's nightdress. Doubled over, the beam ramming her belly, she snagged Jude and was conscious of Handi's anguished white face as the child slowly peeled out of his gown, leaving sturdy little legs dangling bare. Then, with a horrible ripping of cloth, his body slipped.

She gripped a sleeve. He slid out of it, his head disappearing within. Red-faced, straining, Sary braced and let go, pivoting head down. She grasped his arm and hoisted Jude's hefty little body up by her fingertips alone. Painfully balanced, the beam cutting into her stomach, Sary snaked an arm up and back, grabbed a rafter, and precariously levered both of them up. Sitting unsteadily astride the beam, she jammed her face into

Jude's flossy, sweet-smelling curls, breathing deep.

"Put your arms around my neck," she barked huskily, feeling his short arms instantly clamp her neck—*Good boy, sweet boy, smart boy!*—conscious of his big, wondering, trusting green eyes. Then Jude turned his attention to his grandfather, who lay like a broken toy soldier sprawled far below.

"Grampa hut."

"Yes," Sary muttered. "Grampa hurt bad."

****

Sary knelt beside Julian. He was smashed and splintered like a tree rotting from within, yet living as a last leaf clung to its branch. She tried to ignore Ratchet, partially cushioning him, as she listened to each heaving sigh. A gasp, a long silence, a feeble cough, a hitching breath, like he drew a cart laden with rock. He struggled for the next breath every time, each possibly the last allotted, as Jude squirmed, fighting Sary to see him.

She set Jude a safe span away. "Stay," she ordered, pointing with a warning finger to plummeting chunks of charred wood. She searched the pit perimeter for Handi. "Handi! Come get Jude and fetch someone." But Handi still trailed the gun, frozen.

Sary didn't notice Julian painfully reach into a pocket and drag out blood-soaked candy, softly calling, "Jude," amid the implosions and turmoil. "Come to Grampa…"

Jude toddled over, dragging his nighty, happily chortling.

"Canny!"

Julian drew Jude in, enveloped him, and reached for the fallen revolver.

Sary spun back at Handi's horrified expression.

Julian showed yellow teeth, twisting in pain, and held the gun to Jude's head.

"Hutting me, Grampa. Want up!"

Julian gripped him harder in a spasm. His face softened though, as his eyes wobbled to Sary, taking on a look of puzzled wonder. He almost released the heavy revolver.

"Why?" he breathed. "I would've given you *anything.* A fucking queen! All for you…"

Sary winced. A burning scrap sailed between them, landing on Julian's face. Julian let out a gargle and gripped the gun tighter. His hand spasmed. More bits of sparking char sailed down. Somewhere an upright crashed, firing the air. Sary looked up. Handi still stood frozen, as if firing the gun would take her last will.

Townsfolk, reflecting fire like so many demons, peered into the pit now, calculating. They seemed to be betting on the outcome. No help there.

Julian coughed blood and swept away raw blazing pine, chuckling weakly. "Our pyre!" He chuckled as falling timber sailed around her, spitting fireworks into the night. "You, and me, and this misbegotten bastard."

Sary tugged a leg. Julian jack-knifed, howling. Bone poked through. She watched his gun hand. If he *died,* the gun might fire…

His chest seemed caved, his voice thin as a pressed weed, yet he held Jude in a grip to the death.

"Help us!" she called up. Townspeople still merely watched, stoic and condemning as a row of hanging judges. *He's weak. His lids are heavy. Take Jude…soon…not a minute to spare…*Beams landed around her with a shower of red. The cellar was an oven.

I can't just leave him…

She realized the dark world swam with crimson wavering faces, as if she were under water. Her eyes brimmed with wet she could not blink away.

Snaring his eyes with hers, Sary moved in—kneeling, she laid her head to his chest, ignoring the sparks landing soft as hot rain.

Her hand crept to the little boy, the gun now between her and Jude. She smelled Jude's baby scent, next to the stench of old blood and corruption.

"Say…Julian. No thorn in your tongue. Just roses," Julian whispered huskily.

"Julian," she breathed, keeping her eye on the scabrous hand and clawed yellow fingers, mesmerized by those knotted claws tightening the trigger—and kissed him.

"Julian!"

Julian's head snapped back…

His eyes flew open, mouth gaping like a fish, and a hole appeared in his temple as if painted on.

Handi stood above them with the long-barreled rifle. Smoke still curled from the barrel.

Julian's trigger finger clenched. His hand flew up, involuntarily blasting the sky, and there was a howl and curse from the ring circling the pit.

Sary snatched Jude from Julian's arms and raced up a worker's ramp, passing Handi, who was hobbling slowly down, and dashed on through the ominous gathering.

Grace watched Sary, mute, and then followed, picking up speed. Determined now, Grace brushed aside folk drawn to the burning house.

It was evident Julian's liquor stock had been broken into, for many waved bottles, to sounds of breaking glass and pistol fire. They seemed demonic, prancing before the flaming town.

A few doves joined Handi in the cellar, dancing away from the worst of the falling char, staring at Julian, helpless. Daredevils. Two feebly tried to lug him to the ramp. One searched his pockets. Another filched his watch. But the fire seemed to have spent most of its scraps of lumber and hogsheads.

Responsible townspeople, Aaron among them, still manned the brigade with the dwindling water supply.

"Sweet Jesus!"

Sary halted, shielding Jude's face, startled at the scope—the complete morass of black, wet, burned-out hulks of what once was Big Bear.

Grace un-stoppered her mouth, shrieked, and pointed. "It's her! Get her! She done this!"

As they spotted Sary, some dropped containers and joined Grace, who plodded faster after Sary, who was weaving for the bluff. Grace swatted Aaron to follow. The crowd divided as Grace shouldered past. More dropped buckets. It was futile, now the water was below Sary's buckshot holes. They slipped in sludge, excited, vengeful, gaining even though Sary ran flat out, bouncing Jude on her shoulder, coming face to face with—"Tommy?"

Wide-eyed, breathless, and scared out of his wits, two rifles slung over his shoulder, his chest cross-braced with ammo, dragging gun belts and gripping two mismatched revolvers, Tommy appeared through the smoke like an anxious ghost.

She dashed past him.

Lost my wits! Surely! Her fantastical conversations with Tommy must have bloomed into full-flowered lunacy. She faltered, a few steps farther on as she raced for the bluff. *My Tommy, in that ratty purple velvet cape, possibly the warmest garment he possesses. It's tied about his neck, fluttering behind. Tommy.*

Behind her, Tommy scanned the approaching mob, registered Jude, dropped the extra revolvers, and about-faced. Snatching Jude from Sary, he forged ahead, knees high and pumping hard.

"Tommy! What in pluperfect Hades are you doing…here?" Sary yelled.

"Sometimes gettin' walloped with a bottle is like a kiss, in retrospect," he yelled back, dodging and straight-arming a lout determined to make a name.

Sary raced to keep up. "It was—you, idiot!"

Tommy's alarmed face looked back. The entire town was on their heels, at least the ones not ludicrously slip-sliding in muck made from the water tower.

As they reached the bluff, Sary yanked one of Tommy's rifles, fanning it from the hip. Tommy slowed.

"Don't dawdle!" Sary yelled, backing to the bluff. "How'd you get here?"

Tommy slung Jude on his shoulders, grabbed dirt, and climbed.

"Sold it! Knew this was where you'd end up. It was…" He slowed, looking back at the town and the mob overtaking Grace and plowing on ahead. "What the hell happened here, Sare?"

Sary clambered after, huffing. "What? Sold what?"

"Theater. Wagons. Props. Costumes. Malcolm!"

Tommy shouted.

Sary checked the gaining mob. "Malcolm? You sold *Malcolm?*"

"The theater! To Malcolm. He always wanted to play Oberon..."

Sary shoved at Tommy's behind. "Oh. Keep moving!"

Sary slithered backward.

Orvis was two feet away.

She sighted the green bottle—a glinting acid spark winking by a tower strut.

Orvis ducked, chortling as her shot winged past him.

"Never could shoot worth sh—"

She fired past him again.

The bullet plowed earth beside the bottle.

He lunged, encircling her ankle.

She ignored him, aimed meticulously, and blasted the bottle.

Earth moved.

Planks blossomed out from securing bands.

The remaining water exploded in a mist. Slats shot skyward, then clattered to the ground like wooden daisy petals around a giant smoking black epicenter. Orvis leaped in the air.

Sary hung on. Slivers and gouts of earth peppered and pocked the cliff side, and the tower ponderously tipped as the struts buckled, water turning the earth into mud, as the townspeople yet clawed the bluff at her heels.

Tommy, sheltering Jude, watched anxiously as she crested the top and flashed a look back. Flipping his cape, he loped for a horse. Even then, he expected her to follow.

She picked up the pace, sparing a startled glance at the horse and wagon with the battered Gatling gun with the ring of barrels, tilting on two giant wheels, stenciled with US ARMY.

"What?"

Racing past, Sary regretfully brushed the Gatling as if it were a tame beast. "Damnation!" She was reluctant to leave it.

Tommy gasped, clutching his knees. "Always wanted—one—of—those—" He broke into Cockney. "Thought to me'self, you could use 'alf a 'and." And he gestured to the ruined, smoldering town, shaking his head. "Shoulda but known. Blimey!"

Sary shoved him. "Move!" One and then two murderous faces breached the bluff, spilling over, followed by a stream of enraged, mortified ranchers, miners, drunks, gentle mothers, a contingent of soiled doves, and shop owners.

"Sary! Don't stop!" Tommy put on speed, heading for horses awaiting beside the Mercedes. Sary veered back, hopped onto the wagon, and shouldered the broken Gatling. The wagon's list gave it momentum—it moved a grudging inch and centered on the mob.

"Not worth a tinker's farthing, love!" Tommy shouted, scared. "Make haste!"

"They don't know that!"

Sary cranked the gun around.

Faces grew distinguishable. There was Grace, right in front—yet Sary felt no anger or hatred, only pity. Sary *had* her child.

The mob stopped short, focused on the unlikely sight of the Gatling and Sary, who stood with one hand on the crank, the other feeding a half-empty cartridge belt through the slot.

They faltered, staring into multiple snouts of multiple barrels, and backed and spun in their tracks to pelt off. Only a few crouched, arms swinging, waiting to see what would happen next.

"Oh, the hell with it!"

Sary cranked a few rounds over their heads.

The gun bucked and rattled from its braces as Sary forced the balky bent crank into a few more goes. Reverberation stuffed cotton in her ears and rattled up her arms, past juddering teeth, as the mob dove, scrambling, over the bluff's edge.

Sary laughed and jumped from the cart, racing joyously for the remaining horse.

Mounted, Sary looked back.

"Come, sweeting!" Tommy exhorted.

"No, just a bit!"

She and Tommy edged to the bluff, and Sary gazed sadly down at Handi, a miniature old woman slumped over Julian in the cellar among smoldering wood. Pearl stood beside her. Some of the water had run off into the pit, and Sary hoped Pearl would soon lead Handi away.

The fire had bypassed the saloon. A stick figure shoved through the doors with cradled bottles in her arms. It could only be The Hag. *Her* Hag.

"We could buy this lot for a nickel's worth of pinchbeck, Tommy. Rebuild the house. Have a theater. A grand place. Chandeliers. Velvet seats. Pictures in big gilt frames like—"

She stopped. "I owe you," she said simply.

"Oh, Sary! And, miss all the *divertissement?* 'Sides, Malcolm'd never forgive me."

Sary giggled, reaching for Jude. She peered into his trusting jade-green eyes.

"I'm your mama. Forever!"

Jude studied her, round-eyed.

"Pway poker?" he lisped hopefully.

Sary squeezed him, and then Tommy, with Jude squashed between. "Apparently!" She chuckled, and Jude grinned around his thumb as he looked up at them.

They mounted the horses, and Sary cantered ahead, yelling back at Tommy, "'Sides, I hear there's diamonds in Africa…"

She galloped on.

Tommy, laughing, head thrown back, whooped and gave chase.

**If you enjoyed this story,
watch for *SARY'S DIAMONDS,*
as Sary continues her adventures with a trip to
Africa...**

A word from the author...

As all writers with creative monkeys on our backs, after wading through the muck of pottery, hacking away as a sculptor, sucking up paint fumes, dabbling in stunt work, plus years of hurry-up-and-wait background performing...the Art of Writing is an exhilarating medium, beyond blood-spattered laptops and with few tools outside of a feverish brain and a doorstop thesaurus...

I live, play, and write in Pacific Palisades and Big Bear, California.

~Sharon

Thank you for purchasing
this publication of The Wild Rose Press, Inc.

If you enjoyed the story, we would appreciate your
letting others know by leaving a review.

For other wonderful stories,
please visit our on-line bookstore at
www.thewildrosepress.com.

For questions or more information
contact us at
info@thewildrosepress.com.

The Wild Rose Press, Inc.
www.thewildrosepress.com

Stay current with The Wild Rose Press, Inc.

Like us on Facebook

https://www.facebook.com/TheWildRosePress

And Follow us on Twitter
https://twitter.com/WildRosePress